"They took m

"They kill for the sport of it." Jeb clenched his jaw. "You think you're going to find them by yourself?"

Green eyes flashed. "If it's the last thing I do." She halted, her bosom heaving.

"Like hell you will." Jeb released her. He didn't want to be affected by this woman. He didn't want to be needed by her.

Instead, he thought of honor and integrity. Of patriotism. He thought, too, of leaving the country he'd just come back to. One more time. And his plans for California disintegrated like smoke in the wind.

"I'll help you, damn it."

She gaped at him. For a long moment no one spoke.

"Why?" she asked.

"Because I can. And right now you have no one else."

"I don't even know you!"

"You will by the time we get to Mexico…."

* * *

The Mercenary's Kiss
Harlequin Historical #718—August 2004

Praise for new Harlequin Historical author Pam Crooks

"Pam Crooks brings every character, every danger, every ordeal to life through her vivid descriptions and snappy dialogue. This is one author whose star is rising fast."
—*Romantic Times* on *Hannah's Vow*

"Pam Crooks writes westerns like nobody's business! They grab you from the start, and you better hang on for the ride!"
—*The Best Reviews* on *Broken Blossoms*

DON'T MISS THESE OTHER TITLES AVAILABLE NOW:

#715 THE HORSEMAN
Jillian Hart

#716 A SCANDALOUS SITUATION
Patricia Frances Rowell

#717 THE WIDOW'S BARGAIN
Juliet Landon

PAM CROOKS

The Mercenary's Kiss

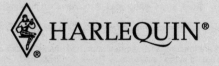

HARLEQUIN®

TORONTO • NEW YORK • LONDON
AMSTERDAM • PARIS • SYDNEY • HAMBURG
STOCKHOLM • ATHENS • TOKYO • MILAN • MADRID
PRAGUE • WARSAW • BUDAPEST • AUCKLAND

ISBN 0-373-29318-6

THE MERCENARY'S KISS

www.eHarlequin.com

Printed in U.S.A.

Available from Harlequin Historicals and
PAM CROOKS

The Mercenary's Kiss #718

To my agent, Paige Wheeler.
Thank you.

Prologue

Texas, 1896

"La-adies and gentlemen! What a singular pleasure it is to bring to your fair city the most dazzling, the most thrilling, the most *renowned* extravaganza this side of the Missouri! Doc Charlie's Medicine Sho-o-w-w!"

The audience packing the wooden benches inside the canvas tent whooped and clapped, their enthusiasm as palpable as the sawdust beneath their feet. Men whistled. Women and children cheered. The calliope player banged the keys in a chaotic medley of earsplitting notes, all to perpetuate the excitement and anticipation of the entertainment to come.

As always, Elena Malone was filled with her own excitement of yet another performance to a crowd who had traveled from miles around to watch.

A crowd with money in their pockets, of course.

The medicine show was her father's production. Doc Charlie Malone carried the responsibility of the entire troupe on his shoulders. As pitchman for his own elixir, Doc Charlie's Miraculous Herbal Compound, it was up to him to sell enough bottles after every performance to support them all.

And there wasn't a better pitchman than Pop.

Oh, but she never tired of watching him. He always dressed impeccably in a smart suit and crisp white shirt, kept his mustache trimmed neat and his graying goatee combed and stylish. He had eyes that were sharp and straightforward. His booming voice inspired confidence. Honesty. Doc Charlie Malone was the picture of professionalism.

A medicine man the crowd could trust.

And why not? He touted his elixir with pride, and while the results he claimed didn't always happen to everyone, most times they did. Elena was shrewd enough to know there wasn't a cure around that could single-handedly conquer the world's ills.

But Pop's elixir came close.

She roused herself from her musings and realized that Jake, the show's blackface comedian, had finished his opening routine. The crowd's laughter attested to their enjoyment of his jokes and his success in delivering them. He was still taking his bow when a trio of jugglers appeared in the ring, plates spinning in the air as they ran.

Elena's gaze swept the crowd and noted the rapt expressions on the people's faces, their happiness and delight. On cue, the performers abandoned the plates and switched to fiery torches. Everyone seemed to wait with bated breath at the jugglers' dexterity, at the danger, fearful they might be burned and fascinated by the possibility.

Everyone except one.

Her attention snagged upon a man openly staring at her. A Mexican with jet-black hair that cascaded down to his shoulders in gleaming waves, and who possessed eyes as dark, as glittering, as polished onyx.

Elena pulled her own eyes away. She was accustomed to men staring at her—women and children, too, of all ages. It was part of performing in front of a curious public. She had learned to distance herself from it.

"Your cape, Elena."

She turned and glanced at Toby, the freckle-faced young man who worked behind the scenes to help keep the show going smoothly and on schedule. A ventriloquist and a song-and-dance team would perform after the jugglers. She had some time yet before she'd take her turn in the ring.

She smiled as he settled the satin fabric around her shoulders. She was inexplicably glad for the covering— not that she was shy wearing her red-spangled costume, which conformed to the shape of her body like a second skin, enabling her to move freely during her trick-riding routine. She still had the uncanny feeling the Mexican watched her. "Thanks."

"Good crowd tonight," Toby commented. He removed his cap and ran his shirtsleeve over his sweaty forehead. He always labored hard for the show. Pop was lucky to have him.

"Yes. The take will be high, I think."

"High enough for Doc?" He grinned, his expression teasing, but knowing.

Her mouth softened. "Is it ever?"

Pop's obsession to sell his precious elixir, *cases* of it, was common knowledge among the troupe. The more money they took in, the happier Pop would be.

But then, everyone knew their expenses were formidable. If Doc Charlie's Miraculous Herbal Compound didn't sell, the troupe didn't eat. Their debts always came first.

"Be careful out there, Elena." Serious again, Toby pulled his cap back onto his head.

She gave him a confident wink. "I always am."

He moved away from her, to the next chore that awaited him. Elena turned back to the ring, her fingers fastening the cape's clasp. Only minutes to go.

The first wave of apprehension went through her, as it always did before she performed. Even though she was only eighteen years of age, Pop considered her the show's top act—the final one before his pitch. He depended on her to leave the audience so thrilled, so awe-struck, they were compelled to buy his elixir out of sheer gratitude for the pleasurable entertainment he'd given them.

At last, it was time. Toby led a pair of white horses into the ring, both unsaddled and wearing red-feathered ornaments on their heads. Elena swept off her cape with a flourish, bowed, then bounded onto the lead horse's back. With an ease she'd earned from countless hours of practice, she performed her routine of splits and cart-wheels, tail and shoulder stands, until the crowd cheered in delight. She slid into the grand finale—a breathtaking choreography of somersaults and back flips on a half-dozen matching white horses.

When the routine was complete, she dismounted in one fluid leap. The applause increased to an even higher crescendo. Exhilarated, she sank into a long, deep bow of acknowledgment.

"Yes-sir-ree, ladies and gentlemen!" Pop's booming voice soared over the applause. "An extravaganza the likes you'll never see again! Doc Charlie's Medicine Sho-o-w-w!"

After another rise of cheers, the clapping gradually quieted. The audience knew the show hadn't ended yet, that there was more to come. No one understood better than Pop that the townspeople had gathered under the tent not only to be entertained but to be cured of their ills, real or imagined.

"Now, you fine folks realize that Doc Charlie's Medicine Show has to move on. By dawn's first light, we'll be on the road west. So tonight is your one and only chance to be healed."

Cheers erupted again. Clearly Pop held the crowd transfixed.

"I don't claim that my elixir is a cure-all for everything. But I'm telling you true, Doc Charlie's Miraculous Herbal Compound is made right from the secrets of the ancients." He held up a bottle for them to see. "This elixir is good for three things. The kidneys, the stomach and the liver. *And any singular disease rising therefrom!*"

Elena had slipped from the ring with the horses to allow her father the audience's complete attention. From her vantage point near one of the tent's entrances, she watched him. She was proud of his honesty, his forthrightness. The people looked to him for hope. And health.

Pop couldn't afford the national advertising many of the patent medicine companies used to sell their products. He had only himself—and the herbal compound he had created—to draw in customers. Thus, his pitch had to be sterling and straightforward.

Riveting.

The audience was indeed riveted to his oratory about a man cured of tapeworms from Doc Charlie's Miraculous Herbal Compound. Pop always gave specifics. He revealed the man's name, his occupation, his hometown. Even the number of children he had.

And the crowd believed.

"Again, I tell you true, ladies and gentlemen. There is not a greater pain remedy on earth than my herbal compound. There is no sore it will not heal, no ache it will not subdue. Why, you can even use it to treat your horses and cattle!"

A collective murmur of surprise rippled through the tent.

"Yes-sir-ree! One dollar for a bottle. That's all, ladies and gentlemen. One dollar. Isn't that a sweet price to pay for an elixir this *miraculous?*"

Men dipped into their pockets. Women reached for their handbags.

"You won't have a chance to buy this wonderful cure ever again. No-sir-ree! We'll be gone by dawn, so stock up now! Buy two bottles. Three or four, if you please."

Along with the show's other performers, Elena took her place at a tent entrance, cases of Doc Charlie's Miraculous Herbal Compound stacked at her feet.

"Step right up, ladies and gentlemen! One dollar a bottle! That's right. Just one dollar!"

The rush of footsteps drowned out Pop's voice. The wooden benches cleared and the aisles filled with people eager to buy their own supply of elixir. Elena had all she could do to keep up with the stream of customers, each waving dollar bills in her face.

Pop had done it again.

Toby dropped the last of the leather bags into the heap piled in Elena's arms. Her muscles strained with the weight of the night's take, but it was a strain she gladly endured.

"Sure you don't need some help, Elena?" Toby asked, picking up scattered crates once filled with elixir.

"No, thanks. The show ran long tonight, and you have plenty of chores to do yet."

"All right, then. See you in the morning."

Giving him an answering smile, Elena stepped from beneath the canvas into the night. Pop was busy with the crew as they labored to take down the tent; he wouldn't be free to count their money for another couple of hours yet.

The crowd had long since headed for home. The field where they'd staged the show was empty except for the pieces of trash strewn among the weeds, trampled flat from the evening's activities. Except for the low drone of the generator keeping the tent's lights glowing, the night was quiet.

Elena's costume provided little warmth from the night's chill, and she hurried toward the gaily painted, high-wheeled wagon she shared with her father—and the safe he'd bolted securely inside. Tomorrow, they would deposit the money into the nearest bank. Pop would be pleased to know the week's bills would be paid in full with enough left over for some much needed extras.

Upon reaching the wagon, she propped one foot on the bottom step and eased the cumbersome bags onto her thigh while she struggled to turn the knob.

A man's hand suddenly covered hers. *"Señorita."*

She froze at the heavily accented voice harsh in her ear, at the tequila on his breath.

At the menace in his presence.

She jerked her hand away and pushed against him to flee, but the cold metal of a knife's blade at her throat stopped her.

Her breathing quickened in fear. In horror. The low

nicker of unseen horses nearby indicated the Mexican wasn't alone.

And she didn't have a chance with any of them.

"You want the money, don't you?" she whispered shakily, a sickening sensation coiling faster and faster inside her at the impending loss.

"Ah, *señorita*. That is not all I want."

Abruptly he spun her about, and she scrambled to keep her balance, her arms automatically tightening around the money. He plucked one of the bags from the heap and tossed it into the darkness, to the men mounted behind them. He did the same with another, and then another.

Until Elena's arms were empty.

Dismay welled up inside her. "No! You can't do this! You can't!"

The Mexican barked an order. Horses' hooves pounded deeper into the darkness, then died away.

She was alone with him. Her chest heaved, and she didn't dare take her eyes off him. She wanted to claw him, to kick and scream at the unfairness of what he'd done.

Of what he was going to do.

But the knife's blade appeared again and prevented her. The flash of metal in the moonlight left her vulnerable and defenseless. Terrified. His long, wavy hair framed the cruel planes of his face.

Never would she forget that face.

Raw, burning fear surged up inside her. She took a step back, but he was too quick. She turned to flee him, but before she could manage it, he had her in his grip again.

Beneath the blade, the straps of her costume gave way. Elena cried out and clutched the fabric to her breasts. He snarled and pushed her to the ground. A savage yank on the red spangles ripped the garment in two. He clamped a grimy palm over her mouth, smothering her scream.

"Silencio!" He straddled her, his weight rendering her immobile. He unbuckled his belt with his free hand. "I will kill you if you make a sound, *señorita*. And not even the good doctor's medicine will help you, then, eh?"

His head lowered; long, wavy hair fell across her cheek. With his mouth and tongue upon her, the stench of his lust, his greed, filled and sickened her.

Afterward, when he left her cold and alone, Elena curled into a tight, miserable ball. And wept.

Chapter One

Laredo. Two Years Later

Jeb Carson wanted a night of hard drinking, wild whoring and a plate full of hot, American food. He didn't care in what order he got them, just that he did. There were times in a man's life when his needs overrode all else.

Now was one of those times.

He'd ridden hard through northern Mexico toward the Texas border for days. The anticipation drove him hour after long, dusty hour. He didn't analyze this need to get back to his homeland, that being in America was where he should be. Now that he was back on her soil, he couldn't wait to have what he'd always taken for granted.

He swept an assessing glance around him. Laredo's streets bustled with commerce and evening activity, signs that the place had grown since he'd been here last. No one seemed to notice a couple of strangers riding in.

"That belly of yours growls any louder, the whole damn town will know we're here."

Jeb glanced at Credence Sherman, the only person he trusted enough to call friend. "Can't help it. Got a strong hankering for a big, thick steak."

"Sizzlin' in its own juices." Creed grunted. "Me, too."

They pulled up at a small saloon at the edge of the plaza and dismounted. The interior was cool, dim and unexpectedly crowded.

Jeb preferred crowds. Easier for a man to go unnoticed.

"What'll it be, boys? A place at the bar? Or your own table?"

He glanced at the first bona fide American woman he'd seen since he left the country six years earlier. She wore an apron around her waist, and she was older than he was by a decade or so, but she was clean and her features were pretty enough to warrant looking at twice. Jeb guessed by the way she was looking back, she was available, too.

"A table," he said, letting his gaze linger. "We're staying a while."

"Glad to hear it." She tossed him a provocative smile and led them toward the last empty table, wedged in a dark corner at the back of the saloon and hidden from view by anyone walking in. By the sway of her hips, she knew what he was thinking.

And wanting.

After seating them, she left with a promise to bring back a couple of stiff whiskeys. Jeb watched her go, his blood warming just looking at those hips.

"Keep your pants fastened, *compadre*," Creed said. "She's practically old enough to be your mother."

Jeb allowed a small smile. He hadn't thought of his

mother in years, and he stifled the thought of her now. "Doesn't matter. She's warm, breathing and female."

"You've always been able to get any woman you want. Take your time. You've got all night."

"I'm not feeling choosy at the moment. Or patient."

Creed's amusement deepened. "Damn, but you're jaded."

Jeb hadn't had a woman since…when? Havana. A little Cuban beauty who'd betrayed him the next morning to her Spanish-loyalist lover.

The incident had nearly cost Jeb his life. But with a fair share of determination and guts, he had escaped the Spanish soldiers holding him prisoner. Within hours a riot erupted, and both the woman and her lover were killed.

Jeb felt no remorse for his part in it. She had double-crossed him—and the United States, which had sent him there to help her people. She'd paid the price for her treason.

As if he, too, remembered, Creed fell silent, and Jeb knew what he was thinking.

War was pure hell. And it was good to be back home.

Creed possessed skin as sun-darkened as Jeb's, his build as tall, as muscular. Fast friends from their days at West Point Military Academy, they'd formed a partnership based on mutual trust, equal skills.

And a shared passion for rebellion against rules.

Jeb had been born with nerves of steel. Few could match his thirst for risk, that ever-present flirtation with danger he found exhilarating. Only Creed was cut from the same cloth. They'd saved each other's necks more often than Jeb cared to count.

But at that point, their similarities ended. Creed was

headed home to a large, loving family, to the childhood sweetheart he hoped was still waiting for him.

Jeb had no one. At least, no one who cared if he came back or not.

The barmaid returned with their drinks, and without sparing her a glance, Jeb threw back a quick swallow. The whiskey burned the bitterness that flared inside him. A second swallow buried it altogether. He reached inside his coat pocket for a rolled cigarette, then tucked it unlit at the corner of his mouth.

"We'll head for San Antonio in the morning," Jeb said, and rooted for a match. "I figure you can take the Southern Pacific to Los Angeles. I'll send word you're arriving, and—"

"Come with me, Jeb."

"No." His mood souring again, he found the box he was looking for.

"You can find work out there. You—"

"We've had this discussion already, Creed."

"Then what the hell are you going to do?"

"I'll think of something. I always do, don't I?"

Suddenly, near his left ear, a match struck flint. He stilled. Creed's attention jumped upward to whoever stood in the shadows beside him.

"Allow me, Mr. Carson."

The sharp scent of sulfur reached his nostrils. An arm appeared. Jeb dared to dip the end of his cigarette into the flame. He drew in deep. Only then did he look to see who held the match.

A tall, burly-chested man, well into his thirties. He wore a military uniform signifying him as a field officer in the United States Army.

Jeb leaned back in his chair. He narrowed an eye. "Have we met?"

"No, sir."

"But you know who I am."

The officer glanced over his shoulder, as if wary someone was listening. "I'd like to join you, if you don't mind."

Jeb's instincts warned he wouldn't want any part of why this man sought him out. But before he could refuse, Creed pulled out a chair, and the officer seated himself.

"My name is Lieutenant Colonel Eugene Kingston." He kept his voice low. "I'm here on direct orders from Mr. Alger."

Jeb put the cigarette to his lips again. He'd been gone a long time, but he made it a point to keep up with the happenings in Washington. Warning bells clamored in his brain. "Russel A. Alger?"

"Yes, sir. Secretary of War for the United States."

Jeb exchanged a grim glance with Creed.

"We need your help," Kingston said.

"I'm not interested."

The officer's lips thinned. "You don't know what I'm asking."

"Doesn't matter. I'm not interested."

"Mr. Carson." Desperation threaded through the words, and Jeb recognized the officer's restraint to keep from showing it. "Perhaps this will convince you of the seriousness of my request."

Jeb didn't bother to look at the paper Kingston slid toward him. "How did you find me?"

The officer met his hard expression squarely. "We've made a point of keeping track of you." His glance touched on Creed before returning to Jeb. "Both of you."

"I've been out of the country for—"

"—five years and eleven months."

"Where exactly have I been, Lieutenant Colonel?" he asked softly.

"South America. Madrid. Havana. Manila. Puerto Rico. Santiago. In that order."

A slow fury simmered inside him. Suspicions surfaced. "How could you have known I'd be here at this saloon? Tonight?"

"We have sentries out watching for you at the border towns. We knew you'd arrived in Mexico on—"

Jeb's arm snaked out and he grabbed the man's shirt hard, yanking him half out of his seat. "My father sent you, didn't he?"

A sheen of perspiration formed on the officer's upper lip. For the first time, his gaze wavered. But only for a moment. "I told you. I received my orders to contact you from Mr. Alger."

"Bullshit." Disgusted, Jeb shoved him away.

Kingston righted himself in his chair and cleared his throat. "It is, er, possible that General Carson would be aware of—" he drew in a breath, clearly uncomfortable with the information he was about to impart "—of Mr. Alger's intent."

Jeb glared at him. "Tell the General he can go to hell."

"I don't think I'll do that, sir."

"And don't call me 'sir!'" Jeb snapped.

He downed the rest of the whiskey in one savage gulp, then raked a harsh glance around the crowded saloon. Where was that damn barmaid? He caught her eye, gestured for another drink. She nodded and winked. Jeb ignored her.

"The document looks legitimate," Creed said, his low

voice penetrating the storm raging inside Jeb. Creed slid the paper closer.

Because Creed wanted him to, Jeb looked at it. He recognized the presidential seal in the letterhead, the signature scrawled at the bottom.

"It's a copy," Jeb snarled. "Could be forged."

"Maybe not," Creed said, and looked at the lieutenant colonel. "And then again, maybe it is."

Kingston shook his head emphatically. "President McKinley wrote the letter to the Secretary, Mr. Carson, but it's about you. Mr. Alger has the original. For obvious reasons, of course. He didn't want to risk the information falling into the wrong hands."

The barmaid appeared, and the conversation halted. Jeb snatched the bottle of whiskey from her and refilled his glass himself.

"And whose hands might that be?" he demanded after she left.

"Mexican rebels."

Jeb breathed an oath. He didn't want to know. Or feel.

"There have been reports of revolutionary activities against the government of President Porfirio Díaz," Kingston said quickly before Jeb could stop him. "The people are angry at his tyranny. The government is getting rich off them. Díaz is taking their land, and they've found hope in a young upstart named Emiliano Zapata."

"Zapata." Jeb recognized the name of the man who was fast acquiring a reputation as a fierce fighter.

"Yes. But the United States has refused to support him, and to retaliate, Zapata's men have been robbing Americans on both sides of the border to fund their activities. One man in particular has shown himself to be unusually dangerous. His name is Ramon de la Vega."

"So?" But the name branded itself into Jeb's memory.

"We've cut off the flow of arms into Mexico, and he and his rebels aren't happy with us. Last week, they stopped a train just outside of Eagle Pass northwest of here, robbed it and killed a dozen people. The month before, they raided a small village and killed another twenty."

Jeb's fingers tightened around the glass. "How do I fit into all this?"

"President McKinley fears a major revolution is forthcoming if Zapata and de la Vega are not stopped."

"And?"

"And we feel that, with your expertise—"

"Find someone else."

"There's none other. I mean, you're highly recommended, sir."

Jeb snorted. Again he thought of his father. "I'll bet."

"By Colonel Theodore Roosevelt. Among others."

He stilled.

Roosevelt.

Jeb had ridden with the man and his troops during an attack on San Juan Hill in Santiago. It had been a privilege to be part of the initiative with them. But Jeb refused to be swayed by Roosevelt's influence, even in a matter as serious as this one.

"There are thousands of American forces who can do a hell of a lot more effective job than I can," he said. "Enlist them instead."

"Mr. Carson." Kingston slid another uneasy glance at Creed, as if imploring his help in convincing Jeb to his way of thinking. But Creed merely leaned back and crossed his arms over his chest, keeping the discussion on Jeb's terms. "Let me be frank here. Your skills as a soldier—"

"I'm not a soldier in the truest sense of the word, am I, Lieutenant Colonel? My father saw to that years ago."

"A mercenary, then."

A cold smile curved Jeb's lips. For the first time since Kingston had arrived, some of the tension eased. "That's more like it."

The officer withdrew a thick packet from inside his uniform. "Mr. Alger promises generous payment for your services and has instructed me to give you the first installment."

Jeb snorted. "And what happens to the rest of the money if I end up dead?"

"We certainly hope that isn't the case, sir."

"Let me explain something to you." Jeb took one last drag on the cigarette, exhaled slowly and crushed the ashes in a small bowl. "I've been gone a long time. In fact, Creed and I have been back only a couple of hours. As you know." His mouth quirked. "I've spent nights in muddy trenches, sweated days in mosquito-infested jungles. I've been shot at, knifed, beaten to within an inch of my life. I've been taken prisoner, and I've escaped. All in the name of my country."

Once, he thought nothing of leaving the United States behind. A foreign country—it didn't matter which one— offered danger and adventure. An opportunity to slake the hurt and rebellion gnawing inside him.

Not anymore.

He'd come full circle. He had traveled the world, seen some things no man should see and done some things no man should do. He'd evolved into a man who made his own rules and lived by them.

He was a patriot. Pure and simple.

But he'd had enough.

"Find someone else," Jeb said again, and took another swig of whiskey.

"Mr. Carson." The lieutenant colonel appeared crestfallen at the finality in Jeb's tone. "You're the best for the job. Your reputation to accomplish where others have failed is…is legendary."

Jeb smirked. Legendary? Would the great and mighty General William Carson think as much of his son?

Never.

"Jeb has plans, Lieutenant Colonel," Creed said, speaking up for the first time. "Chasing after Mexican revolutionaries doesn't fit into them."

"Plans?" The officer frowned.

"That's right." Jeb grabbed onto the line Creed tossed him. "Heading west first thing in the morning."

Going to California wouldn't be a bad idea after all, he decided. Creed's family would accept him for the man he was. No questions asked. Something his own father had never been able to do.

"Is there anything I can offer you to make you change your mind?" Kingston asked. "More money, perhaps. I'm sure Mr. Alger would understand."

"No." He slid the packet back to the officer, who reluctantly returned it to the pocket inside his uniform. Jeb stood, and Kingston did the same. "Now, if you'll excuse us. Creed and I plan to celebrate our return to this fine country."

Jeb watched the officer go. He steeled himself against thoughts of revolutionaries. Of war and death.

Of being needed.

Instead, he forced his thoughts ahead to the pleasures

that awaited him. Plenty of whiskey. A willing woman. And that thick, juicy steak.

For the first time in a hell of a long time, life was good.

Chapter Two

The Next Day

The deeper they traveled into the Texas woodlands, the more Elena became convinced they were lost.

"Pop, are you sure we're going the right way?" she asked with a frown. "We haven't seen anyone for a couple of hours now. Not even a ranch or farmhouse."

The woods seemed to be getting thicker, too. She glanced up at the sky, gauged the sun's location and determined it was more westerly than it should be.

From his place next to her on the wagon seat, Pop looked at the sky with her. "I'm sure this is right, Lennie. And if it's not, we'll still find our way to San Antonio."

"San Antonio is north. We're heading west."

"There's more than one road to take us there." He patted her knee in gentle reassurance. "Soon as we get into open area, it'll be easier to see where we're at. Don't you worry none."

But Elena *did* worry. She didn't like the eeriness she felt from being in the woods alone. A stop for some much-needed supplies had given them a late start, and the troupe had ridden ahead. She missed the protection that traveling with a large group provided.

They would be miles ahead of her and Pop by now. With every hour that passed, it seemed less and less likely they would meet up with them in time for the next show.

She sighed, leaned forward and cupped her chin in her hands. The road was rough, hardly more than a rutted trail, and it bounced the wagon continuously.

She tried not to think about being lost. Pop knew what he was doing. He always did. They'd traveled together for her entire life, and he had an uncanny knack for direction. Not once had they missed one of his shows because he made a wrong turn somewhere along the way.

But today could be the first time.

She eyed him covertly, and her worry deepened. He'd begun to show his age these past months. He tired more easily, moved a little slower. Countless hours riding on a hard wagon seat in all kinds of weather was beginning to take its toll.

Only his medicine shows invigorated him. Doc Charlie *thrived* on them.

Not so, Elena. Once, the crowds exhilarated her. The smells and sounds. The opportunity to travel and see parts of the country she might never see otherwise.

It was all she knew, this traveling, and she had grown weary of it. She longed for a home—a real *house*—of her own. With a yard and a garden and neighbors to wave to when they passed by.

She sighed again. Pop wouldn't understand this change in her. In fact, he'd be devastated if he knew.

Winter would be upon them soon. As always, they'd

find someplace to stay for the coldest months, work on new routines, and Pop would make plenty more of Doc Charlie's Miraculous Herbal Compound. Come spring, he'd be ready to go again.

Except Elena wouldn't be with him.

She simply had to tell him her decision. The sooner, the better.

Even more important, she had to convince him not to go, either. She wanted him to settle down with her so she could take care of him in more comfortable surroundings. He could even open his own apothecary. He could find plenty of new opportunities to sell his elixir. Lots of patent medicine companies did.

She drew in a breath. "Pop?"

"You've got something on your mind, Lennie. Have now for a while, haven't you?"

She straightened. Had it been so obvious? "Yes."

"If you've got a problem, we can't solve it if I don't know about it. Isn't that right?"

Elena gave him a rueful smile. Pop might be slowing down physically, but his mind was sharp as ever. "Yes."

He covered her clasped hands with one of his. "Well, go on. I'm listening."

She opened her mouth to speak, but a soft noise in the back of the wagon closed it again.

"Is that who I think it is?" Pop asked, his eyes twinkling at the timing of the intrusion.

"I'll only be a few minutes. We'll talk then, okay?"

Pop winked. "I'll be right here on this wagon seat."

Bracing herself against the jerky motion, Elena slipped through the narrow door leading into their living quarters. She pulled back a tiny curtain over the window.

Daylight filtered inward, enabling her to see the dark-eyed baby wiggling in the crib.

Her son, Nicholas. The love of her life.

"Hello, sweet-cakes," she cooed, scooping him into her arms for a hug. "You took such a good nap, didn't you?"

"Ma-ma-ma."

She kissed him on the nose. The warmth from his chubby body soaked into her as he cuddled close, laying his head on her shoulder. But in the next moment his head came up again, and he peered at her, his grin happy and expectant.

"Are you hungry?" she asked, laughing.

Nicky was *always* hungry, but then, he was growing so fast. She could hardly believe they'd already celebrated his first birthday.

She laid him in the little crib. "Mama will change you, and then you can eat, okay?"

Stepping to the small bureau where she kept his clothes in a drawer with hers, she retrieved a fresh diaper. By the time she returned to the crib, he'd already pulled himself up and was trying to climb over the rail.

Elena laid him back down again. She could barely keep up with him anymore. He had boundless energy and curiosity. He delighted in staying just a step ahead of her and found it all great fun when she was forced to give chase during his adventures.

She removed the soiled diaper and replaced it with the clean one, her fingers deftly maneuvering the pins while her thoughts drifted to when he'd first learned to climb out of his bed. They were traveling somewhere in western Louisiana, and it'd been pure chance she peeked into the wagon to check on him while he napped.

She nearly had heart failure seeing him toddle toward

the back door. His pudgy hand turned the knob, and by
the time she clamored through to reach him, he'd pushed
it right open.

A shudder went through her just thinking of it. One
lurch from the rig and he could have fallen out. He could
have become entangled beneath the heavy wheels.

He could have been killed.

Of course, they kept the door locked after that. Still,
a traveling wagon was no place to raise a child.

Settling him on her hip, she found a box of crackers
and returned to the driver's seat with Pop. She wouldn't
be able to warm anything until they stopped to build a
fire, and given their urgency to catch up with the rest of
the troupe, Pop wouldn't be stopping anytime soon.

"Why, there's my little man!" Pop boomed in greeting.

Nicky wiggled with excitement at seeing his grandfather. Pop lavished him with his usual round of kisses
against the curve of Nicky's neck, which never failed to
send him into shrieks of laughter. Pop lifted his head
and pried his goatee from little fingers, then sat back in
his seat. His eyes gleamed with pride. And love.

"What a joy that boy is to me, Elena," he said.

A surge of emotion welled inside her. She hugged
Nicky close. "To both of us."

She centered her world, her every thought and action,
around him. He'd been conceived in a few horrible moments of violence, that cruel twist of fate which had torn
apart her virginity and planted him in her womb, a tiny
human being innocent of the horrors of the outside
world.

But a constant reminder of them.

Haunted by the hate which threatened to destroy her,
Elena had had every intention of ending the pregnancy.

She wanted no part of the brutal Mexican who had shattered her innocence and tormented her with nightmares. How could she bear it?

How could any woman?

But the days passed, and slowly she healed. Pop's devastation from her attack ran deep, but he loved her unequivocally, and the rest of the medicine show troupe—the only real family she'd ever known—surrounded her with overwhelming warmth and support. From them, the people who loved her most, she drew courage and went on.

The hate eventually died, buried beneath the hope and anticipation that unexpectedly grew in its stead. She began to realize the baby growing inside her was her own, and no one could ever change that. Perhaps it was God's way of helping her survive the ordeal; she thanked Him every day for giving her Nicky.

"Ma-ma-ma."

After finishing his cracker, he patted her chest and plucked at the buttons of her blouse. He didn't nurse much these days, and the thought that he'd be fully weaned soon saddened her. Another sign of how fast he was growing and that he didn't need her as much. Pop handed her a baby blanket and Nicky's favorite stuffed horse from the basket tucked beneath the seat; she cuddled her son close, and he began to nurse.

He lifted his hand and curled his fingers around her thumb. Elena pressed her lips to the warm skin, shades darker than her own, then gently brushed the wavy hair away from his temple—hair thick and gleaming black.

Like *his*.

The differences between mother and son were striking. Nicky was as dark as Elena was fair. Someday he'd question her about it, and she'd have to tell him the truth.

Until he was old enough to understand the circumstances surrounding his heritage, however, she wouldn't dwell on them.

Instead, she marveled at what a handsome little boy he was in his red shirt and denim dungarees. As if he knew what she was thinking, he grinned up at her as he suckled, and she laughed at his impishness.

"Elena, honey."

At the seriousness in her father's voice, she darted a quick glance toward him. He stared over his shoulder at something that clearly alarmed him.

"Looks like we got trouble." He pulled his Winchester from behind the driver's seat and laid it on his lap. "Hang on to Nicky. I'm going to try to outrun 'em."

"Outrun who?" Her gaze clawed through the woodlands. "Why?"

And then she saw them. A group of a dozen or so heavily armed Mexicans. They were everywhere in the trees behind them—and gaining fast.

"Hee-yah!" Pop yelled, and slapped the reins against the team's backs.

The wagon lurched forward and picked up speed. Elena held Nicky in a death grip with one arm and clutched the edge of her seat with the other. The sound of horses' hooves pounded in her ears, but nothing matched the terror thundering inside her heart.

She and Pop had heard of these men. Fierce revolutionaries who thought nothing of robbing innocent Americans of their money and then killing them for their trouble—ordinary citizens who had little to do with their cause but who found themselves helpless against their ruthless tactics.

The rebels followed no pattern. They killed at whim, whether it was a train or a stagecoach, large or small.

Oh, God. Pop's medicine wagon would make easy pickings.

The rig careened wildly as the team sped over the narrow, rutted path, and Elena braced her feet to keep from toppling over the edge.

"Pop!" she gasped. "Slow down! We'll upset if you don't."

"I can't let them get us, Lennie!" he said tersely.

Elena heard his desperation, and her fear increased tenfold. Pop wasn't a fighter, and while she knew how to handle a gun, she'd never shot at a living thing in her life.

"They're closing in on us," Pop said.

The men were close enough now she could see the gleaming rows of bullets in their ammunition belts.

He did all he could to handle the team as they lunged and lurched between the trees. Elena ducked to keep from being struck by low branches; she held Nicky so tight he squealed in complaint.

Suddenly a group of the revolutionaries broke away and formed a blockade in the road ahead of them. A formidable row of ruthless men, fanned out and impenetrable with their rifles cocked and leveled right at them.

"Pop! Stop! You have to stop!" she cried.

To crash through the wall of men and horses was unthinkable, and her father swore in frustration. He yanked hard on the reins, and the team reared, their shrill screams piercing the air.

One of the men barked an order, and the revolutionaries took up position on both sides of the wagon. Elena's focus locked on him, and the blood froze in her veins.

Two years had passed, but she recognized the wavy-haired Mexican as if it were only yesterday.

"It's him!" she whispered in horror.

She knew what he was capable of, and if she did anything, *anything,* she had to keep him from seeing Nicky.

She averted her head and frantically covered him with his blanket. Every inch of him. And though he had long since lost interest in nursing and wanted only to sit up now that the wagon had stopped, she kept him tight against her, pressing his face to her bosom to muffle his protests.

As if the past two years had fallen away for him, too, Pop snarled and whipped out the Winchester.

"You son of a bitch!" he bellowed, and cocked the rifle.

But the leader was too quick. A shot exploded. Pop jerked and toppled from the wagon seat with a sickening thud.

Elena screamed. She bolted toward the edge of the rig, her free arm reaching for him though he was sprawled on the ground, too far to touch. Blood bloomed on his shoulder and stained the fabric of his suit coat. She cried out his name on an anguished sob. Ashen-faced, Pop gripped his leg, twisted at an unnatural angle.

"Get into the back, Elena! Now!" he grated through clenched teeth.

He wanted to spare her from seeing what would happen to him next, she knew, and the wagon's interior would help her protect Nicky.

But Elena wouldn't leave Pop. She *couldn't.* And she'd be a fool to think the men would let her out of their sight if she tried.

"You should have killed him for his insolence, Ramon," one of the men grunted, dismounting and taking the rifle, which had skidded out of Pop's reach.

"There is still time for that, eh, Armando?"

The male voices swirled around Elena. Ramon had controlled her once, left her hurting and humiliated, as helpless then as Pop was now. A fury unlike anything she had ever experienced before erupted inside her, and she spun back toward the Mexican.

"Leave us alone, damn you!" she snapped.

He dragged his glance from the side of the wagon, as if he only now had taken the time to see the colorful lettering proclaiming "Doc Charlie's Medicine Show" and his infamous herbal compound. Beneath the brim of his sombrero, something flickered in those cold, black eyes.

And a slow smile curved his lips.

"Señorita," he purred.

A thousand times, she'd heard the taunt of that word in her nightmares. Her nostrils flared with hate. "We have no money. Search the wagon. You'll see the safe is empty!"

Pop had deposited the last show's take two days ago. The rebels would be disappointed in the small amount of cash he'd kept back for them to live on until their next performance.

Ramon made a slight gesture, and one of his men circled toward the back. The locked doorknob jiggled; in the next moment a gunshot exploded. Within moments, the rebel could be heard thrashing among her and Pop's belongings.

Nicky squirmed, and his arm shot up out of the blanket. Horrified that he'd managed it, Elena snatched it back down again.

Ramon's gaze sharpened over her.

Her defiance died.

"Let me see the child, *señorita.*"

Raw fear clawed through her and stole her ability to speak, to provide a logical reason why she kept her baby hidden beneath a blanket.

Ramon drew closer. Elena's pulse pounded. She eased away from him toward the far edge of the wagon's seat.

"You know what will happen if you disobey me, *señorita,* do you not?"

Her foot found the step that would help her get down. She'd run from him. As fast and as hard as she could.

"Elena. Oh, God, honey." Still sprawled on the ground, too badly wounded to help, Pop sobbed her name, his anguish as real as hers.

But she ignored him.

Instead, she moved away from the wagon. And toward the woods. One step at a time.

Armando turned his mount as if to give chase. Ramon spoke sharply in Spanish, and he halted.

Ramon himself rode toward her, his horse's gait slow. Lazy. Calculated.

"I want to see this child you keep from me." His voice held a suspicious edge.

"No." She shook her head, her panic rising in leaps and bounds. "No, no."

Abruptly she turned, but too soon he was there, in front of her, his horse blocking her path. She pivoted and darted into the trees. Nicky squirmed and wiggled against her, and Elena shifted her grasp, her concentration momentarily broken in her need to hold him better. She stumbled over the splintered branches scattered over the ground.

By the time she righted herself, Ramon loomed in front of her again. Lightning quick, he yanked the blanket from Nicky's head.

Nicky blinked up at him.

Ramon stared downward.

"Por Dios." His glance dragged to Elena. "You were an innocent—the child's age—he looks like—"

Elena cried out and spun around, but Ramon swore viciously and grabbed Nicky by the back of his shirt, plucking him from her arms with more force than Elena could fight without hurting her son in the process.

"No-o!" she screamed. She lunged toward Ramon, her fists pounding against his thigh. "Give him back to me. *Give him back!"*

As if he were a trophy to show off to his men, Ramon turned and held Nicky up high, out of her reach. The resemblance—the thick wavy hair, the black eyes and golden skin—could not be denied.

A moment of stunned silence passed through the revolutionaries.

"Ramon, the *gringa* speaks the truth. There is no money." The rebel who had been searching the wagon poked his head out the door.

"I have found something more valuable, Diego." Ramon settled Nicky in front of him and slid an arm around his waist. "My son."

"No-o!" Elena screamed.

"Armando!" Ramon snapped. "See that the wagon cannot give us chase."

"He's mine!" She lunged toward him, her arms tugging at Ramon's thigh as she tried to pull him from the saddle. "Nicky is *mine!"*

"Ramon, she is the child's mother," Armando frowned. Clearly, he didn't approve.

"You can't take him from me!" Elena pulled on Ramon's thigh again, this time with a Herculean strength dredged from deep inside her. He jerked sideways, almost losing his seat. With a savage epithet, he regained

it again and kicked out. The toe of his boot slammed into Elena's temple. She staggered backward from the blow.

"Ma-ma-ma!" Nicky shrieked, his fear and panic rising to match hers. His arms strained toward her. "Ma-ma-ma!"

"Nicky! Oh, God! Nicky!" Frantic, Elena catapulted toward Ramon yet again, her hands reaching to grab her son, but in a blinding flash, the butt of his rifle swung toward her.

Pain exploded in her head.

She crumpled and everything went black.

Chapter Three

Jeb had one hell of a hangover.

A night with too much whiskey and too little sleep had left him paying the price for his indiscretions. The journey from Laredo north to San Antonio wasn't helping his affliction any, but Creed had been insistent.

They had a train to catch.

Taking a shortcut through the woodlands lining the Nueces River helped. At least the trees shaded the sun, and the air was cooler. Quiet. Jeb was in no mood to be civil to anyone who happened to come his way.

Even Creed knew to keep his mouth shut. Not that he was in any better shape than Jeb. Years of friendship kept them suffering in companionable silence.

The river looked inviting, though, and Jeb craved a smoke. Their mounts needed rest and drink. He figured they could spare the time, and Creed acknowledged his gesture to pull up with a curt nod.

After dismounting, Jeb stretched muscles tight from too many hours in the saddle, then led his horse to the bank. He removed his hat and raked a hand through his hair. He'd have to get a haircut when he got to San Antonio. A shave and a good, long bath. After being out of the country so long, he'd have to learn how to act in polite society all over again.

He squatted at the river's edge and caught a glimpse of his reflection on the glistening surface. He refused to speculate on what the General would say if he saw Jeb now—hungover, bleary-eyed and looking barely civilized.

The General wouldn't approve. But then, he *never* approved of anything Jeb did.

Jeb splashed cold water over his face and scrubbed all thought of his father from his mind. Cupping his hands, he poured water over his head. The liquid felt good against his scalp and helped ease the steady throb in his temple.

Creed hunkered beside him and handed him a rolled cigarette, then lit one for himself. Jeb drew in deep on the tobacco and squinted an eye toward the treetops. The silence enveloped him. The peace.

He felt the rumble of horses' hooves moments before he heard them. Creed twisted, searching for riders. Jeb saw them first, just beyond the woods.

He reached for the Colt strapped to his thigh and leapt to his feet, all in one swift motion. Instinct warned a group of men riding as hard as this one was either looking for trouble—or running from it.

He slipped behind a sycamore tree for cover and heard Creed do the same. Back pressed against the trunk, weapon raised, Jeb glanced over at him. His grim expression mirrored Jeb's unease.

Jeb gauged fifty, maybe sixty yards separated them from the riders. Mexicans, heavily armed. A dozen of them, led by one man. Jeb glimpsed a flash of red, but the trees and distance marred a clearer view, and he couldn't see what the leader held in front of him.

"What do you make of 'em?" Creed asked in a low voice.

"Damned if I know," he muttered.

One look this way would reveal the horses Jeb and Creed had had no time to hide, but none of the Mexicans bothered. Within moments, they were gone, leaving behind only cloud of dust in their wake and a bevy of unanswered questions.

Questions Jeb had no intention of answering.

"Could be those Mexican revolutionaries the lieutenant colonel was telling us about last night," Creed said, returning his weapon to its holster.

"Maybe."

But Jeb didn't want to think about Kingston or what he needed. He hadn't wanted to think of it last night, and he didn't want to think of it now. He strode toward his mount.

"Whatever those men are up to doesn't concern us anymore, Creed," he said firmly. Unable to help it, he looked across the woodlands to the path that had fallen silent. "They're heading south." His mouth curved, cold and determined. "And we're heading north."

To San Antonio. To a new beginning.

And nothing was going to keep him from either one.

At the sight of the overturned medicine wagon wedged between the trees, Jeb drew his horse up abruptly.

Creed reined in beside him. "An ambush?"

"Looks like it."

The team had been cut from their harnesses and set free. Jeb spied them drinking at the river. He removed his Colt from the holster, just in case, but it seemed whoever had attacked the wagon had left.

"I'll check the rig," Creed said. Weapon drawn, he crept toward it and inspected the interior, then gestured that no one was inside.

Still, the stark silence troubled Jeb. He urged his horse closer, saw a woman lying on the ground and half-hidden among the tree's shadows. Dread rolled through him.

A gray-haired man lay a short distance away. Jeb took in the crimson stain on his shoulder, the contorted leg. The man moaned, appeared to fade in and out of consciousness. Creed rode toward him and dismounted.

Jeb sheathed the Colt, his attention on the woman again. He slid from the saddle and knelt beside her to check for a pulse.

She was still alive. Blood oozed from an angry gash on her forehead. The wound appeared fresh, and he figured her assailant hadn't been gone long. Minutes, most likely.

The band of armed Mexicans had been riding hard from this direction. Jeb studied the wagon. It wouldn't have been easy to overturn a rig that size. But a dozen men on horses could do it. Easy.

He suspected these were the men Lieutenant Colonel Kingston told him about, revolutionaries so ruthless even the President of the United States was concerned. And Jeb suspected, too, they were hightailing it home, to the relative security of their own country against possible retaliation from this one.

He ran a grim glance down the length of the woman. Her blouse was partially unbuttoned, revealing the creamy flesh of a breast, but her clothing wasn't dirty or torn, and he made a cautious guess the band hadn't added rape to their abuses.

He slipped an arm beneath her shoulders, but she

whimpered, and he halted. Her head lolled toward him. In the filtered sunlight, he noticed the swelling from a purpling bruise on her cheekbone.

She'd put up a fight against whoever hit her, and a compassion he didn't often feel stirred inside him.

Her hair had fallen loose from its ribbon. He brushed the long, golden strands from her cheek and noted its satin texture, the warmth and softness of her skin. The delicate bone structure of her face.

Even bruised and bleeding, she was a beauty.

She whimpered again and shifted a little against him. Her lashes fluttered, as if she tried to open her eyes but couldn't.

"Easy," he said in a low voice. "You're going to be all right."

Her eyes flew open. She struggled to focus on him. He'd been knocked out a time or two himself and knew how she clawed her way out of the blackness. Suddenly she gasped and pushed away from him.

A wildness filled her expression. She twisted back and forth, searching, her features frantic. "Nicky! Where's my baby? *Nicky!*"

Baby?

He exchanged a quick glance with Creed, then reached out to touch her, to calm her, but she flinched violently, and he drew back.

"There's no baby here," he said carefully.

She stared at him. She made a sound of anguish, of unadulterated grief, and the depth of it cut right through him.

"Oh, my God. Oh, my God!" She wavered on the edge of hysteria.

"They kidnapped him?" Jeb asked, stunned.

She nodded, her fist pressed to her mouth.

"Christ."

"Elena, honey," a hoarse voice rasped.

She swung toward the man lying on the ground. She scrambled to his side and buried her face in his chest. "Pop, he's *gone*."

The man shook with a silent sob. "I know, honey." His trembling fingers speared into her hair, holding her to him. "God help us, they took him."

Her head came up again. The wild look in her face had returned. "We have to find him. We have to go *now*."

"Lennie—"

"Come on, Pop." She tugged on his suit coat. "You have to sit up. I'll get the horses, and we'll go after him."

Jeb rose and walked toward her.

"He's not going anywhere," he said quietly. Firmly. He squatted beside her. "He's hurt too bad."

Eyes as green as leaves in the jungle seemed to stare right through him. As if Jeb had never spoken, she turned away and appealed to her father again.

"I can't leave you here," she said, her tone growing more desperate. "You have to come with me, Pop. We have to find Nicky."

He moaned. "Lennie, honey. I—" He swallowed. "I can't go with you. I—I need a doctor, and—and—"

"We'll get you a doctor," she said, the hysteria creeping in on her. "After we find Nicky. I mean, we have to find him first and—"

"I might not make it, Lennie. I'm hurtin' bad."

"You *will* make it!" She drew back suddenly. "The elixir."

She darted to the wagon and disappeared inside. Jeb could hear her scavenging through the contents, and just when he thought she might need some help finding whatever she was looking for, she appeared, wielding a wooden crate.

She dropped it on the ground and knelt beside her father. Working quickly, she wrenched the top open, snatched one of the brown bottles and whisked off the cap.

"My elixir," Pop wheezed, watching her as if his life depended on it. "Yes, give me some."

She slipped her arm behind his neck to help him sit up. "Take a double dose, Pop. It'll help you feel better."

He drank the stuff right out of the container.

Skeptical, Jeb took a bottle from the case and scanned the label proclaiming the amazing benefits of Doc Charlie's Miraculous Herbal Compound.

"Medicine," Creed said as he read one, too, and pursed his lips.

Quackery was more like it, but Jeb kept the thought to himself. He'd never put much faith in patent medicines or the men who sold them—scam artists who preyed on ailing citizens who'd give away their hard-earned money for the promise of good health and a clear mind.

He tossed the bottle aside. But if this man and his daughter believed in the herbal compound, damned if he would tell them otherwise.

A trickle of the coffee-colored liquid slipped from the corner of Pop's mouth, and he ran his sleeve across his chin to wipe it away. He exhaled a slow breath and eased back down on the ground.

"Thank you, Elena," he whispered.

She recapped the bottle. "I'll get the horses. I'll be right back. We've lost too much time already."

Jeb had heard enough. His arm snaked out to grasp

her wrist, keeping her right where she was. Her startled expression made Jeb wonder if she even comprehended he and Creed were there.

"You can't take your father with you," he said slowly, succinctly. She yanked against Jeb's hold on her, but he held her fast. "You can't go, either. You're bleed-ing, and you—"

"Let go of me," she snapped.

"You need a doctor, just like he does."

"Let *go* of me!"

Again she strained against him, and Jeb marveled at her strength after everything she'd endured.

But he was still a hell of a lot stronger than she was. And he wasn't letting her go anywhere just yet.

"Ma'am, he's right," Creed said. "You need some medical attention before you—"

"They have my son," she said through clenched teeth.

"Yes," Creed said. "And we're real sorry about that. But the fact is, you're hurt bad. Both of you are."

Creed was the pragmatic one. Diplomatic and even-tempered most of the time. But impatience shot through Jeb. He cut right to the chase.

"You have any idea who you're up against?" he de-manded.

Her nostrils flared. "Yes! I do!"

"Those men are dangerous."

"They took my son, damn you!"

"They kill for the sport of it."

"I don't care who they are or what they'll do. I want him back."

Jeb clenched his jaw. Of course, she did. What kind of mother would she be if she didn't? He had to try a different tactic, convince her she couldn't go off half-cocked on the revolutionaries' trail.

"They're long gone by now," he said. "Headed for the border, most likely. You think you're going to find them by yourself?"

Green eyes flashed. "If it's the last thing I do."

"You need some help," Creed said. "Surely you know that."

Creed spoke the words Jeb rebelled against saying. Or thinking. An image of San Antonio slid into his brain. The train waiting there. California and all his newfound plans.

"My father and I will go after Nicky," she said defiantly.

A brilliant, flickering flame appeared over those plans....

"Like hell you will." Jeb released her.

She rubbed her wrist. "I'm not leaving Pop behind."

Her father peered up at her. Some of the color had fused back into his cheeks. From the elixir? Or from hope?

"Maybe these gentlemen will help us," he said.

She turned to Jeb. If she thought he looked nothing like a helpful gentleman, she didn't say it.

But her contemptuous look confirmed it.

"They could get us to San Antonio," Pop went on. "We can contact the authorities when we get there."

"No." She returned the bottles of elixir to their crate in jerky movements. "It'll take too long to arrange a search party. Tomorrow at the earliest. I won't consider it."

"Elena."

"I'm not going to San Antonio. I'm going after

Nicky. And I can't leave you behind, *so you're going to have to come with me, do you hear?*"

The shrill tone of her voice revealed the panic billowing inside her. Jeb steeled himself against it.

"Are you going to set your father's leg before you go?" he asked softly.

Her glance darted to the twisted limb.

"He can't ride a horse with a bullet wound. And that bullet needs to come out. All the blood he's lost will make him too weak to even stay in the saddle."

She swallowed.

"Guess you could have him lie down in the wagon. But then, you'd have to right it first."

Her head swiveled toward the trees, to the wagon wedged on its side between them.

"The harnesses need mending before you could even think about hitching the team. By then, it'll be dark. *Pitch-dark.* Going to be hard to find your way."

Her lower lip quivered. Jeb steeled himself against that, too.

"I can't leave my father," she said. "He's all I have, besides Nicky, and I need Pop to help me find my baby and—"

She halted, her bosom heaving. Jeb clenched his teeth.

He didn't want to be affected by this woman.

He didn't want to be needed by her.

He thought of Lieutenant Colonel Kingston. The General. He thought of honor and integrity. Of patriotism. He thought, too, of leaving the country he'd just come back to. One more time. And his plans for California disintegrated like smoke in the wind.

"I'll help you, damn it."

She gaped at him. For a long moment, no one spoke.

"Why?" she asked.

"Because I can. I've been chasing men like them for years for the United States government. And right now, you have no one else."

"I don't even know you," she said.

"You will by the time we get to Mexico." He rose and headed for his horse. "Creed can take your father to San Antonio."

"Why should I trust either of you? How do I know you won't kill us or—or something along the way?"

"Elena, honey." Pop took her hand, and she clung to his so hard her knuckles turned white. "If these gentlemen had a notion to hurt us, they would've done so by now."

"Oh, Pop." Her eyes welled with tears, and she burrowed her face against his neck. "I don't want to go with him. I want to go with you."

"Did you hear him, Elena? This is what he *does*. For the United States government."

"I can't leave you."

"Nicky needs you more than I do."

Her eyes met his, and her shoulders squared fiercely.

"All right, then." She swiped at the tears on her cheek and took in a long breath, then rose and strode toward Jeb.

He glanced down at her. The top of her head barely reached his chin.

"Tell me what needs to be done first," she said.

He untied a coil of rope from his saddle horn. "You're bleeding. We need to stitch you up."

"No. I'm fine." With her thumb she swiped at the blood trailing down her temple and smeared it on her skirt. "The next thing."

She was pale, and she'd taken a hell of a hit against the side of her face. The gash on her temple looked nasty. But neither was life threatening. She was anxious to get moving. Jeb decided not to push the issue.

"Get the horses," he said. It was the easiest of the jobs for her. "We'll need them to get the wagon back on its wheels."

She nodded and began walking toward the river.

"Then find a sturdy branch," he called after her. "Strong enough for a splint."

Her hand lifted, acknowledging his command without turning. She broke into a run, her urgency a tangible thing.

An urgency Jeb was beginning to feel, too.

He could only hope she understood all that lay ahead for them.

Dusk had nearly settled by the time they finished. The wagon sat on all four wheels again. The team was harnessed and ready to go. The old man lay on a cot on the ground, resting comfortably enough, his leg set and strapped to a splint.

But then, Elena had given him a generous dose of Doc Charlie's Miraculous Herbal Compound. Jeb figured the man was pretty much numb from it.

She hovered over him, fussing, as much for his sake as her own. But the old man couldn't be in better hands than Creed's. He'd promised Elena he'd drive all night to San Antonio, that once they rode out of the woods and got back onto the main road, the trip wouldn't take long. He even offered to send word to the rest of the troupe explaining what happened. His sincerity went a long way in appeasing her.

"You're sure about all this?" Creed asked in a low voice.

"She can't go hunting for those men alone," Jeb said

grimly. "I'll catch up with you in California later. See that the old man is taken care of before you board that train. Find him a good surgeon to take out the bullet."

"I will." Creed hesitated. "Lieutenant Colonel Kingston will want to know what happened here."

Hell, he *should* know. Jeb hoped the officer and his superiors ordered the whole United States Army to war against the revolutionaries.

"Report the incident. Just keep my name out of it," he said.

"The General will find out sooner or later," Creed said.

"Not if I can help it."

"You ever going to reconcile with him, Jeb?" he demanded. "Now might be as good a time as any."

Jeb glared. Creed knew better than to even suggest it.

"Well, you're taking a hell of a chance going after the rebels," Creed went on, glaring back. "With a civilian, no less. And a woman at that."

Jeb heard his worry. It wasn't often he and Creed disagreed. "You have a better plan?"

"Go back to Laredo. Find Kingston. Enlist his help."

Jeb considered Elena. Her baby. The hours already gone.

"No," he said. "There's no time."

"You'd both be safer."

"Going to Kingston first would be the smart thing to do," Jeb conceded. Not that Elena would have agreed to it. His mouth quirked. "But then, when have I ever done the smart thing?"

"Damn, you're stubborn," Creed said, shaking his head.

Jeb grunted. That had gotten him into trouble more times than he cared to count.

He glanced at the sky. He wanted to see Creed on his way before it got dark. And they still had to load the old man into the wagon. He pulled on his gloves.

"Elena."

Her head lifted. At Jeb's unspoken command, she bit her lip and nodded, then bent to drop a kiss to her father's forehead. "It's time, Pop."

"I know."

She pressed her cheek against his. "I'm afraid. For you. For Nicky. For all of us."

"Me, too, honey." He stroked her hair, over and over. "But you have to be strong. No matter what happens."

"I'm not sure I can be."

Her head lifted, and Jeb saw that her cheeks were wet. She stepped away, allowing Jeb and Creed to lift the cot into the wagon, taking care as best they could not to jar the injured leg unduly. By the time they came out again, she'd mounted her horse. Her gaze found Creed's.

"Thank you," she said quietly. "For everything."

He shrugged off her gratitude and climbed onto the driver's seat. "Be real careful. Both of you."

She nodded once, then tugged on the reins. By the time Jeb lifted a foot into the stirrup, she'd spurred her horse into a hard turn and galloped out of the woodlands.

Heading south.

Without him.

He muttered an oath and tore off after her.

Chapter Four

Too soon, darkness fell. The need to find Nicky consumed Elena, drove her with a relentless desperation that quelled fatigue or hunger and blinded her to the needs of her mount.

Or the man who kept pace beside her.

She kept her sights on the horizon. On Mexico. On getting to her baby as soon as she could.

But as the hours fell away, the black night grew more disorienting. A halfhearted moon barely provided enough illumination to keep them on the trail, and clouds rolling in threatened to obliterate even that.

It would be easy to lose their bearings. What if they found themselves heading north, *away* from Mexico? From Nicky?

She refused to think of the possibility. She had to find him, no matter what.

"Time to pull up, Elena. We've ridden long enough."

Elena started at the low voice of the man she knew only as Jeb. It was the first time he'd spoken to her since they had left her father in the woodlands.

"No," she said. "I want to keep moving."

But she slowed her horse to rest, just for a few moments. Again she studied the horizon. She could barely discern the narrow ribbon of water ahead, but the shimmer of the moonlight on the surface confirmed it was there. A westerly tributary of the Nueces River, she realized, and an opportunity to water the horses.

In the silence of the night, a gun cocked. Her heart began a slow pound. Slowly, carefully, she turned.

And faced the wrong end of Jeb's Colt revolver.

"It's best that you understand right now, Elena," he murmured. "I give the orders. And I expect you to follow 'em when I do."

She couldn't see his unshaven face in the shadows beneath the broad brim of his hat. But she could feel him watch her with a cold cunning that left the blood faltering in her veins.

He could kill her right now. And no one would know. Except Pop, and by then, it'd be too late.

She refused to show her fear. Her vulnerability.

"Even when a defenseless woman just happens to disagree with you?" she taunted softly.

The calm in her voice amazed her. Steadied her. She held that dark gaze of his without flinching. In the shadows, his teeth gleamed. It chilled her, that smile.

"You learn fast, Elena. That's good. Real good."

"My son has been kidnapped by a vicious band of rebels. The longer it takes to find him, the harder it will be." A sudden surge of emotion welled up inside her. "For both of us."

"Doesn't matter. We have to rest. You want to kill your horse?"

Panic flickered inside her. It was harder to control, to hide, than the fear.

"It *does* matter, damn you!" she said, her breath quickening. "I can't stop. Not yet."

"It's after midnight. We'll get an early start in the morning." The Colt jerked toward the river. "Until then, we'll camp by the water where the horses can drink their fill."

Elena hated the harsh truth of his logic and debated taking off in a hard run southward—away from him. After all, she didn't need his services, despite what Pop said. She could find her way to the nearest border town without him. She could find help with the local lawmen, too. The sheriff. The chief of police. She'd wire the governor of Texas if she had to.

But the revolver was proof Jeb intended to do things his way without a care to hers.

"He's my son," she said through her teeth. "If he were yours—"

"—I'd do the same thing." The interruption was swift. Impatient. "You'll do him no good when you're too exhausted to think straight."

"I'm not exhausted!"

"You will be when the adrenaline stops. Now let's go." The revolver waved toward the river again.

He was wrong. She could ride for hours yet. All night, if she had to. And then again all day.

Nicky would be missing her right now. Was he crying? Calling her name? He wouldn't understand who the men who'd taken him were or why she wasn't there with him. He'd never gone to sleep before without her cuddling and rocking him first.

Elena bit her lip. The need to hold him in her arms again stole the very breath from her lungs. She *ached* from it.

She sat straighter in the saddle. She had to keep looking for him, but for now she'd do what Jeb commanded her to do. She'd ride to the river so they could rest. Then, when he fell asleep, she'd slip away and resume her race to Mexico.

The plan soothed her. Gave her focus. Allowed her to turn her mount toward the water without further protest. Elena watched Jeb dismount and tie his horse to the shrubbery growing wild along the bank.

Despite her plan, she couldn't bring herself to do the same. The minutes ticking away tortured her with the knowledge she should be chasing after her son instead of sitting here going nowhere.

Jeb glanced at her. ''Get off the horse, Elena.''

She suspected he knew what she was thinking. But did he have an inkling of how much it hurt to have Nicky stolen from her?

He couldn't possibly. And what did he care anyway? He didn't even know her or her baby.

The self-pity rolled through her in waves. She blinked hard at the tears that surfaced with a vengeance, and swallowing convulsively, she swung out of the saddle.

But once on the ground, her knees threatened to give way. With the horse and the night's shadows to shield her from Jeb's view, she gripped the saddle horn and sagged against the horse's neck. She buried her face against the warm hide.

She just needed a few moments to compose herself. She needed control. Strength. She needed—

''Elena.''

She whirled toward Jeb with a gasp.

''Sit down while I light a fire.''

His fingers closed over her elbow, but she jerked free. She didn't want this man touching her when he was so determined to keep her from going after Nicky.

''I don't want to sit,'' she said. ''I want—''

''I know damn well what you want.'' In the silence

of the night, his voice sounded rough. "You just can't have it yet." He took her elbow again, but this time his grip remained firm. "Sit over here." He pulled her with him away from her horse. "I'm going to start a fire. We'll eat. Then we'll sleep. When it's morning, we'll get up, eat breakfast and ride again."

She stiffened at his condescending explanation. Did he think she wouldn't understand the routine? He released her, but she remained standing. "You needn't talk to me as if I were a child."

"I'm just telling you the way things are going to be."

She glared at him. "Have I no say in any of this?"

He kicked pieces of wood into a pile with the toe of his boot, then lit a match. In the glow of the flame, his hard eyes met hers. "No."

"Nicky is *my* son. Not yours."

"Which is why I'm giving the orders. I can think better than you can." He hunkered over the firewood. In moments, flames hissed and snapped. He straightened again. "So until you can step back from being afraid for him, I'm going to do your thinking for you."

He strode toward the horses. Clearly he considered the conversation at an end. Elena's mouth opened to protest.

But she closed it again. He didn't even spare her a glance as he bent to uncinch the saddle on his horse. Why would he bother to listen to anything she had to say anyway? He hadn't so far, had he?

She folded her arms and shivered, more from worry for Nicky than the chill in the air. Energy coiled through her, a tight, nervous energy that threatened to spiral out of control.

She began to pace. Jeb expected her to trust him. Why should she? She knew nothing about him—his skills, his background, his credibility. Yet she was supposed to let him lead her around by the nose? Place in his charge the daunting task of finding her precious child? What would he know about confronting the ruthless Mexican, Ramon?

Then again, what would she?

Jeb expected her to step back from her fear and worry. Ha! Easy for him to say. She couldn't imagine a hard man like him ever having a child of his own. How would he know what it was like? What could Pop have been thinking, insisting that she go with him?

But what choice did she have at the moment?

The first ragged edges of fatigue seeped into her muscles. With it, doubt. And a whole new round of worry raised its ugly head. What if she failed Nicky? What if she never saw him again? What if—

Elena stopped short. She had to stop thinking like this. It'd destroy her if she didn't.

"If it's any consolation, the men who kidnapped your baby are holing up somewhere," Jeb said from behind her. "Just like we are."

Elena whirled. "We have no way of knowing that."

"It's the middle of the night. Their horses have to rest, too."

Elena was no stranger to the care of them. She knew the importance of keeping them watered and fed, that a tired horse could soon be a lame one. And without strong mounts to help them flee with Nicky, they'd be vulnerable to the repercussions.

"Yes, of course." She tiredly tucked loose strands of hair behind her ear. It was an angle she hadn't thought of, and the knowledge that, at the very least, she and Jeb weren't losing ground in their chase was somewhat reassuring.

"I've got beans warming on the fire." He opened one

of his saddlebags and removed a leather case, slim and rectangular in shape. "Let me have a look at that cut on your head."

His words reminded Elena how the Mexican had struck her with the butt of his rifle. She touched her fingers to the tender spot, the blood from the gash long since dried.

She spied her valise on the ground, laid there by Jeb when he had unsaddled her horse. The small suitcase bulged from all she'd hurriedly stuffed inside—essentials for Nicky, along with a few things for herself. She lifted the lid and took out a bottle of Pop's elixir.

"What're you going to do with that?" Jeb stood on the other side of the campfire, feet spread, hands on hips. The broad brim of his hat kept his features in shadow, but the hard set to his mouth made his disapproval clear.

She latched the valise. "The injury needs to be disinfected."

"I've got whiskey for that."

"Pop's elixir is better."

"That so?"

"Yes." She refused to defend Doc Charlie's Miraculous Herbal Compound to him. Except for her father, no one knew its benefits better than she did. "I always carry some with me. I never know when it'll come in handy."

"And now is one of those times."

She ignored his sarcasm. "Yes."

Folding a washcloth, she saturated a corner, then dabbed the wet fabric against the laceration. The slight sting indicated the elixir was working its magic.

"I'll do that." Sounding impatient again, he took the washcloth from her and indicated a fallen log he'd dragged closer to the fire. "Sit."

She hesitated. She truly did need his help, she supposed. Without a mirror, it was impossible to see what she was doing.

But she fully expected his method of cleaning the wound would be as brusque as his manner. Bracing herself for it, she gave in and perched on the log warily. He straddled it, his body at a right angle to hers.

"Turn toward me," he said. He cupped her chin and tilted her face toward the fire.

It'd been a long time since she sat so close to a man other than Pop. Elena didn't move while Jeb studied the laceration first, then the swelling on her cheekbone.

She could smell horse on him. Tobacco and leather.

Raw masculinity.

The strength of it rocked her. It was all she could do to keep from pulling back, to distance herself, a defense mechanism that had slammed into place the night of the Mexican's brutal attack.

"You're going to get a shiner out of this," he said, his words dragging her from her discomfiture. He ran the pad of his thumb over the puffy skin beneath her eye, his touch far more gentle than she had anticipated. "You'll need a few stitches, too."

"We'll find a doctor for that later," she said firmly as he took the washcloth and began wiping away the old blood. "I don't want to delay finding Nicky for something so frivolous."

The washcloth halted. "Frivolous?" Jeb grunted and resumed cleaning. "The gash is deep. He hit you hard."

Elena swallowed. Jeb was right on that count.

"The wound needs to be closed," he went on. "And I never intended to waste time finding a doctor. I'll sew you up myself."

Startled, she drew back. "You?"

"Yes. Me."

The apprehension grew in leaps and bounds. "I've never had stitches before."

"You think I'll botch the job? Or hurt you?"

Her lips clamped tight. That's exactly what she thought.

He tossed aside the washcloth and reached for the leather case lying on the ground next to him. "Then you'd better understand one more thing between us, Elena. Besides following my orders, you're going to have to trust me."

He opened the container. Firelight glinted off an assortment of surgeon's tools—knives, tweezers, pliers. And an ominous-looking saw.

An amputation kit, Elena realized, taken aback.

He removed a needle and spool of thread, pulled out a length and broke it off.

"Are you a doctor?" she asked.

"Far from it."

"But you have knowledge of medicine? Surgery?"

He threaded the needle deftly. "What I've learned about treating injuries, I learned in the field." His gaze, dark and shadowed, met hers. "The hard way."

The field?

"This will hurt some," he said, distracting her from the question of how he had acquired his experience. And where. "But I'll work as fast as I can. You want a shot of whiskey first?"

"No." She reached for Pop's elixir. "I can numb the skin with this. It'll only take a few minutes." Again she drenched a clean portion of the washcloth and pressed it over the laceration.

"What's in that stuff anyway?" he demanded.

"Only Pop knows. He's never told anyone. Not even me."

"Why not?"

"Doc Charlie's Miraculous Herbal Compound is a solution he's formulated himself from the secrets of the ancients."

"The secrets of the ancients."

"It doesn't matter what the ingredients are. All that's important is the elixir is therapeutic." She considered him and the disdain he didn't bother to hide. "Your opinion of it is irrelevant."

"You'll think differently when you feel the needle going through your skin when you could've had whiskey instead."

"The pain will be minimal, I assure you."

He sighed and shifted his position. "Sit on the ground and lean against my leg."

He nudged her off the log and directed her to sit sideways between his spread knees, then eased her head back to rest on his thigh. The position gave him clear access to the laceration.

"This will only take a few minutes, so don't move." He took the washcloth from her and tossed it aside. The needle and thread hovered above her. "I'll work as fast as I can."

He brushed the hair away from her forehead and began closing the wound, each dip and pull of the needle practiced and smooth—and as pain-free as she'd predicted. Again Elena wondered about the circumstances from which he had acquired his skill. He seemed to have learned from them well.

In her close proximity, she dared to study him. His dark eyes were narrowed in concentration. Beneath her head, the muscles in his thigh were firm, his strength a palpable thing. She noted the days' growth of beard and hair hanging too long past his collar—and how they gave him a dangerous look.

Yet she felt no fear of him. Not now, at least, though the memory of his long-barreled Colt pointed at her earlier clearly indicated he wasn't a man to be crossed.

He tied off the thread, and Elena quickly lowered her lashes. True to his word, the suturing had only taken a few minutes.

"Eight stitches," Jeb said grimly, snipping off the ends with small scissors taken from the amputation kit. He straightened, and Elena pulled away.

"Thank you." She sat cross-legged in the grass and tentatively probed his handiwork with a fingertip. He'd closed the wound neatly.

He regarded her for a long moment. "Who took your son from you?"

For a little while, her worries for Nicky had faded under the distraction of Jeb's doctoring. Now they came crashing back all over again.

"I know him just as Ramon," Elena said. "And I only learned that when he and his men ambushed us."

"Why would he take the boy?"

She strove for the calm she needed to discuss the situation. Given his intention to help her, Jeb was, after all, entitled to know. "I can only speculate. Ramon never knew he existed until today."

Jeb's features hardened in suspicion. He leaned forward. "There are a hell of a lot of babies in this country, Elena. Why would he take yours?"

She tamped down the ugly memories that reared up, as she always did when they returned to haunt her. She drew in a breath. "Ramon raped me two years ago. I haven't seen him since. Until this afternoon, that is."

A moment of stunned silence passed.

"Nicky is his."

"Sweet Jesus."

"So I'm quite certain he will not give my baby back…very easily."

"No." Jeb's gaze didn't waver. "He won't."

"I don't even know who he is," Elena went on, the words pouring from her now that Jeb had turned the spigot. "That—that night, he robbed us of the entire take from one of Pop's shows. The fact that he—Ramon— came upon us today was pure chance."

"You know nothing about him, then?"

"No." She considered Jeb, his unexpected willingness to change his travel plans to go after the Mexican and his men. "Do you?"

"Not for sure."

"But you have an idea?"

"A speculation."

This time Elena waited. By the tight set of Jeb's mouth, it was easy to see he knew more than she did.

And what he knew wasn't good.

"His name is Ramon de la Vega," Jeb said, pulling no punches. "He's a follower of Emiliano Zapata. They're revolutionaries. They intend to overturn the government of the President of Mexico."

Her heart began a slow, thundering pound. "Oh, God."

"They're cold-blooded killers, Elena."

"How do you know that?" she said, her voice a hoarse whisper. Her first instincts screamed—*prayed*— he was lying to her. That he only wanted to scare her. That this whole conversation was a terrible nightmare he'd dreamed up to torture her.

But one look at his expression revealed he was dead serious.

"I've worked for the United States military a long time. I kept track of men like de la Vega."

"Why would he want a baby with him? Nicky will only slow him down. He'll—he'll—"

Something flickered in Jeb's features, something shadowy and distant, but it disappeared before she could define it.

"Probably intends to have the boy follow in his footsteps someday," he said.

"What?" she gasped.

"It's what fathers do," he added, his tone sarcastic.

"No. I won't allow it. I absolutely refuse—" Elena clamped her mouth shut. The idea of Nicky becoming a revolutionary like Ramon was so ludicrous it didn't warrant discussing further.

Jeb rose, went to the fire and stirred the beans with a knife.

"Do you have a husband?" he asked. "Someone we should notify of the boy's kidnapping?"

A husband. Elena stiffened. What man would want her? A woman with an illegitimate child, violently begotten by a man as lawless and despicable as Ramon de la Vega. A woman whose innocence had been destroyed by his lust.

"No," she said. "Besides my father, Nicky and I have no other family."

Except for the medicine-show troupe, and they'd find out soon enough what happened. She didn't want to think of the worry they'd all endure when they did.

Jeb slathered a tortilla with the beans. "So it's just you and me, then." He rolled the thin bread and held it toward her. "Name's Jeb Carson, in case you're interested."

Her stomach revolted at the thought of food. "I'm not hungry."

"Eat anyway."

His low voice held the command she'd begun to associate with him—a man who was accustomed to giving orders and having them obeyed.

She quelled the urge to refuse and took the tortilla from him. The thin bread was warm against her hand, but she didn't take a bite.

"So what's yours?" he asked, spreading beans on several more. "Besides Elena?"

"Malone. Elena Malone. My father's name is Charles."

He nodded, as if he'd already guessed that much. "The label on the elixir claims he's a doctor. Is he?"

Jeb sounded skeptical again. Her chin hiked up a defensive inch. "If you're inquiring if he has a certificate stating his degree as such, then no. But he's a doctor in the truest sense of the word, if one considers his dedication to healing people of their ills with his medicine."

Jeb grunted, his mouth full of tortilla. Watching her coolly, he swallowed. "The elixir making him rich?"

She made a sound of exasperation. "My father's financial affairs are none of your—"

"Just answer the question, Elena."

She thought of the bills incurred with every performance, of how imperative it was to sell enough bottles of Doc Charlie's Miraculous Herbal Compound to pay them. She thought of how they lived from show to show. Hand-to-mouth. And how she'd grown to tire of it.

"No," she said. "Not hardly. Why?"

"Might be de la Vega is thinking of ransom for the boy." Jeb took another bite of tortilla and beans.

Oh, God. The notion had never occurred to her.

"Costs money to buy arms and food for his men," he added. "Revolutions don't come cheap."

"I'll pay any price he demands. I'll rob a dozen banks if I have to."

"Let's hope it doesn't come to that."

"I'm prepared to do anything to get Nicky back," she said, just in case he needed reminding. "Are you?"

The last of the tortillas he'd made gone, Jeb reached inside his jacket, withdrew a small bottle of whiskey and took a quick swig. He held out the bottle to her. She shook her head in refusal, and he recapped it.

"I expect finding your son will be one of the hardest things you've ever had to do." He strode toward his saddle and bags and tossed a Winchester rifle onto the ground. A gunbelt with two revolvers. An extra Colt pistol. Several knives.

The man was a virtual weapons arsenal. She had no idea he was so heavily armed.

"That's all we have to defend ourselves with against the whole damn bunch," Jeb said. "We have a lot of ground to cover to find them. And they've got half a day on us."

Elena's spirits sank. His perception of their ability to fight their way to Nicky was, obviously, more realistic than hers.

"But am I prepared to do anything to get him back for you?" Jeb squatted next to her. The firelight splashed over his unshaven features. Dark danger emanated from him. A ruthlessness that could stagger the fiercest of his enemies. "Yeah. Ramon de la Vega will pay the price."

A sudden apprehension skidded down her spine. She

didn't yet know what Jeb Carson was capable of, if his words were false bravado or deadly conviction.

But, oh, how she wanted to believe him.

He had no more power to see into the future than she did. How would he know with any certainty that he could steal her son back from the Mexican rebel?

Jeb tossed a bedroll toward her, then laid a second one out on the other side of the fire. He stretched his lean length over it, then dipped into his pocket for a cigarette.

He seemed to have dismissed their conversation in favor of a leisurely smoke, but her stomach churned with worry. Did he expect her to relax as easily as he did?

He turned and caught her staring. He indicated the beans and tortilla she still held. "Eat up, Elena."

She eyed the food with distaste. "I don't want it."

"Eat so you can get some sleep. I want to pull out at dawn."

She rebelled against the command. Saying nothing more, she arranged the blankets. Before crawling beneath them, she tucked the tortilla into a fold where he wouldn't notice. She'd eat later when she had more of a mind for it.

She settled onto her side, facing away from Jeb, and pulled the edge of the blanket to her chin. Heat from the fire warmed her back, and she stared out into the black night beyond their camp.

Had Pop arrived in San Antonio yet? Had Creed kept his word and gotten him to a hospital safely? Was he in pain, or was he taking doses of his elixir regularly to prevent it?

And, oh, God, what of her baby? She missed Nicky so much. The ache soaked clear into her bones.

Where was he? Tears stung her eyes. Was he safe?

Was he sleeping peacefully? Was he warm enough? Had he cried himself to sleep, wanting her?

But even more important, would she ever hold him again?

Chapter Five

Jeb came awake instantly. Somewhere deep in his subconscious, his instincts told him she was gone.

He breathed a fervent oath and rolled to his feet. Only low-burning embers remained of the fire he'd lit, and he strained to see past them in the dark. Elena's blankets were still there, but no womanly form lay beneath.

He turned toward the horses, his brain racing to determine how long she'd been gone and formulating a plan to go after her. But both their mounts grazed near the river. The saddles and valise still lay on the ground, and he began to suspect she hadn't left after all.

Then where was she?

A faint nicker jerked his attention to the river again. The sound came from Elena's mare, a palomino and part of the team they'd unhitched from the medicine-show wagon. The low, throaty sound conveyed concern, the kind when an animal senses trouble for his owner.

Jeb drew closer, his hand on the butt of his Colt. Moonlight peeked through a gossamer veil of cloud cover and provided enough illumination for him to search one side of the bank, then the other. He found her huddled near the water's edge, her head bowed over her drawn-up knees, her body still.

Jeb frowned. She had probably sought out the river for the solace it could give her. He'd done the same thing himself a time or two over the years.

His hand fell away from his gun. She was thinking of her baby, he knew. Anyone could see how much she hurt from being separated from him, that the worry and anguish cut deep. She needed time to sort through the pain. To get a hold on it.

But Jeb couldn't leave her just yet. Some unseen force kept him right where he stood, watching her, his concern building the longer she sat there looking so damned alone.

Maybe he should go to her. Lend a shoulder. Listen, if she needed to talk.

But he hesitated. Emotional women left him feeling inept, even one as hurting—or as deserving of a good cry—as Elena. Hell, he'd rather face a firing squad.

She hadn't noticed him, so he lingered. Just a few minutes to assure himself she'd be all right sitting there at the river's edge in the middle of the night.

When her hand lifted to cover her mouth, when she curled in a tight ball, his reluctance to go to her slipped. She began to rock, back and forth. She didn't make a sound, not with her hand pressed to her face to stifle any she might make, and only then did he realize she didn't want him to hear.

He started walking toward her. He didn't want to scare her—she wouldn't expect him to come up behind her— but he didn't stop until he stood right behind her, an arm's length away.

He hunkered down to her level. Now that he was this close, little sounds came from behind her hand, the sobs she tried so hard to hide. His fists clenched to keep from touching her; to do so would startle her even more.

"Elena," he said gently.

The rocking stopped. She twisted around to face him, bolting to her feet in one fluid motion. Her speed and agility surprised him, left him still squatting and looking up at her.

He rose slowly. Her bosom heaved as she fought for the control that seemed so important to her.

"Elena." This time when he spoke her name, he laced his tone with a thread of command. She needed to know she didn't have to go through this alone. That she shouldn't be afraid of him. That he was with her to help her.

"I woke you. I—I'm sorry," she said shakily, her fingers swiping at the moisture streaming down her cheeks.

"You didn't. And even if you did, it's nothing to be sorry for." His voice sounded rough. Rougher than he intended, and she flinched. His mouth tightened, and he reached an arm toward her. "Let's go back to camp."

"No," she said with a shake of her head. "I will. Soon. But not yet."

"You have to get some sleep."

"I can't. I tried—"

He had expected her argument. Determined to over-rule it, he took her elbow, but she jerked away with a step backward into the river. The water seeping into her shoes would be cold and uncomfortable.

"I keep thinking of Nicky," she said, her arms folded tight against her. "How can I sleep when I don't know where he is?"

"We'll find him," Jeb said. "I swear it."

Her chin trembled. "You don't know we will. Not

really. You're just being nice and telling me that so I don't worry, but I am worrying and—''

A choking sound smothered whatever else she intended to say, and she angled her head away, her eyes closed tight. She stood in the water, her body stiff and proud but her grief tearing her apart.

It rankled that she fought to keep her pain from him. Why it bothered him he couldn't fathom, but it did, and he reached for her again.

''Don't, please,'' she said, stepping around him. ''I'll be fine in a minute or two.''

Jeb's stride was longer than hers. He took her arm and turned her toward him.

''Cry it out,'' he growled. ''Damn it, you'll feel better.''

Her mouth opened, as if she intended to argue, but instead, her features crumpled and her shoulders hunched. She sank into his chest with a strangled sob.

His arms took her in. Her body felt heavy and vulnerable against him, as if it was all she could do to hold herself upright, and something surged through him, a protectiveness, a *possessiveness,* that left him shaken and teetering on new ground.

He couldn't recall holding a crying woman before, and a fierce need arose in him to fix all that made her hurt. He vowed to find her baby and exact a fitting revenge on Ramon de la Vega if it was the last thing he did.

His embrace tightened. She shifted against him, her forehead pressed to his shirt, her fists clutching the fabric. She kept her arms folded between them, a shield, he guessed, to keep herself from touching too much of him.

Hot, violent sobs racked her body as the volcano of emotion she'd kept suppressed inside her until now spilled over in churning waves. Jeb held her until the storm had passed, until her sobs quieted into shuddering hiccups.

When even those grew silent, she still didn't move away, as if she was too spent and needed a few minutes to pick up the shredded pieces of her composure and put them back together. But, hell, he didn't care.

She felt too good to let go just yet.

Probably had to do with him being needed again, but he didn't dwell on it. Main thing was she'd purged herself of the hurt, for now, at least, and if she clung to him a little longer than he expected, that was fine with him.

"Forgive me," she said finally, her voice muffled against his shirt. "I didn't mean to fall apart like that."

"Nothing to forgive," he said, and scavenged inside his back pocket. He pulled out a bandanna, crumpled but clean. "Here. Use this. And don't tell me I'm being nice again."

She drew back, dried her cheeks and nose.

"You are, you know. Being nice," she said. "Thank you."

He grunted. "You ready to get some sleep now?"

"I think so."

"Go on, then." He gestured toward the campfire that was dying a slow death. He'd have to get it going again for her. The night carried a chill. "Take your shoes off. The leather needs to dry before you wear them in the morning."

"I know."

"I'm going to have a quick smoke, then I'll turn in, too."

She nodded and began walking toward their camp. While his attention lingered on the sway of her hips, he thought once more of her baby. Nicky. Jeb made a fervent wish the boy was still safe, that de la Vega intended him no harm.

It could be the one thing in Elena's favor, that she shared her son with him. The one thing that could keep her baby safe.

Or it could be the one thing to destroy her.

Amazingly enough, Elena slept. She didn't think it could've been possible, but when she awakened, a rosy-hued dawn flirted with the horizon.

She felt stronger. More alert. And as determined as ever to find Nicky.

Her head swiveled. She found Jeb on the other side of the ebbing fire, his back to her, his breathing deep and even. She hadn't heard him return to camp after her emotional breakdown, and memories of his compassion toward her rushed forward.

She hadn't thought him capable of it, that compassion. But his arms had been solid and warm, the strength in him a tangible thing. She had stolen from his strength shamelessly, replenished her draining supply. He'd offered, and she had taken. She'd needed him, and he had been there.

It wouldn't happen again.

She had to remain clearheaded and focused, for Nicky's sake. A hard man like Jeb Carson had no time for a weeping, sniveling woman. The sooner they could resume riding, the better it would be for everyone concerned.

Jeb would insist upon breakfast first, though. That, too, would be for their benefit. Elena had learned he had his own way of doing things—and a reason for doing them.

Well, breakfast she could do. The gnawing emptiness

in her belly concurred the plan was sound, and she quietly slipped from beneath her blanket. She rigged a fishing pole, found the skillet and coffeepot Jeb had brought. By the time she had rolled up her bed, cleaned her teeth and brushed her hair, a pair of trout sizzled in the pan.

Suddenly Jeb's eyes flew open. Sitting cross-legged on the ground, Elena nibbled on the tortilla and beans she'd rescued from the folds of her blanket and watched him. He shifted to his back, his glance jumping to where she'd lain.

"I was beginning to think you'd never wake up," she said.

He twisted and found her. He took in the snapping fire and brewing coffee, and scowled. "How long have you been up?"

"Long enough to get some things done."

"Damn." He sat up and plowed a hand through his shoulder-length hair. "I didn't hear you."

He appeared irritated, as if he'd failed in some way. Elena hid a smile. "Mothers learn to be quiet from sleeping babies."

His expression hardened. "I'm no baby."

"No." Her stomach did a funny slip. *Far from it.*

"I'm responsible for you."

"Are you?" Odd that he would think so. He barely knew her. She rose and strode toward the fire. "Since when?"

"Since I decided to help you. And I take my responsibilities seriously."

"Hmm." She poured coffee into a cup. "So if I decided to leave you and go after Nicky on my own, you'd feel compelled to come after me."

He took the cup without thanks, his dark eyes on her. "Don't even think it."

Elena found a fork and poked the fish in the skillet. The meat flaked easily. "Well, I did. Last night."

"Why?"

"Because Nicky isn't your son. He's mine." She slid one of the fish onto a plate and handed it to him. He accepted with his free hand, his coffee still untouched.

"What difference does that make?" he demanded. "Him not being my son."

"Our perspectives."

"We both want him back from de la Vega."

"Me more so than you."

"Meaning?"

She sat back, the fish steaming on her plate. "Meaning I'll stop at nothing to find him. And if our opinions differ on how we shall go about it, then—" She shrugged.

"Then what?"

"I'll do it my way. Without you."

He made a sound of derision and sipped his coffee.

"I want you to know that," she added, her chin tilting.

"You still don't trust me."

"I have no reason to."

He scowled. "You got a plan in mind?"

Elena turned and studied the road they would soon travel, the same one she fervently hoped de la Vega planned to use, too. How far ahead was he? Would she and Jeb be able to catch up with him? Or had the band's flight taken a completely different course by now?

"No," she admitted. "Except to keep riding until I find my baby." She turned back and met Jeb's shadowed eyes. "Do you?"

"Yes."

By the confidence she heard in that single word, Elena

realized he wouldn't ride without one. She set her plate down, found a long stick and handed it to him. ''Show me.''

He set his plate down, too, then began drawing lines in the dirt. ''This is the Nueces. This is Laredo and San Antonio.'' He made a pair of X's in the dirt. ''We're here, heading west. And Eagle Pass is here.'' He glanced up at her. ''I figure de la Vega will lead his men to the border the fastest way he can. But there are a dozen of them, and their horses need water. They'll stick to the Nueces as much as possible.''

Elena frowned, her attention riveted to the crude map. ''They could turn south at any point along the river. How would we know where?''

''There's a village not far from here.'' The end of the stick tapped the dirt. ''Carrizo Springs. Did de la Vega take anything with him? Clothes? Supplies for the boy?''

''No.'' Elena bit her lip. ''Nothing.'' No diapers. No milk. Not even a single cracker for Nicky.

Jeb eyed her valise, bulging from everything she'd packed for her son. He nodded and tossed the stick aside. ''Could be they'll stop there for what they need.''

''Maybe.'' A glimmer of hope formed.

''Could be, too, someone's seen them in the area. We'll go into the village, ask questions.''

The hope doubled. She pressed a hand to her chest to contain it. ''All right.''

''But we're not going anywhere until you clean your plate.''

There he was, nagging her to eat again. Elena took a good-size bite of fish just to appease him. After swallowing a second, she stood up.

''I'm full, really.'' Upon noticing his own meal was almost finished, she met his disapproving glower head-on. "I just had the tortilla and beans you gave me last night. Do you want this? I'm going to throw it away if you don't."

Elena had no intention of discarding perfectly edible food, not when it could be easily wrapped and saved for later, but she suspected Jeb's appetite hadn't been satisfied yet. Before he could refuse, she slid what remained on her plate onto his. "Eat fast, Jeb. I'm going to start cleaning up."

"Bossy, aren't you?" he muttered, but shoveled a forkful into his mouth.

"Just impatient to get moving." She took the cooled skillet in one hand, her empty plate in the other, and headed toward the river. Kneeling at the bank, she scrubbed the dishes with sand, then rinsed them.

"You want any more coffee?" Jeb asked, approaching her with the pot. He'd rolled up his shirtsleeves, and she noted how tanned his skin was.

She shook her head and reached for a towel. "One cup is all I usually have in the morning."

"Most days, I can't get enough of the stuff." He emptied the last of the brew into his cup, then set about washing the pot and his plate.

Covertly Elena watched him work, taken, in spite of herself, with the way his hands moved. He had lean fingers, blunt tipped and long. Thick veins corded his forearms. For the second time that morning, she thought of how strong, how warm, those arms had been. And how comforting they'd felt when he had held her last night.

When he had held her. Her pulse dipped, and she jerked her glance away. Grim reality rolled into her. She should never have let him do it. If she hadn't broken down, if she had retained control of her emotions, the embrace never would've happened.

Nor would she be thinking of it now. Again.

It had been infinitely worse after her attack. Men she didn't know...shadows and darkness...

They'd left her terrified. Ramon de la Vega had done that to her.

She had lived through a hell filled with panic and fear after he raped her. Inch by inch over the past two years, she had managed to claw herself out. But sometimes, when she least expected it....

"You okay, Elena?" Jeb asked, frowning.

A long moment passed before she allowed herself to speak. "Of course," she said and rose. "I'll make sure the fire is banked. Whenever you're ready, we'll leave."

She forced herself to walk at an even stride back to camp. She couldn't think about Jeb or how he made her feel. To dwell on him would distract her from finding Nicky, and she refused to allow anything to do that.

After dousing the fire, Elena found the tack Jeb had hooked on a tree trunk. The horses were hobbled side by side, and she stepped between them to drape the reins over her mare's back. She held the horse's head with one hand while she slipped the bit into the mouth with the other, all the while keenly aware Jeb had returned to camp.

Too aware.

The clank of metal against metal revealed he'd packed the dishes with the rest of his gear. She forced herself not to listen to him moving about. She concentrated instead on slipping the bridle over the mare's head, adjusting the headpiece around the ears, buckling the throatlatch, tasks she could do as much by feel as by sight, having done it a thousand times over throughout her life. Now, however, she gave the job her full attention, as if it were the first time.

"Elena."

The low sound of Jeb's voice, the unexpected feel of his fingers on her chin, startled her. She pivoted, and his nearness startled her even more.

He stilled, then drew his hand away slowly. "Easy," he said. "Just want to check those stitches of yours. That's all."

Elena hadn't given them a single thought all morning. She was foolish to be so skittish. Or was she?

His eyes—dark, shadowed, long-lashed—watched her. A rough beard stubbled his cheeks. If she had thought him dangerous last night, seeing him now, in the light of the morning, convinced her of it.

He was capable of great violence. She felt it in him, the power he kept coiled inside until he allowed it to be unleashed. But he didn't move, as if he waited for her permission to do so.

Somehow that reassured her.

He seemed to sense when her apprehension crumbled, and his hand moved to lift the hair on her temple. His head tilted in perusal.

"Looks good," he said. "Better than I expected."

"My father's elixir," she said, not moving, not looking at him.

"The secrets of the ancients."

"Yes." She heard his sarcasm and ignored it.

Her hair settled back into place, but he didn't move away. For a wild, irrational moment, neither did she.

Jeb's scent surrounded her. The vibrancy of his maleness. Refusing to be swayed by it, she stepped around him and began saddling her horse.

The rain that had threatened the night before never materialized, but instead left a blanket of humidity that hung thick and heavy over the state of Texas.

Jeb lifted his hat, swiped his arm across his forehead. The oppressiveness reminded him of northern Africa, when he spent a brief stint in the Sahara. There he had learned to live in the heat. Survive in it. Enough days of sweat and blazing sun forced a man to cope or die trying. He donned the hat again, tugged the brim to its usual place low over his forehead and glanced over at Elena.

She didn't complain, but he knew the heat was getting to her. Perspiration dampened her blouse to her back; her cheeks were flushed pink. She wore a scarf over her head, but the thin fabric did nothing to protect her face from the wind or sun. She needed a real hat—one as broad brimmed as his. When they reached Carrizo Springs, he intended to buy her one.

She dabbed a handkerchief to the open vee of her blouse. She'd undone a couple of buttons to catch what little breeze they had, but she dabbed gingerly as if she hurt somewhere, had for a couple hours now, and that concerned him.

"You okay?" he asked finally.

"I'm fine."

He didn't believe her. "You want to stop again? There's a small stand of trees—"

"No, no. Thank you, but let's keep riding. The village isn't that far."

"It's far enough if you're sick."

She glanced at him then. "I'm not sick."

"You're sure about that?"

It seemed to Jeb her cheeks grew a little pinker. She turned her head, avoiding his scrutiny.

"My son is still nursing," she said. "He's been weaning himself so he doesn't nurse often, but he always does at night, and—'' she lifted a shoulder helplessly ''—I'm feeling a little—''

''Full,'' Jeb said, and pursed his lips.

''Yes.''

He didn't have an inkling how she'd go about rectifying the situation. No baby. No suckling. How the hell was she supposed to get her milk out?

Infection could set in. Mastitis. It happened in animals all the time.

He'd always considered himself a problem solver. Put him in a difficult situation and he'd find a way out. But with Elena…

Maybe he should get her to a doctor. Find a midwife or something. Another female would know what to do.

''Your father's elixir,'' he said, the thought coming to him like a thunderbolt. ''Would that help?''

God knows she believed in the stuff. A cure-all for everything, or so it seemed. But the startled way she looked at him revealed that the idea wasn't as helpful as he hoped.

''I don't think so.'' She shook her head. ''I'm not sick.''

''Yet.'' She worried him. ''What do you want me to do?''

''You?''

She looked so taken aback at his question, amusement rolled through him. He suppressed the burgeoning fantasy of how he'd find a cure for milk-swollen breasts. Or that she'd interpreted his offer as such.

''Yeah, me,'' he said.

''Nothing,'' she said quickly. Her chin lifted. ''I just need some hot packs is all. Perhaps when we get to Carrizo Springs, we could spare a few minutes—''

''You'll get them.''

She actually looked relieved. Did she think he'd deny her?

Annoyed, he scanned the horizon and discerned the shapes of miniature rooftops. The village was just ahead. If Elena felt compelled to delay going after her son for even a little while, she must be feeling damned uncomfortable.

He frowned. Because of the delay, she'd be more anxious than ever to find him. But to do that, Jeb needed information, information he hoped someone in Carrizo Springs would provide.

Chapter Six

Just as when he arrived in Laredo a couple of days earlier, the changes that had taken place while he was out of the country amazed Jeb. Carrizo Springs had flourished from a village into a little town, complete with a courthouse, a couple of churches and a small business district. More people, too. He could slip in with Elena without drawing too much attention.

He gestured to pull up in front of a grocery store. Next to that, a druggist had set up shop. Between the two, he'd find her some help for her delicate condition.

Jeb dismounted, tied the reins to a hitching post. He didn't bother to hide his curiosity from all that transpired around him; instead, his gaze floated lazily, just as anyone's would. But beneath the cool facade, he studied anything that moved. If someone was watching for them, someone like Ramon de la Vega, he couldn't see it.

He grasped Elena's waist and swung her from the saddle. He didn't step away once she was on the ground, but used his body as a shield, keeping her between him and her horse—and hidden from speculative stares.

"Let me do the talking when we get inside," he murmured, noticing for the first time how long her lashes were, how thick and golden. "Do anything I tell you to, y'hear?"

Those lashes lowered. He wondered if his closeness flustered her. She pulled off her scarf and shook her hair free.

"Sure. But within reason, of course." She finger-combed the long strands, caught the wind-tossed tendrils. "Where are we going?"

"The grocery store first. The druggist, only if we have to. And I'm not going to tell you to do anything unless I have a damn good reason for it. So you'd better do it."

Her eyes lifted, met his. He sensed her impatience, the desperation that never left her.

"One more thing," he said. He studied her face, the fine structure of her bones, the smoothness of her skin. "Stop being so skittish. Act like we know each other... well."

The pulse in her throat leapt. "Like I said, Jeb. Within reason."

His lips thinned, but he slid his hand to the small of her back. He wasn't going to argue the issue, not here, not now, but she'd have to accept they were going to do things his way—or not at all.

At his touch her muscles tensed, but he didn't give her a chance to move away from him. He nudged her toward the boardwalk and through the mercantile. The door swung closed behind them.

He paused a moment to allow their vision to adjust. The dim interior was a welcome respite from the day's heat and bright sun. Pungent scents surrounded them—onions, chilies, pickles, garlic. One corner of the store contained dry goods, another hardware. A glass-covered case carried an assortment of pistols, revolvers and rifles.

Next to it, a showcase for perfume and jewelry. The place carried just about anything people around these parts could want.

A cross-looking storekeeper stood behind the counter, his attention absorbed by the shoppers who stood in line, waiting for their purchases to be tallied. At Jeb and Elena's arrival, he glanced up with a scowl, then turned and yanked back a curtain leading to the back room.

"Margarete!" he yelled. "Customer!" He fixed his frown on Jeb again. "She'll be right with you."

Jeb acknowledged him with a curt nod. "No hurry."

"Hell, that girl don't know how to hurry. She's lazy as they come." His scowl deepened, but he returned to the numbers scribbled on the pad in front of him.

Elena turned toward Jeb with a sniff. "His manners certainly need polishing, don't they?"

"Forget him," Jeb muttered. He strolled to a table stacked with women's straw hats and chose one with a wide pink ribbon and chin cord. "Try this on." He put it on her head, pulled the cord snug under her chin. Bending a little at the knees, he squatted down to her level and considered the fit.

"How does it look?" she asked.

Her hair flowed from beneath the crown and tumbled over her shoulders, hair that was rich and golden and so shiny he had a sudden curiosity of how the strands would feel sliding between his fingers. He almost regretted having to buy the hat and cover up all that hair.

"Looks good," he said, and straightened.

Yeah. Elena looked real good in the thing.

"It's nice." She found a mirror and contemplated her reflection.

"It's necessary."

"Do you want to buy it?" A young girl of about

seventeen years of age walked toward them from the direction of the back room, her arm extended to take the hat from Elena.

She was pretty enough, Jeb thought, her chocolate-brown hair done up with fancy curls around her face, but given the paint job she'd done on her lips and cheeks, she had to work at it.

"Yes," he said.

"But we don't even know what it costs, Jeb," Elena said in quiet protest, removing the contrivance from her head and looking for a price. "I didn't bring much money with me."

"Doesn't matter," he said firmly. "You need one. And I'm buying." He turned back to the girl, Margarete. "The lady isn't feeling well. If you could help her, I'd be much obliged."

Margarete eyed Elena suspiciously. "What's the matter with her?"

"My baby—"

"She lost him," Jeb interrupted. He didn't want Elena revealing too much information. If Margarete thought her son had died, that was fine with him. "And she's got too much milk."

The girl eyed her with uncertainty and a notable lack of sympathy. "There's nothing *I* can do about that."

It was all Jeb could do to keep his irritation in check. "She knows what needs to be done. Just help her do it."

"If you could boil a little water and find some cotton towels for me, I'd be most grateful," Elena said quickly. "I'll pay you for your trouble."

The girl's glance bounced between them. "All right," she said with a sigh. "We have a room you can use. Follow me."

The storekeeper was busy measuring a bolt of cloth. Margarete led them behind the counter and through the curtain to the back room, living quarters, it appeared, for him and his family. Jeb wasn't ready to relinquish Elena to the girl's care until he knew for certain Elena would be properly tended to, and he slipped behind the curtain with them.

Margarete opened a door. A barely made bed sat along one wall; on the other, a cluttered bureau and washstand.

"This is my room," she said, and indicated a chair for Elena to use. "I'll go to the kitchen and get what you need."

"Thank you," Elena said.

The door closed behind her. Elena suddenly whirled toward him.

"I did *not* lose my son," she hissed, thumping a finger against Jeb's chest with every word. "He was *taken* from me, and I will get him *back* as soon as I possibly can."

Jeb had never seen her so riled. He pressed a thumb to her lips. "Quiet," he said. "These walls are thin."

She pushed his hand away. Her eyes welled with tears. "She thinks Nicky died. He's *not* dead. I'd know it if he was. I'd *feel* it."

"So let the girl think otherwise."

"Why?" Elena demanded, blinking furiously. "What does it matter what she thinks?"

Jeb blew out a breath. He was making a mess of things and had to scramble to right them. "It's not uncommon for a baby to die. But having one kidnapped is fodder for gossip. I don't want folks talking about us now, or after we leave. Ramon de la Vega could catch wind of it."

She bit her lip and glanced away. Gripping her chin, Jeb forced her to face him again. "Understand?"

A long moment passed.

"Yes," she said.

He wondered if she truly did. His hand fell away. "If de la Vega knows he's being chased by me—by us—he could hole up somewhere so deep it'd be years before we found him."

She paled. "Years?"

"Mexico is full of mountains. And it's a hell of a big country. He's got followers who'll protect him. He'll disappear, for his son's sake."

"Oh, Jeb." She raked a trembling hand through her hair.

The pain and anguish in those two words tore at him. A sharp need to take her into his arms burst inside him, but before he could move to satisfy it, the door flung open.

"Here are the things you asked for," Margarete said, strolling in with a bowl of steaming towels hooked in her arm. "You want anything else?"

"Yes," Jeb growled. "Privacy."

She set the bowl down with a thunk. "You can stay here as long as you want, I guess. Pa's got things for me to do, so I won't be in here for a spell anyway."

"Thank you," Elena said.

Margarete left and Elena waited, obviously expecting Jeb to follow her out.

"I'll be in the store if you need me," he said.

She didn't look like she needed him at all, not for whatever she had to do to ease her discomfort, and certainly not now that she'd gotten a hold on her feelings.

"I won't be long," she said.

He pulled the door closed behind him and found Margarete tending to a shelf of untidy fabric bolts.

"Check on her now and again," Jeb ordered. "See that she's all right."

The girl glanced at him, then at the curtain. He suspected she thought Jeb could check on Elena himself, but she shrugged. "Sure."

Two men were sitting around a barrel. Whiskey, if the spigot was an indication, and since he had a few minutes to kill, Jeb headed over to join them.

One of the men dozed in his chair, chubby legs stretched out with ankles crossed. A glass of the amber liquid perched on his portly belly. He sported a snarled beard that fanned over his chest, and as dusty and disheveled as his clothes were, Jeb decided the old geezer had been planted in his seat and taken root.

A second man sat next to him, this one as tense as the first one was relaxed. He looked Apache, but wore American clothes. Ex-military, Jeb noted. Army blue, with the trimming long since torn off. He glanced up at Jeb's approach.

"Mind if I have a drink?" Jeb asked.

The Apache shrugged. "Grog's free for the taking."

"Generous of the owner," he said, just to make conversation.

The man grunted. A tin cup hung from a hook on the barrel. Jeb filled it halfway; he took a swallow and felt the familiar burn down his throat.

A small window rimmed with dirt provided a view of the street. Wagons drove by. Buggies and horses. People strolled on the boardwalk. As far as he could tell, it was business as usual in Carrizo Springs.

Jeb needed to find out if de la Vega had passed through this morning or last night. He took another swig of whiskey and scanned the store. Several customers remained, but one woman took up the storekeeper's time—and patience. She appeared fussy, undecided on a leather belt she planned to buy. The Apache watched them, the tension in him palpable.

Jeb wondered at it. "You from around these parts?"

"Just traveling through."

"Makes two of us." The Apache wouldn't have been in town long enough to know if the revolutionaries had stopped in, then. "What brings you here?"

"Business." A stream of tobacco juice landed in a pan of ashes at his feet.

Jeb sipped again. The Indian didn't look prosperous or trustworthy. But hell, he could trade with the devil for all Jeb cared.

"Will that be everything, Mrs. Pennicutt?" the store-keeper asked. The array of belts they'd been looking at landed in a box he hurriedly shoved back onto a shelf.

"Yes, thank you, Henry. Norbert will look quite the dandy on his birthday."

"Margarete!" the storekeeper snapped, striding back to the counter. "See to Mrs. Pennicutt. There's something I got to do."

"Yes, Pa." She abandoned the fabric bolts and dawdled her way to the counter. Mrs. Pennicutt rooted in her purse for payment.

The Apache's eyes met Henry's. Without a word or a glance in anyone else's direction, he rose and left the store. Henry riffled through a drawer, removed a key and left the same way.

"Humph. Them two's up to no good," the old man muttered, one eye squinted open, as if he'd been peeping at them all along.

"That so?" Vaguely curious, Jeb stepped to the window but couldn't see anything. "Why do you say that?"

"The Injun comes through every now and again. Hauls somethin' he don't want no one to see." Mrs. Pennicutt left, her purchase wrapped and clutched to her bosom. "My name's Roy Marsh, in case you're interested."

"Roy," Jeb said with a curt nod and declined to give his own. "A store like this, the owner would do business with lots of different suppliers," he said. "Could be the Apache is a dealer of some sort."

"He's a dealer all right."

The disgust in Roy's tone challenged Jeb's curiosity further, but he shrugged it off. How the storekeeper stocked his inventory—and with what—had nothing to do with him. Or Elena.

Another time, another place, he might have pursued the oddity to get the answers he wanted. But not today. And considering his intention to move to California as soon as he could, not ever again.

The store had emptied of customers. Margarete meandered back to the dry-goods section. Jeb gestured to her to check on Elena instead and, with a roll of her eyes, the girl complied.

"Don't believe me, do you, boy?" Roy demanded. He straightened in his chair with great effort, reached toward the barrel's spigot and topped off his glass.

"Doesn't matter to me one way or the other."

"I'm in this store every dang day. I see what comes in. What goes out. And who. I'm tellin' you, what he's buyin' from that Injun ain't on any of these shelves."

Jeb threw back the last of the whiskey, returned the cup to its hook and wondered if the man was delusional from too much whiskey.

''What's it to you, old man?'' he asked.

A faraway look stole into the rheumy eyes, lucid in spite of the liquor. ''Place used to be mine. Started it in an ol' shanty back in '66. Took me thirty years to build up to the size it is today. My store was the only mercantile in town then, just as it is now. If folks can't get what they want, they got no place else to go.'' He roused himself with a shake. ''Henry bought me out, but lets me sit here as much as I want. Hard to let go, if you catch my meanin'.''

Jeb couldn't imagine devoting his entire life to one endeavor. Not after the past six years, anyway, when he'd moved around so much he rarely slept in the same place twice.

He'd wanted to, once. Devote his life to one thing. But the General had destroyed that dream.

''Mr. Carson?'' Margarete's voice yanked Jeb from his musings. ''Your wife needs a fresh blouse. She asks if you'll bring her valise in.''

He nodded, not bothering to correct her assumption of his marriage to Elena, and strolled outside. He had no desire to be married anyway. And what woman would want him?

Not Elena. Not if she knew what kind of man he really was.

He shook off the thought and paused on the boardwalk. After the dimness of the store's interior, stepping back into the sunshine took some getting used to. He tugged his brim lower and slid his glance up one side of the street, down the other. Not a sombrero in sight.

He strode toward Elena's mare and untied one of the straps securing the valise to her saddle. A narrow alley separated the mercantile from the druggist's shop, and as he started on the second strap, he noticed the Apache and the storekeeper on the far end.

Strange place to do business.

This time his curiosity refused to be quenched. Jeb slipped into the shadows, out of sight from anyone who might be looking his way. The men spoke in low tones, too low for him to hear, but he could see Henry reach into his apron pocket and withdraw a wad of bills as plain as the sun in the sky.

The Apache counted each one before stuffing the bundle into his boot. Henry dropped the key he'd taken from the drawer into the Indian's palm and pointed into the distance, to a location Jeb couldn't discern. The Indian strode away.

Jeb debated going after him. But within moments, the low rumble of wagon wheels made the decision for him. The rig lumbered past the entrance to the alley, giving him only a fleeting glimpse, but whatever the team hauled, they labored from the weight of it. He waited until the sounds died away and the back door of the mercantile slammed shut before inspecting the tracks the wheels made. The depth confirmed his suspicions of a heavy load.

Well, hell. Nothing he could do about it, not with Elena waiting on him. He returned to the street, tilted his head back and read the sign overhead: Bell's Groceries and Fine Sundries. Henry H. Bell, Proprietor.

He committed the name to memory. It was a habit of his, remembering details. Might be he'd have to recall this one some day.

Valise in hand, he reentered the store and strode toward the back room. Margarete was nowhere in sight, and he didn't give the storekeeper a backward glance. He knocked once, then walked in.

Elena sat on the bed, her back to him. She wore only her chemise with her skirt, her blouse tossed aside in favor of the clean one she waited for. The chemise had been unlaced. One strap fell over her shoulder, and the garment sagged against her spine.

He closed the door. His eyes clung to the bare curve of her shoulder and wouldn't let go. She was almost completely dressed, but the part of her that wasn't stirred his blood.

"Thank you, Margarete," she said, half turning toward him. "I—oh, Jeb!"

She bounded off the bed with a squeak of horror, one hand yanking her chemise closed while the other snatched her blouse from the mattress and pressed it to her chest, right over the warm towels she was using. "I thought you were Margarete!"

The shock in her tone amused him. "I know."

He walked closer and set the valise on the bed. She took a hasty step back.

"What are you doing here?" she demanded.

"I couldn't find Margarete. And you wanted your valise."

"You shouldn't be in here."

"No rule against it." And if there was, he wouldn't care.

She backed up until she couldn't go any farther. "Get out."

She looked less flushed now that she'd been out of the sun for a while, but the rising color in her cheeks revealed the slow burn of an inner turmoil.

"You're acting like you're afraid I'm going to hurt you," he growled. He moved closer, defying that turmoil. "Are you?"

She angled her face away and drew in a quick breath. "Yes," she said. "No, I mean. No, not at all."

He reached out and gently lifted the hair off her shoulder, his fingers lingering over the satin texture as he brushed the strands aside. The chemise's strap slipped down, gifted him with a glimpse of her upper breast before she jerked it back up again.

"I could, I suppose, hurt you," he mused. "But if I was so inclined, I would've done it last night. Or this morning. Maybe this afternoon. Any damn time I wanted to before now."

She shifted her stance, as if she were ready to bolt, but he kept his body in front of her, preventing it.

"You're safe with me, Elena." It became imperative he convince her of that. He had no intention of freeing her until he did. "All right?"

She avoided looking at him. "All right."

Still he didn't move. "You feeling better yet?"

"Yes. The hot packs helped. My…milk let down so, yes, I'm feeling better."

"Good."

"I'll be ready to ride again as soon as you leave."

She looked at him then, her features accusing him as the reason for delaying her. Reluctant to, he stepped away.

"I'll wait for you out front," he said and remembered the hat he intended to buy her. "You want any extra groceries? Might be awhile before we see another town."

She adjusted the paraphernalia she clutched to her chest. "You're low on coffee. And if you want to get some vegetables, I could make a stew for us."

He realized he'd buy her anything she wanted. "That it?"

"A few tins of peaches? For dessert."

He filed the items in his head and marveled at her efficiency.

"Now, please go."

Another time, another woman, he would've rebelled. He had little tolerance for being told what to do by a high-handed female.

With Elena, it was different. He left, not because she'd told him to, but because she was so anxious to find her son and he was keeping her from it.

In the narrow hall outside her room, he noticed Margarete eating a sandwich in the kitchen. She stared out the window, her expression wistful. She'd forgotten all about Elena, he was sure, so deep were her thoughts. No wonder her father called her lazy.

He pulled back the curtain and reentered the main room. After making his purchases, he paid his bill, leaving a little extra for Margarete's help, then packed the supplies on his horse. Elena still hadn't appeared, and he was left with the unfamiliar task of waiting on a woman.

He leaned a shoulder against a wooden post and lit a cigarette. Behind him, the door slammed.

"Saw somethin' out there, didn't you, boy?" Roy said. He carried a checkerboard under his arm. Evidently it was time for him to head home.

"Nothing to get excited about," Jeb said. "No proof of anything."

"There usually isn't. That's how they get away with it." A loud exhalation revealed his disappointment. "Been a pleasure talkin' to you."

He began to shuffle down the boardwalk. Jeb contemplated the old man's stubborn curiosity about the storekeeper's business dealings.

Could be his need to know was just natural, since he once owned the place. Or maybe he had a grudge that needed satisfying. Still, if the man spent his days sitting in the store, no one would know better than he what transpired in Carrizo Springs.

After all, folks needed to eat. Henry Bell's mercantile was the only one of its kind in town. They'd come here for their groceries and sundries. Especially someone with a baby who needed milk, diapers, soft food to eat.

"Hey, Roy?"

The old man slowed, turned back to Jeb.

"You ever hear of Ramon de la Vega?" Jeb asked. "A revolutionary. Supports Zapata and his cause."

"Humph. Who hasn't? He and his men have folks scared plenty with their killin' and thievin'." The rheumy eyes narrowed. "Why?"

"Just wondering if he's been around, is all."

"Nope. I'd know it if he was. All of us would."

"Reckon so."

"Anything else you been wonderin' about?"

"That's it."

His hand lifted in a wave. "Good day to you, then."

Roy resumed his trek down the boardwalk. Pensive, Jeb scanned the Texas horizon and the land it encompassed. Land that sprawled for hundreds of miles in any direction.

The revolutionaries were hiding out there.

Trouble was—where?

Chapter Seven

Elena slid the last of the chopped vegetables into the pot of stew, added salt and pepper and replaced the lid. It'd be at least another half hour before they ate dinner. What was she supposed to do until then?

Dusk would settle soon. She'd resisted stopping to make camp when there was still daylight left in which to ride. Their stop in Carrizo Springs had cost valuable time, but there'd been no help for it.

Tomorrow, though, they would cross the Mexican border. Surely, once there, they would learn something of the revolutionaries' whereabouts. And if they didn't…

Her disappointment had been swift and cutting when Jeb told her there'd been no sign of them in Carrizo Springs. She knew, then, de la Vega was too shrewd. Stopping in the little town would've been the easiest, most logical thing to do. Carrizo Springs had whatever he might need for Nicky.

The worry nagged at her that her baby wouldn't be properly cared for. That she and Jeb would fail to find him quickly, that de la Vega was far too cunning for her, or Jeb, or the entire United States. What if he just disappeared with her son, as Jeb feared could happen?

The worry worsened every hour she was away from him. It was killing her, this worry, and she simply couldn't let it. What good would she be for Nicky then?

Leaving the pot to simmer, she strode toward her horse. Pop had always claimed plenty of honest work was as therapeutic as his elixir, and she rummaged in her valise until she found the leather-backed brush she used to groom her horses. Jeb had already removed the saddles and hobbled their mounts next to a stalwart cottonwood, and with long front-to-back strokes, she slid the soft bristles through the mare's coat, over and over again, until the mare nickered in pleasure.

"Feels good, doesn't it, girl?" Elena said, patting the long neck. She thought of the endless hours of riding they had put in today, of how the mare had pushed on in the heat, a credit to her loyalty and docile nature. "You deserve to be pampered tonight, don't you?"

The mare swung her head toward Elena and nickered again, as if she agreed. Elena smiled and resumed the brushing, taking comfort in the familiarity of the routine.

"You've got a way with her," Jeb said. "She likes you."

He approached from the stream where he'd bathed while she cooked supper. He wore no shirt, but carried a clean one in his hand and was in no hurry to put it on. He was bootless, too, his hair wet and combed back without a care to the neatness of it.

Her brush strokes faltered. His masculinity overwhelmed her. He made her feel flustered and unsteady.

She didn't like feeling flustered and unsteady.

She avoided looking at him and bent to the task of grooming the mare with renewed vigor.

"I was there when she was born," Elena said. "I've raised her since she was weaned."

"That so?" He paused a few feet away.

Elena moved to the other side, away from him.

"Yes," she said. "I've trained her to perform in my father's shows. She's gentle enough that I can ride her with Nicky in my lap."

Jeb tossed aside his shirt, took a metal pick from his saddlebag. Angling his body and lifting one foreleg, he began cleaning the mare's hoof of dirt and stones.

"Tell me about your father's medicine show," he said.

Elena dared a quick look in his direction. His interest surprised her. "Have you ever been to one?"

"Never."

"That's a shame, then. They're fun."

His mouth quirked. "If you say so."

"They are." She refused to stoop to his level of sarcasm.

"You have a part in it?"

"Yes." She could feel his expectant gaze on her while she worked the bristles back and forth, side to side.

"You going to tell me about it, or am I going to have to drag every word out of you?"

She finished her brushing and glared at him over the horse's back. "Are you going to listen proper, or are you going to be snide?"

"Snide? Me?"

He looked so charmingly taken aback, she had to struggle to hide her smile. "Yes, you."

"I wouldn't have asked if I didn't want to know."

She'd forgotten her decision not to look at him. Taking a soft grooming cloth, she wiped down the mare's coat and gave all her attention to it.

"Well, some medicine shows are more elaborate than

others,'' she said. ''Pop has always strived to bring his audiences the best entertainment he can.''

''Such as?''

She shrugged. ''Song-and-dance acts. Juggling. Comedy. Animal tricks. Sort of like a miniature circus.''

He finished cleaning the last hoof and moved over to his horse to do the same. She finished wiping down her horse, took her grooming brush and repeated the process on his.

''As for my part in the shows, I've done just about everything there is to do, one time or another. My specialty is trick riding, though.''

''Yeah?'' He seemed intrigued at that.

''I've performed in the show since I was five, so I've been doing fancy tricks a long time.''

''Five years *old?*'' He gaped at her in amazement.

''Yes. It's all I've ever known,'' she said.

The memory of her intention to tell Pop she wanted to quit and settle down flashed in her brain—and how Ramon de la Vega and his men had violently denied her the opportunity.

Well, she *would* tell Pop. Soon. When she found Nicky and got herself to San Antonio.

Finished with the pair of hooves on the left, Jeb moved to the right. Elena changed sides when he did.

''You ever want to do anything else?'' he asked. ''Quit traveling? Lead a regular life?''

She gave him a rueful smile. ''Yes. More lately than ever before.'' He didn't say anything, but she sensed him waiting for her to explain. ''You see, my routines are the show's final act before my father does his pitch for the elixir.'' She sighed, her grooming of the horse complete. ''He depends on me to—''

''Get the crowd fired up. Loosen their purse strings.''

"Yes." She refused to defend Pop's strategy. She folded the grooming cloth into a neat square. "I don't know what he'd do without me," she said simply. Worriedly. "He's not ready to give the show up, and I am."

"You have your son to think about."

Her head lifted. She hadn't expected Jeb to understand. "Yes. I want Nicky to have a normal life."

"Convince your father to open an apothecary or something. Sell his elixir that way."

Elena blinked. How could Jeb have known that was her dream? That she and Pop settle down in a nice, quiet town and open their own shop.

Jeb strolled toward her. It took a moment to realize what he was doing; she moved back a step but found her way blocked by the horses on one side and the big cottonwood tree on the other.

She was starting to feel flustered and unsteady again.

A panicky need to escape before he got too close gripped her. Slipping between the horses seemed her only chance, but Jeb's long arm shot out before she could.

He leaned a hand against the tree trunk, trapping her. His wrist touched her hair, he was so close. She stared at his collarbone, at the droplets of water that lingered there. He smelled cool. Clean. He smelled of strong soap and man, and her heart beat so fast she could barely breathe.

"Why are you always running from me?" he asked, his voice a low rumble of frustration.

"I'm not."

"You are."

She pressed her lips together and refused to look at him. She could feel him studying her, his dark eyes intense, probing, as if he strained to reach the innermost recesses of her mind. As if she were an intricate puzzle he was determined to solve.

"You're a beautiful woman, Elena," he murmured. "Men are sure to want you. Touch you. Do you never let them?"

She didn't want to hear him say any of this. She'd long ago buried a desire to be touched, to be wanted by a man. She refused to let Jeb resurrect the pain she'd worked so hard to forget.

"Go ahead, deny me the truth," Jeb growled when she didn't answer. Barely suppressed anger darkened the command. "Hell, deny yourself, too, while you're at it. But tell me a woman like you doesn't want a man inside her at night, and—"

Elena's head snapped up. "Damn you!" She planted both hands against his chest and pushed. Hard. He stumbled back, and she was free. "That's exactly what I would tell you," she snapped. "I don't need a man, do you hear me? Not ever. I have Pop. And I have Nicky. They're all I *need!*"

"You're wrong." The words were low. Fierce.

"Don't you tell me what I do and don't need!"

"Someone has to, damn it."

Her jaw dropped at his audacity. "What would *you* know of any of this? How could you possibly—"

"I know that you're entitled to a husband to warm your bed and help raise your son," he shot back. "Any woman is. You're a fool to keep telling yourself you're not."

Her lip curled. "But I'm not just any woman, am I, Jeb? Certainly not a foolish one. Not anymore. I'm different, and any man who sees Nicky knows it."

"Different."

"Yes."

"Because you were raped."

She'd never known a man so callous and blunt. *"Yes!"*

"And now you're wallowing in self-pity because you think de la Vega ruined your life."

Sharp-edged rage exploded inside her. She'd only hated one man in her life before this moment, but right now she hated Jeb Carson with her every breath. Her arm swung out to strike him, to inflict the pain he inflicted on her, but he caught her wrist and hauled her roughly against him.

"Let go of me," she said, her voice hoarse.

"Not until I'm ready, sweetheart."

She yanked at his grip, her fist clenched tight. "You have no right to do this to me."

"I've got something to say, and you're going to listen."

"Let *go* of me!" Again she tugged, but he held her fast.

"You have any idea how lucky you are, Elena? De la Vega could've killed you. He could've sliced you into ribbons or shot you full of lead after he'd taken his sick pleasure. But he didn't, did he? He walked away. He let you live so you could go back to your father and your trick riding in his medicine show." Jeb halted, his features hard. "And that wasn't all he did, was it?"

Elena's bosom heaved. His words circled around her, fast and furious.

"No," she whispered.

"He gave you your son."

She swallowed hard. Her precious baby.

"That's more than a lot of women who've suffered what you have can boast about. Believe me."

She stared up at him, his perception humbling her. "You speak as if from personal experience."

"Yeah, I've seen it. And more."

"Have you?"

"War is hell."

She could only speculate about his past, where he'd been, what he'd done, but whatever atrocities he had lived through shaped his thinking. Allowed him to look at her pain from the outside, even when she kept it buried on the inside.

For too long.

She'd thought of all those things he spoke of. Oh, God, many times. Had the reality, the self-pity, clouded hope? Gratitude? Did she dwell more often on what she'd lost, instead of what she'd gained? Or what had always been hers? Important things, like her life with the medicine show. The troupe she'd grown up with, the people she called family. Pop. His love and devotion.

And Nicky. Of course, Nicky most of all.

"Let the shell you've built around yourself crack open, will you?" Jeb said. "Enjoy the life you've been given, because once it's gone, you'll never get it back again."

At some point, he'd loosened his grip upon her wrist, but his fingers still circled her forearm. She felt the strength in those fingers. The surprising gentleness.

"Are you finished yet?" she asked, though her tone had lost its sting.

"No." His gaze drifted over her face. His anger appeared to have spent itself, but his opinions clearly ran deep. "One more thing."

She stood very still—and waited. His fingers moved over her wrist, as if he tried to soothe whatever pain he might have caused.

"I don't mean to make light of the humiliation de la Vega put you through," he murmured. "No woman deserves what he did. And, I swear, just say the word when we catch up with him, I'll string him up by his—" He halted, jaw clenched. "Damn it, Elena. I'll make him pay."

No man had ever offered to avenge her before. No one except Pop, and hearing Jeb's avowal touched her clear to her soul.

He made her want to weep.

She blinked furiously to keep from it, and angled her head away so he wouldn't see the struggle. He gripped her chin and carefully brought her back again.

"You're not going to cry, are you?" he asked. He sounded worried.

"No." She shook her head for emphasis. "No, I'm not."

It wasn't like him to be worried over a silly thing like a woman crying. She squared her shoulders. Jeb Carson had more important things to fret over. Like finding Nicky.

"Ramon is not worthy of my tears." She pulled her arm from Jeb's grasp and stood determined before him. "However, if I learn he has harmed my son in any way, you have my full and absolute permission to make him pay in any manner you wish."

Jeb's mouth curved in a cold smile. "Is that a promise?"

"On one stipulation."

His brow arched.

"That I get to string him up by his balls first."

Jeb finished off his third bowl of stew and sprawled onto his back with a moan. "I ate too much."

Elena's mouth softened. "You were hungry."

"You're a good cook."

His compliment pleased her. "All I did was put it in the pot. You bought the vegetables, shot and skinned the rabbit."

"That's the easy part."

Rather liking this relaxed side to him, she smiled. "I'll open a tin of peaches if you want dessert."

He moaned again. "Don't have room. But thanks."

Elena decided against the fruit, too. She'd barely managed a bowl of the stew. Once she had Nicky back in her arms, she'd eat all the stew and peaches she could handle. She rose, began gathering dishes.

"Leave 'em," Jeb ordered, his head swiveling toward her from his prone position. "You cooked. I'll clean up."

"I don't mind." She needed something to do anyway.

"Elena." He used that firm tone of voice again, the one that meant he intended for his command to be obeyed. "I don't expect you to wait on me hand and foot," he said, frowning.

She hesitated, then gave in. "All right."

Elena tried not to think how quickly she'd have them done rather than see them sit in the grass unwashed. She sat back down again and hugged her knees to her chest.

She tilted her head, squinted into the sky. The sun moseyed closer to the horizon; the night loomed long ahead of her. Would Jeb consider a few hours of riding toward Mexico in these cool hours of evening? They'd be that much closer by morning.

Seeing how relaxed he looked, she declined to even suggest it. She doubted he'd agree anyway. He appeared to doze, and her stare lingered.

He certainly was a fine specimen of a man, she had

to admit. Lean belly. Chest darkened with just the right amount of hair. Thick, corded muscle that rippled over his shoulders and biceps every time he moved.

A man, through and through.

Heat curled in some deep, hidden part of her, the womanly part Ramon had all but destroyed. The feeling was unfamiliar but not offensive. Perhaps merely a fascination.

An ache.

Her heart pumped a little faster. It frightened her some, if that's what it was. An ache for what she'd never had before. For what she'd never allowed herself. She wasn't sure how she should respond—tolerate or ignore it—but one thing she knew for sure.

Jeb Carson was responsible.

Let the shell you've built around yourself crack open, will you?

His words plopped into her memory like cream into chocolate. Perhaps her protective shell had begun to crack, after all, and she had no idea if she should shore it up again.

"You okay, Elena?"

Jeb's words startled her, and she looked away. Had he noticed she was staring at him?

"Of course." She swung her head, feigned concentration on a pair of green-feathered kingfishers playing on a branch of the cottonwood. "Why wouldn't I be?"

"You're looking mighty serious."

"I didn't mean to be."

"You bored?"

She shrugged. "No. Restless, maybe."

He rolled to his side, propped himself up on an elbow. His chest seemed even broader this way. More powerful.

The heat inside her curled hotter.

"Know how to play poker?" he asked. "We could go a few rounds, then you won't be restless anymore."

"If you want." Pop had taught her all sorts of games over the years. She could hold her own in most.

"I have a better idea."

She rested her chin on her drawn-up knees. "What is it?"

"I want to see you perform."

Her head came up again in surprise. "Trick riding?"

His mouth curved. "I can think of a number of ways you could...perform for me, but trick riding was what I meant."

She blinked. His comment threw her off-kilter. Was he teasing her?

"Sorry. You're not used to a man flirting with you, are you?"

He didn't look sorry. She huffed a breath. "That was flirting?"

"Best get used to it, Elena. I intend to teach you the ways a man can talk to a woman. Flirting and otherwise."

She eyed him with grave suspicion. "Why?"

"You might like it."

Her brow arched. Would she? Ever?

"So do some tricks for me," he said, grinning at her.

"Jeb." Elena could barely hide her exasperation. "It's almost dark."

"I can see you fine. But you'd better hurry while I still can."

"My horse is bedded down for the night. It's silly to undo the work we just did."

"Not silly at all."

"And I don't have a costume. My skirt will get in the way."

He made a vague gesture. "Tie it between your knees or something." He rolled to his feet and stepped over the dirty dishes. "While you're doing that, I'll saddle your horse."

Elena had run out of excuses. She sighed and got to her feet.

Elena sat straight in the saddle, her body loose and relaxed, and waited for the mare to hit her stride. The ground was flat, with no obstructions. Plenty of room to move around. She didn't have much daylight left, but she had enough to give Jeb a pretty good idea of what she could do.

Knowing he watched from the fringes of camp added a layer of nervousness to the adrenaline building inside her. She'd performed in front of hundreds of people at a time, too many times to count. Why did having an audience of one man make her as jittery as a june bug?

She decided to perform her newest routine for him. One of Pop's favorites. Fast and exhilarating, the stunt included a half-dozen tricks strung together into a tight package of vaults, spins and scissors that always left her—and the spectators—breathless.

When the mare was ready, Elena began the combination with a single vault. She lifted her right leg over the saddle horn and kicked free of the stirrup. Hanging on to the horn, she tucked her feet for the drop and hit the ground with a jump. The springing motion propelled her upward through the air; she twisted her body and landed back in the saddle seconds later, then threw her right leg over the horn again and spun in the saddle to a backward position. She grasped the handholds specially built for her saddle, dove headfirst over the horse's tail, kicked her legs high and straight into the air, then held the stand for a count of five before she swung her legs down and straddled the rump again.

In the next breath, she swung her legs high, crossed them and spun around to land forward. A quick move back into the saddle and she slid into the next trick of the routine, a horn spin where she swung around the saddle horn in one continuous pivot that brought her facing the front again.

She saved the most difficult routine for last—a neck scissors. Riding backward, she hung on to the horn with both hands, swung her feet up and twisted to bring her left leg up high enough over the neck, while at the same time lifting her right one up and over, then raising herself again to a sitting forward position. She ended with a second vault, just like the first.

The mare galloped toward Jeb, then slowed to a stop. Elena jumped to the ground, raised her arm with a flourish and sank into a low bow.

Jeb applauded with gusto. "Damn, but you're good."

The admiration in his words warmed her. "Thanks."

"What else can you do?"

"Somersaults. Drags. Handstands. Cartwheels. Backbends. Just about anything I want to do, I guess."

"All on the back of a horse."

She nodded and righted her skirt again. Jeb took the mare, and they fell into step back to camp.

"Ever count all the tricks you know?" he asked.

"Once."

"And?"

"A hundred of them. But that was a while ago."

"You think you know more than that?"

"Maybe a hundred and fifty."

A slow whistle slid between his teeth. They reached

camp. Elena noticed their supper dishes, still lying in the grass. Still unwashed.

Jeb noticed them, too. He pushed his hat higher onto his forehead. And frowned.

Elena took pity on him. "I'll wash them if you bed down my horse."

"I'll do both chores," he said. "It's my fault your horse needs grooming all over again. I already said I'd do dishes, and I will."

"You'll do them in the dark," she warned.

"Yeah." He glanced at the sky. "Seems so." He seemed annoyed by the situation he found himself in. "Go on," he said before she could offer to do dishes again. He gave her a swat on the behind with his hat. "Get ready for bed. I won't take long."

He set to work pulling the saddle off her mare. Elena watched him a minute before she gave in and headed to the stream to wash up.

Jeb Carson was a hard man.

But a fair one.

And if she wasn't very careful, she would find herself liking him much more than she should.

Chapter Eight

Something yanked Jeb from deep sleep into instant awareness. For a long moment, he didn't move. Didn't breathe. The intrusion was elusive. He couldn't pinpoint it, but it was out there. Beyond their camp.

Someone.

Elena lay a dozen yards away, her back to him, her breathing slow and even.

A dozen yards too far. He should've bedded right next to her. Kept her close. He reached for his gun, gauged the hour at well past midnight, well before dawn.

Anyone out this time of night meant trouble.

He moved silently to Elena and clamped a hand hard over her mouth. She jerked awake, her throat working up a scream. Seeing him, she froze, eyes wide.

He could taste her fear. Her confusion. He motioned her to keep quiet. She nodded, once, and he removed his hand from her mouth. She sat bolt upright and he pressed a pistol into her palm. Her fingers closed around the weapon. She looked terrified, but he didn't take time to reassure her.

Most likely, things would get worse before they got better.

The sound came again. Closer. He remained crouched beside her, his brain working to discern the sound's location. She touched his forearm and pointed to the stream.

At times like these, his senses turned razor sharp. It was uncanny what he could hear, see, in the dark of night. Creed claimed he turned into a damn beady-eyed hawk. A predator hunting the unsuspecting. Saved his butt more than once.

Two men on horses took shape. They made no attempt to be quiet. Their voices rose and fell in what sounded like a drunken song. Could be they didn't know Jeb and Elena were near.

Could be they did.

It wouldn't be the first time an unknown enemy had used a ruse like this to draw him out. Jeb had learned the hard way to leave nothing to circumstance. He bent close to Elena's ear.

"Get to the horses," he whispered. "Anything happens to me, ride out of here as fast as you can."

She drew back with a tiny gasp and an emphatic shake of her head.

"Go." He pulled her to her feet and gave her a firm shove toward their mounts.

She went, but reluctantly. He left camp, slipped deeper into the night, closer to the stream, each footfall soundless. The men moseyed to the water, dismounted and led their horses to drink.

They hadn't yet detected his presence. Had they come alone? Or were they traveling with a band of comrades, scattered and hiding somewhere nearby?

One of the men unbuttoned his pants to piss. Jeb made his move, a Colt in each hand.

"Well, now, if I'd known I was going to have callers

this late at night, I'd have prepared a right proper welcome,'' he drawled.

They spat startled epithets and spun toward him, both scrambling for their weapons.

''Touch 'em, and you're dead!'' Jeb snarled.

''All right! All right!'' One pair of hands shot up.

He kept his attention on the pair that didn't. ''Whatever you've got in mind, forget it, *amigo*,'' he warned. ''I can shoot faster than you can think.''

''We ain't done nothin' wrong.'' Gravelly voiced, he was clearly the older of the two. The leader. Jeb's eye narrowed at his hostility.

''Never said you did. But I might need convincing you don't plan to.'' His Colt jerked. ''Get your hands up, I said.''

''You got claim to this part of godforsaken country that says a man can't take a piss when he needs to?'' The hands slid skyward.

''Never said that, either.''

''We got a right to be here, same as you,'' the other said. He spoke with a faint lisp, brought on by several teeth missing at the front of his mouth.

''I'll decide that.'' He returned one of the Colts to the holster. With his free hand, he disarmed the men and threw their weapons into a pile in the grass.

''See here, boy. Name's Sergeant Calvin Bender. This is Corporal Nate Martin. We're with the United States Army.'' Bender's chest puffed from his superiority. ''I could have you thrown in jail for this.''

Thin moonlight enabled Jeb to see they were dressed in Army uniforms all right, but where were the rest of the men in their company? Were these two lost?

Or had they deserted?

He gestured with the Colt toward camp. ''I like to see

who I'm talking to. Start walking. A fire will give me all the light I need.''

The two men exchanged tense glances.

''Relax. Nobody's going to get hurt,'' Jeb said. After all, he knew what it was like to be taken captive. To not know if he'd be shot on the spot. Or tortured. Or released with his hide intact. ''Just want some answers, that's all.'' He pinned his stare on the one who'd tried to answer nature's call. Sergeant Bender. ''By the way, there's a lady with me. Fasten your pants before you meet her. You might make her blush.''

The man glared with a noticeable lack of amusement but did what he was told. Jeb stepped back in indication they should go before him.

''Don't walk too fast. Or too close. Don't do anything stupid, and we'll all be just fine,'' he said.

The men shuffled forward, their hands high.

''Elena,'' he called.

''I'm here.'' Her voice reached him from the dark vicinity of the horses.

''Throw some wood on the fire and stoke it high,'' he ordered as they entered the camp. ''We've got company.''

She hurried to the embers and soon transformed them into spitting, snapping flames. In the firelight, he studied the faces of his captives, noted how disheveled and dusty their clothes were. They'd been too long from a hot bath and a good laundress, and once again he wondered where they'd been.

''Name's Jeb Carson,'' he said, standing back and finally sheathing his own gun.

''Carson?'' The corporal stared, jaw agape, the holes between his teeth more evident. ''*The* Jeb Carson?''

Jeb's mouth formed a cool smile. What was it Lieutenant Colonel Kingston had called him back in Laredo? Legendary.

Ah, yes. A legendary soldier.

Seemed his reputation had reached beyond the steaming jungles of war-torn countries clear into the scattered ranks of the United States Army.

"Last heard you were in Santiago," Bender said, watching him, one thick-browed eye narrowed. "What brings you back to the States?"

Jeb debated telling him he had retired as a soldier-for-hire. That his plans called for a normal life somewhere in California.

But he held back. Let them think he was still on the government's payroll as a hired gun.

"Business," he said.

"We're looking for a man named Ramon de la Vega," Elena said suddenly. "Have you heard of him?"

"The revolutionary?" Bender asked. "Reckon most folks around here have." His frosty gaze fastened on Elena. "What do you want with him?"

"Elena," Jeb growled, stopping her when her mouth opened to reply. "That's enough."

He didn't yet trust these two men. Though they wore the uniform proclaiming themselves as defenders of the United States, their presence this close to the Mexican border, alone and in the middle of the night, was too suspicious for Elena to innocently explain their own presence.

"Perhaps they've heard something about Nicky, Jeb," she said. "If Ramon and his men have been seen in the area, then—"

"You're the baby's mother, ain't you?" Martin said, stunned.

Elena whirled toward him. "Yes! Yes, I am. How did you know? Have you seen Nicky?"

"We saw him all right," Bender said, and a slow, calculated grin appeared on his lips.

Jeb recognized the meaning in that grin. A thunderous rage began to build inside him.

"You saw him?" she gasped, turning back to Bender.

"Yep, de la Vega was mighty proud of that boy, too," he drawled. "Carried him in his arms, as bold as you please. Told everyone in the village about his new son."

Elena's hands flew to her mouth. "When? What village?"

"Depends how bad you want to know."

"What's that supposed to mean?" she asked, clearly taken aback.

"Means everything comes with a price, lady," Martin said, his voice carrying a thread of amusement.

"You expect me to *pay* you for that information?" she demanded in shock. She strode closer to Bender. "Where did you see my son? Tell me! Where was he?"

"Elena! No!"

Jeb lunged toward Elena before she could grab the sergeant by the front of his coat. But the soldier grabbed her first—with enough force to send her falling into him with a cry of surprise.

"Let her go!" Jeb roared. His hand closed around the man's wrist like a vise. Elena kicked out, fists flailing. Bender had all he could do to hold her squirming body and struggle free of Jeb's grasp at the same time.

"Nate! Take her!" Bender yelled. He flung Elena with a suddenness that had her tripping over her skirts into the corporal. He was unprepared to take her weight, and they tumbled to the dirt, alarmingly close to the fire.

Jeb had a fleeting glimpse of them rolling in a tangle

of arms and legs as Elena fought to free herself. His fist drew back. The hit snapped Sergeant Bender's head back and hurtled him spread-eagled to the ground.

Elena screamed. Jeb spun toward her. Flames licked at her skirt hems, and she batted them frantically. Corporal Martin's expression turned ugly. He lunged toward her and battled to haul her to her feet.

Jeb snarled and threw his weight into him. Martin's grasp yanked free, and Elena scrambled away from the fire with a sob.

"Make a run for it, Nate!" Sergeant Bender bellowed, heaving himself, swaying, to his feet. "I ain't waitin' for you!"

The corporal's struggles faltered. "Cal!" He swore violently. "Damn you, Cal!"

Jeb took advantage of Martin's distraction to pull a knife from the sheath at his waist. He had no choice but to let the sergeant go. He wasn't in any position to abandon the corporal, and he sure as blazes couldn't leave Elena behind.

Horses' hooves confirmed Sergeant Cal Bender had escaped.

But Jeb had his accomplice at his mercy.

His weight held the smaller man down on the ground. The blade pressed against Nate Martin's scrawny neck. His round, panicked eyes revealed his fear.

Jeb's lips curled back in a feral smile. He liked it when the enemy showed fear.

"Ever feel a knife sliding across your throat, Corporal?" he taunted. "Only burns for a few seconds, but all that blood pouring out makes you forget it even hurts at all."

Martin lay perfectly still, his breathing wheezy.

"I'm going to ask you questions," Jeb said. "And

you're going to answer them with the truth. I've never been much for rules, so you'd better play the game right, y'hear me?''

He let Martin take all the time he needed to think the warning through. Finally Martin nodded.

"Where did you see the boy?" Jeb demanded.

"In a village, south of here."

"There's a hundred villages south of here," he snapped. "Which one?"

"San Ignatius," Martin said quickly. "A morning's ride past the Rio Grande. Southwest of Eagle Pass."

Jeb committed the directions to memory. "When did you see him?"

"This afternoon."

That would explain his and Sergeant Bender's travel-worn appearance. They'd been riding hard since then.

"You with a patrol down there, Corporal?" he crooned. "Or just doing some leisurely sight-seeing?"

Martin's hesitation lasted long enough to convince Jeb he was doing some serious soul-searching. And with every second he did, Jeb knew the Army soldiers had been up to no good.

"We had a meeting with de la Vega," Martin admitted.

"A meeting." Jeb hid his surprise. "What for?"

"He's hurting for arms. Guns. We knew where he could get some, and—" the corporal ran his tongue around his lower lip "—we set up a deal with him."

"To sell him *guns?*" Jeb demanded in disbelief.

"Yes, sir."

His control began to slip. "I had you and the sergeant pegged wrong, Corporal. You're even more stupid than I thought."

"De la Vega's aiming to help his people. He wants to overthrow Díaz. Help them get their land back."

"You're helping him start a damned war!" Jeb roared.

"What do I care what they do down there?" Martin shot back. "Long as they keep their troubles on their side of the border, they can shoot themselves up all they want."

Jeb fought to keep his voice even. "When are these guns expected to reach the rebels?"

"Not sure," Martin hedged.

"Soon?"

"I said I don't know for sure."

Jeb's glower darkened. The blade pressed harder against skin.

"Soon, then. Don't know exactly, but—" Martin released an uneasy breath "—soon."

"Who's bringing the guns? Where're they coming from?"

"Someplace up north. Denver, I think. I swear I don't know who's bringin' 'em in. Cal handled all that. Some deal he made with a friend of his. A quartermaster."

A quartermaster in the Army would have access to supplies like rifles. Would know just where to order them, keep them stored until they were ready to sneak out.

A quartermaster as greedy, as traitorous, as Cal Bender or Nate Martin.

Jeb had heard enough. He roughly jerked the corporal to his feet, the knife plain in his hand.

"They'll hang you for treason for this," he growled.

Sweat glistened on Martin's brow. He watched Jeb close. He was ready to bolt. Jeb could feel it.

"What of Nicky?" Elena said. She crouched a few

yards away, her face pale. She rose slowly. ''Tell me everything you know about him.''

Jeb wondered how much she understood of the danger her baby was in. That with all the corporal told them, the stakes had just gotten a hell of a lot higher for everyone.

Martin's gaze raked her, from the top of her golden head down to the burned edges of her skirt hems.

''He don't look nothin' like you, does he?'' he taunted.

''Answer me,'' Elena said, desperate.

''That dark, wavy hair. Dark eyes. Yep, Ramon's his daddy, all right. How did he get under your skirts anyway?''

''Shut up!'' Jeb said, giving him a vicious shake.

Elena hiked her chin higher. ''I'll ask you one more time, Corporal. Was my son all right? Was he crying or—or anything?''

The pain was there—in the faint quiver of her voice— and Jeb glanced at her, words of assurance on his tongue. Words that would tell her if it was the last thing he ever did, he would find her baby and return him safe to her arms.

His mantra, finding her baby.

Suddenly her eyes rounded, and she gasped.

''Jeb,'' she screamed. ''He's got a gun!''

He never saw where Martin pulled the pistol from, but he reacted to her warning with pure instinct, honed from years of hard fighting. His fist shot outward, connected with the other man's wrist. Bone snapped. The bullet went wild, the bark still sharp as Jeb swung the knife's blade in a lethal arc.

Blood spurted from Corporal Nate Martin's neck. A

thin and perfect line of crimson that ended his life in an instant.

For a moment, Jeb didn't move. In slow motion, the soldier sank to the ground.

"Oh, my God," Elena whispered. "Oh, my God."

Jeb dropped the knife, turned full toward her, and saw the horror on her face.

"It had to be done," he said.

"You killed him."

"Yes."

She had probably never seen anyone killed before. Jeb had seen it, had done it, too often. She couldn't seem to stop staring at Martin. Or maybe she couldn't look at Jeb anymore.

"He was the enemy, Elena. A traitor. You, of anyone, should know that."

"A traitor?" Finally she looked at him, the color gone from her cheeks.

"He betrayed our country to de la Vega. So did Sergeant Bender. They're both traitors." He watched her close. "They betrayed Nicky."

"Because of the guns."

Jeb stiffened against the bitterness. How could she understand when she'd never lived as he had?

"Yes," he said. He wanted to make her understand. It was imperative she did. "Ramon de la Vega has killed Americans for his revolution. Their lives mean nothing to him, only their money. President McKinley has ordered him stopped." Jeb took a step closer to her, but she sucked in a breath of protest, and he halted. "Thousands of people will be killed if this revolution of his begins. Villages and cities will be destroyed. The Mexican people will suffer."

Her throat worked but she said nothing.

''Nicky could be caught in a cross fire.''

Jeb didn't want to scare her. But she had to know the facts. The harsh reality.

Her eyes closed. She trembled.

''Corporal Martin and Sergeant Bender have betrayed the president's orders,'' Jeb said. ''As soldiers of the United States Army, providing the rebels with arms is inexcusable.''

''Yes.'' Her voice was barely above a whisper. ''And what of Sergeant Bender?''

''He'll pay the price, too. When I find him.''

Jeb must prevent the rifles from falling into the rebels' hands. He had the knowledge. The need.

He could do nothing else.

''What of Nicky?'' Elena asked, as if she read his mind. ''Is another man's treason more important to you than him?''

''Elena.''

She asked questions he had no answers for. Both situations needed solving. Each as important as the other.

He reached out, slid his fingers beneath her hair, curled them around her neck. Smooth and warm, her skin. And so damned soft.

She trembled at his touch. Would she skitter away from him as she always did?

He braced for it. She didn't, but she wanted to.

He could feel the want.

''Don't be afraid of me,'' he murmured. ''I'm not a monster, Elena.''

''You just killed a man,'' she said shakily. ''What am I supposed to think?''

''He would've killed me. And you. Both of us, first chance he got.''

She bit her lower lip. ''Maybe.''

"He'd spilled his guts. We knew too much."

Her eyes closed, then opened again. She took a breath, let it out. "Yes."

"Look at me."

Her head tilted and her lashes lifted. In the firelight, her eyes mesmerized him. Pools of jungle-green so deep, so dark, he'd drown in them if she let him close enough to climb in.

He'd never hurt her. He wanted to assure her of that. Make her believe it. His fingers tightened on her neck, just enough to bring her nearer. She had to know what he wanted. She had to know, too, she could push away if she had to.

She didn't.

His head lowered.

He touched his lips to hers, moved over them ever gently to soothe the ugliness of what she'd seen, what he'd done.

The kiss lingered, allowed him to learn the feel of her lips, their incredible softness. Her mouth trembled. Her vulnerability, he knew. The courage his kiss cost her.

And then her lips began to move, too. Tentative. As if she explored the sensation he gave her and found it not unpleasant. He let her discover what it was like to kiss a man, gave her time to know she wouldn't be hurt from it.

He ended the kiss as gently as he had started it. Before she was ready, he suspected, seeing how slow she was to open her eyes again. And when she least expected him to.

"Get back into your bedroll, Elena. Try to sleep." He withdrew his hand from around her neck and stepped back, the warmth of her skin lingering on his palm. "I'm going to take care of the corporal, then I'll turn in, too."

"All right." She touched her tongue to her lower lip.

He couldn't tell if her behavior embarrassed her. Or if she simply wanted one last taste of him. He left camp and disappeared into the darkness, taking Corporal Nate Martin's body with him.

Chapter Nine

The soldier's death forced a detour in their journey the next morning. There was no help for it, Elena knew. Traitor or not, they just couldn't leave his body behind to feed the wolves.

Not that he didn't deserve it.

She was only beginning to understand the political repercussions of what he'd done. Sergeant Bender's escape had certainly worsened matters. Where had he gone? Back to Mexico? De la Vega? Certainly not the army! Especially when he realized the corporal wouldn't be joining him ever again—and why.

Would he suspect Martin had confessed?

How could he not?

The possibility of the arms deal going through remained strong. Was there any hope the shipment of guns could be intercepted and stopped before they reached Mexico? Elena had no idea. If only Jeb had learned of it sooner, he could've gone to the proper military authorities and demanded action.

Or taken care of matters himself which, she suspected, he had a deep need to do. Except Sergeant Bender held all the cards, the information of when and where the guns would be delivered. And by whom.

Besides, they had to think of Nicky. They had to keep riding. They had to find him as fast as they could.

Before they resumed their search, however, they rode into Fort Duncan outside of Eagle Pass with the corporal's body draped over his horse and tied to the saddle. Jeb left firm instructions with the officer in charge to call for a coroner and keep the body under heavy guard. A brief explanation wired to a certain Lieutenant Colonel Eugene Kingston finished the matter.

Elena was only too glad to leave the corporal behind. After leaving the fort, they crossed the Rio Grande, skirted the Mexican town of Piedras Negras and rode hard toward San Ignatius.

They halted on a ridge overlooking a gently rolling valley. At last, the village sprawled before them, a quiet farm community surrounded by grassy pastures and fields of wheat and corn.

Nicky had been here. Just yesterday.

The knowledge made him seem closer, within reach, and stirred her flagging hope. She scanned the hills beyond the village, and beyond those, the pine-and-oak-covered Sierra Madres.

How far into the country had Ramon taken her baby? There were so many hills and mountains, she couldn't begin to fathom which direction the revolutionaries might have fled. How could she and Jeb possibly locate them?

The night Nicky had been kidnapped, she had been sure she could find him all by herself. In her anguish at learning he was gone, she'd been convinced she could.

How foolish she'd been. So utterly naive.

Without Jeb…

She turned to look at him. Her glance drifted over his profile, the strong line of his jaw, roughened with dark stubble. Engrossed in his thoughts, he wasn't aware she studied him, and she recalled last night when he had kissed her.

All day, the memory had popped back into her head when she least expected it. Jeb Carson was a dangerous man. He'd ruthlessly defended himself, defended her, and the sobering result would be forever branded into her mind.

But he'd been gentle in his kiss. Incredibly so.

An enigma, Jeb Carson.

Unable to help it, her glance lingered. He chewed absently on a toothpick, his dark eyes sweeping the area in slow assessment, then lifting, as hers had, to the mountains miles beyond.

He said nothing for long moments. Just chewed on his toothpick, rolled it from one side of his mouth to the other.

"What are you thinking, Jeb?" she asked finally.

He glanced at her. "About you."

"Me?" Her head swiveled back toward the valley. Had he been remembering their kiss, too? "You should be thinking of my son instead."

"I am. Indirectly." He leaned from the saddle and plucked her new hat off her head. "I was thinking how to sneak you down into the village without everyone seeing all that blond hair of yours."

The hat dangled from its cord against her back. She didn't bother replacing it, though the late-afternoon sun still shone bright and hot.

"What's the matter with my hair?"

"Too conspicuous. The whole town will be talking about the green-eyed, blond-haired *gringa* who rode in."

"Hmm." She'd probably be the only American woman in the place. "And we don't want word of me reaching Ramon."

"No."

"Do you have a plan in mind?"

"I'm working on one."

"Care to let me in on it? My hair, you know."

He reached out, fingered the strands. "Got to cover it all up."

"Why can't I just wear my hat?"

His hand drew back. He shook his head. "Not good enough."

"I'll pin my hair up so it doesn't show."

A corner of his mouth lifted, and he tossed aside the toothpick. "And you'll still look like a green-eyed American *gringa*."

"So you want to disguise me?"

"Yep."

"How?"

"Going to have to steal something for you." His focus returned to the village. "Bet you never stole anything before, did you?"

"Never."

"Times like these, it's okay."

She couldn't help a disbelieving laugh. "You're making your own rules as you go, aren't you?"

"That's how a man survives. Making his own rules." He straightened in his seat. "We'll ride down to the village and ask some questions. Before we do, see that line of clothes over there?"

He pointed to an adobe structure in the distance, a lone farm an easy ride away. A few sheep grazed in the yard, and a sorry-looking burro, but the place seemed otherwise deserted.

"Yes. Some poor peasant's laundry."

His expression turned serious. "Listen up, Elena. This is what we're going to do."

Berto eyed the two riders approaching his cantina with grave suspicion. There were not many people who bothered to ride out this way. San Ignatius was only a poor village, isolated and boring. With Piedras Negras not too far away, there were more exciting places to visit than this.

He set his hammer aside, kept them in view through the adobe's window. They rode slowly. In no hurry. A *gringo* sitting straight, proud, on his horse. A woman, hunched and weary on a burro.

Curiosity threaded through Berto's suspicion. Maybe they would not be too much trouble. The woman looked old and feeble. Her rebozo covered her head, her clothes faded and worn. He could not see her face the way she kept her head bent. And maybe he did not want to. How could the *gringo* not feel sorry for her, eh?

They drew closer and halted. The gringo dismounted first, and Berto could see he was very tall. Dark. He had not shaved for a while and he wore his hat low, but he did not appear nervous, did not even glance through the open door of the cantina to see who was inside.

Berto wondered if the *gringo* had come to the village sometime in the past. But he did not think so. He had lived in San Ignatius all his life. He would have remembered this one.

The *gringo* helped the old woman off the burro and pressed a walking stick into her hand. She moved as if her bones hurt, and compassion stirred inside Berto. If she was tired and aching, she was probably thirsty, too.

He abandoned the table leg he had been trying to fix,

broken with so many others last night. *Por Dios,* he had been fixing tables all day and he welcomed the diversion a couple of strangers would bring.

"Who are they, Berto?"

Wiping her hands on a towel, his wife of nearly forty years peered around the curtain covering the doorway to the cantina's kitchen. Strangers made his Alita nervous, and after yesterday's trouble she was more nervous than usual.

"I have never seen them before," he said, tying an apron around his waist. He had not had a customer for a couple of hours now, and he had removed the apron while he repaired his furniture. Now it was time to put it back on again.

"She looks sick," Alita said, frowning.

"Maybe she is. Go back to the kitchen. Find them something to eat."

Hearing footsteps, Berto turned. The old woman entered first. She leaned on her walking stick, each step shuffling, slow. Berto could not tell how tall she was, or how thin. The rebozo covered too much of her, but anyone could see how frail she was. Did she suffer from disease?

The *gringo* followed her in. He filled the doorway, shutting out the sun for a moment when he strode through. He paused, let his eyes adjust to the dim interior. He pointed to a table near an open window. Berto could barely detect the woman's nod of acknowledgment.

His curiosity about them ran stronger than ever. A mismatch, if he ever saw one.

"Buenos días!" he said, hurrying forward. He had stared long enough. Whatever their relationship, it was none of his business, only that they carried money in

their pockets. "Sit, sit!" He pulled out a chair, helped the old woman in. "What would you like? A cold drink? You have traveled far to our little village, eh? And it is hot this afternoon."

"What do you have?" the *gringo* asked. He sat across from her and spoke before she could reply.

"Alita makes good lemonade. Not too tart. Not too sweet. Just right."

"Lemonade for her, then," he said. "I'll take a beer. And bring us two plates of whatever it is that smells good in the kitchen."

His voice was low, deep, his Spanish flawless and smooth. Few would argue with a voice that carried such command, and the woman did not seem to care he ordered without consulting her. She just stared at the tabletop, her hands in her lap.

"Sí, sí. Uno momento."

Berto hurried to the back and nearly collided with Alita, eavesdropping behind the curtain.

"What is she doing with him?" Alita demanded in a hiss, stealing one last peek before she let the covering fall back into place. "He is too dangerous-looking for one so frail."

"It is better to know what business he would have with *her*," Berto retorted in a hoarse whisper. "She will only slow him down for wherever he needs to go. Why would he bother?"

Alita grunted in agreement and handed him two plates heaped with steaming rice, frijoles and tortillas.

"Try to find out, Berto. We cannot have any more trouble. Everyone in San Ignatius will expect us to find out who they are and why they are here."

Berto sighed. Sometimes it was a burden owning the only cantina in the village where strangers stopped first to slake their thirsts and fill their hungry bellies. Gossip would spread quickly. There would be many questions about these two, and it would be up to Berto and Alita to learn answers.

"They are probably harmless," he said. "But I will visit with them and see what they have to say. They have asked for lemonade and beer. Bring their drinks out quickly."

He left the kitchen and slid both plates onto the table, then added silverware. The *gringo* nodded his thanks. Berto thought he heard the old woman whisper hers, but he could not be sure.

After Alita brought the lemonade and beer, the stranger picked up his fork. Berto noted his shadowed gaze lingered on the woman; when she did not follow suit, he pushed her plate closer, a silent command for her to eat. Only when she did, did he do the same.

He cared about her, Berto realized, and the knowledge only increased his curiosity further. He found his broom and hoped it did not look too obvious when he swept the floor on their side of the cantina.

He listened, but they did not converse. They ate their meal in no hurry, though there were only a few hours of daylight left. Did they intend to spend the night here, somewhere in San Ignatius?

Who were they?

Alita gestured sharply in their direction as she scrubbed the bar he had already scrubbed this afternoon. Her curiosity was as strong as his—and his wife could be an impatient woman sometimes.

Now was one of those times. He could wait no longer.

"My name is Berto, *señor.*" Pasting on a broad smile, he stopped sweeping and inclined his head toward the bar. "My wife, Alita. We are happy you stopped by to see us this afternoon."

The *gringo* slowed his chewing long enough to incline his head in acknowledgment of the introductions. But he said nothing by way of his own.

Disappointed, Berto tried again.

"And this is… I am afraid I do not know what to call her, *señor*. She is a friend of yours? Or a relative…?"

His voice trailed off. He had to be careful. She was an old woman. He did not want to anger the *gringo*. Or insult him.

"Neither," the stranger said. "I found her."

"Found her!" As if she were a stray dog? Berto could not hide his surprise. "But where?"

"Wandering along the Rio Grande."

Berto clicked his tongue in sympathy and wondered if she had gone *loco.* Had she no home? No family? No friends to watch over her?

"I hope you do not mind me asking, *señor,* but what was she doing there?" His gaze slid toward the woman. She had shifted in her seat so that her body angled away from him. She huddled over her food, as if she wanted to disappear under the plate.

Maybe she did not like them talking about her. Berto felt guilty for asking so many questions.

"She was looking for someone," the dark-eyed stranger said.

Berto resumed sweeping. Mexico was a big country. Texas, too. How would she find anyone in such a large area? It would be impossible if she did not know just where to look.

"We're hoping you can help us." The *gringo* finished his beer, set the glass down and, for the first time, gave Berto his full attention.

He stopped sweeping again. "Me?"

"Ever hear of a man named Armando?"

His blood froze. He exchanged an uneasy glance with Alita, then cleared his throat. "There are many Armandos in Mexico, *señor*. I could not possibly—"

"Heard he was seen around here yesterday. Rides with Ramon de la Vega."

Just hearing the rebel's name set Berto's blood to boiling. He spat on the floor. *"Bastardo!"*

"Ee-aa!" Alita cried out. She hastened from around the bar and clutched his arm. "He is a Federale, Berto!" she hissed. "He is using us to find them."

"No," the *gringo* said sharply. "I'm not. Not like you think."

"De la Vega will punish us if he finds out we talked to him," she said as if the stranger had never spoken. She gave Berto's arm a panicked shake. "Can you not see that, Berto? After what happened here last night?"

"Alita! Enough!" he said.

He loved his wife dearly, but she was prone to dramatics. Besides, he did not like to air his troubles to the *gringo* and the old woman. What would they care of a brawl that took place in his cantina, anyway?

"Did what happened have anything to do with that pile of broken tables and chairs over there?" the dark-eyed *gringo* taunted.

Berto's glance jumped to the corner of the cantina where he had been working most of the day. Clearly, he had misjudged the stranger. He was not as aloof as he appeared.

Berto gave in. He hugged Alita to his side, comforting her.

"Sí, señor," he said. "They were here. Yesterday. De la Vega's men."

"De la Vega with them?"

Berto hesitated to reply. He could not be too careful. Or too trusting. In that regard, Alita was right.

"But you want Armando, eh?" he hedged.

"*Sí.*"

"Why?"

The *gringo* touched the woman with his eyes. "Like I said, she's looking for him." He shrugged. "She has her reasons."

"A relative?"

"In a roundabout way," he murmured.

"But Armando is not expecting her."

"No."

"So he would be surprised if she found him, eh?"

The *gringo*'s mouth curved. "If you're worried I'll reveal you as my source of information, don't be."

"Certainly you see my situation, *señor.* If I tell you where I believe Armando might be, Ramon is sure to be with him. He will not be happy to have unexpected visitors to his camp."

The *gringo* considered Berto for a long moment. Finally he shrugged. "You're right. He won't." He rose with a scrape of the chair legs across the floor. "If I would've known you were so afraid of him, I wouldn't have bothered you. Just thought you could give my friend here a little help, that's all."

Berto stiffened at the slur, given so smoothly he almost missed its sting. But a man did not like to be told he was weak, not with his wife beside him to hear the words.

"They are desperadoes," he said in his own defense. His arm swept outward, indicating the pile of battered furniture in the corner. "They do not care who they hurt or what they destroy, even when they do not drink tequila.''

"You're right about that, too.''

If only the *gringo* would have argued with him.

Berto's glance took in the old woman, hunched and feeble inside the threadbare rebozo. Again compassion stirred inside him. She did not look as if she had the strength to ride another mile.

She wanted to find the revolutionary named Armando. He guessed she would not stop looking until she succeeded. What business was it of his what she did? Or why?

His resistance crumpled. Alita was watching him. As if she sensed his apprehension and understood it, she lifted her shoulder in a shrug, then lowered her eyes. Forty years of marriage told him she was thinking of the old woman, too. She would not be too angry if he revealed what he knew to the *gringo,* after all.

"Whenever Ramon returns to Mexico with Armando and his men, they hide out in the hills. That way.'' He pointed out the cantina's window, toward the west. "There is a small cemetery. When you see it, turn south. You will find their camp nearby.''

"You're sure?''

The *gringo*'s tone sounded sharp. It was not easy for this one to trust everything he heard, Berto guessed.

"*Sí.* Very sure. I have seen their camp myself. When they are not there, of course.''

"Much obliged, *señor.*''

The dark-eyed stranger pulled a bill from his pocket and tossed it onto the table, the cost of their meal and a generous *propina* included. The amount compelled him to impart one more piece of information, in case they were interested.

"Ramon had a baby with him," he said. "He and Armando sat at this same table and fed the little one his supper."

A tiny sound escaped from beneath the folds of the rebozo, the first real one the old woman had made since she arrived. She dipped her head and pressed her fingers to her mouth.

Berto feared he had said something to upset her, but the dark-haired stranger merely thanked him again, then helped her out the door and onto her burro.

"Do not look so worried, Berto," Alita said softly, patting his arm after they left. "She is not upset. I think you have told her just what she wanted to know."

Chapter Ten

Their fabricated story could not be avoided. Elena regretted obtaining the information on Nicky's whereabouts under less-than-honest pretenses, but Jeb had done what he could.

And he had done it well.

The day the rebels had kidnapped Nicky in the woodlands near the Nueces, only the one named Armando had expressed concern for Elena, and for that reason she remembered him. But she'd been skeptical Jeb's ploy to seek information on him would yield the information they needed on Ramon.

Thank God, he'd been right. He believed by disguising Elena and asking about Armando's whereabouts, they would raise less suspicion. The cantina's owners would be more inclined to talk about one of Ramon's men rather than Ramon himself. Jeb had been careful to make no mention of Nicky. It'd been sheer luck that Berto even spoke of him.

Sheer, perfect luck.

Regardless, it'd been a risk. Elena worried Armando had parted ways with the band at some point during their return to Mexico. She feared she and Jeb would be sent on a wild-goose chase, that her disguise would fail and Berto and his wife would guess who she really was.

So many things could have gone wrong.

Nothing had.

After they returned the burro to his rightful owner, they had hurried toward the hills and the cemetery that would be their landmark. A rutted path led them straight to it.

"Looks like we turn south from here," Jeb said, reining to a stop.

"Yes." She pulled up beside him.

But they both lingered, their attention snared by the rows of simple crosses that comprised the burial ground, each one bearing a name painstakingly carved into the wood, some more recent than others. The grass had been mowed back. Pots of blooming flowers brightened the graves.

With the shade provided by oak and pine trees, the cemetery had a serenity about it. Peaceful and cool.

"Seems out of place, doesn't it?" Jeb said, thoughtfully scanning the perimeter.

"Yes." Amid the wilds of the Mexican countryside, the burial grounds offered a form of carefully tended civilization honoring loved ones. "Someone spends a great deal of time here, don't they?"

"Whoever it is, he's nowhere around." Jeb took the reins again. "Let's keep moving. All these trees will make it too dark to ride soon."

They turned southward. The horses' hooves crunched over fallen acorns and dried pine needles as they climbed higher, deeper into the hills. Elena concentrated on keeping her bearings and dodging the branches of more varieties of oak trees than she could name. The air turned cooler, dryer. The woodlands grew thicker, the terrain rougher. Just when she began to despair at Berto's directions, that they'd been led on a wild-goose chase after all, the trees parted into a cozy, sprawling valley, and Jeb whistled, long and low.

Ramon de la Vega's hideout.

Plain wooden cabins had been erected in no apparent order and gave the valley the look of a tiny village. Smoke curled from chimneys, and the faint scent of roasted chilies hung in the air.

Elena stared. Several women worked together grinding corn—wives, most likely, of the men who kept families. Dogs slept deep, warmed by the fire and oblivious to the activity around them. On the fringes of the encampment, a remuda of horses grazed, and a passel of barefoot children chased each other in a game of tag.

But it was the men she studied the hardest. She counted a dozen rebels sprawled around campfires smoking cigars and drinking tequila. All wore ammunition belts and broad-brimmed sombreros. All were relaxed. And none of them knew they'd been discovered.

"I want to get a better look," she said, dismounting. "I don't see Nicky, do you?"

"No." Jeb swung down from his horse.

"I don't see Ramon, either. Or Armando."

Which could mean there were even more of the rebels inside the cabins. How many did they number? And was their leader among them?

Jeb and Elena left the horses and crept from tree to tree in a zigzag pattern that brought them as close as they dared to the hideout. There were probably guards posted somewhere, and she was grateful for the shadows that gave them the advantage.

Here, deeper in the valley, the smells of cooking food were stronger, voices less muffled. The firelight illuminated faces, glinted off bullets and revolvers in holsters.

But Nicky was nowhere to be seen.

Her heart pounded in a growing conviction the cantina's owner had been mistaken. But how could he be wrong about a little boy eating his supper with Ramon and Armando?

What if Berto had seen through their ruse and lied?

Jeb touched her shoulder and pointed, scattering Elena's thoughts. Tall, lean, dressed all in black, a Mexican emerged from the shadowy interior of one of the cabins. He paused on the step, inhaled deep on a cheroot. From beneath the crown of his sombrero, thick, wavy hair fell to his shoulders.

Oh, God. There he was. Ramon de la Vega, chest crisscrossed with ammunition belts, a holster slung low on his hips. The blood skipped in her veins at how heavily armed he was, how arrogant he looked. How cold. This was the man who had ruthlessly killed innocent people for his revolution. Whose ideals overrode all else and allowed for no compassion for those who carried a different view.

The man who had stolen a little boy from his mother's arms without a thought to anyone but himself.

An elderly woman followed him out. Plump, gray haired and smiling, she carried a baby in her arms, his chubby body so achingly familiar, so heartwrenching precious that Elena's feet propelled her forward to snatch him into her own.

But Jeb yanked her back with one arm tight around her shoulders. His hand clamped over her mouth to stifle the cry of Nicky's name in her throat.

"No, Elena," he whispered against her temple. "Not now."

Her breath came in frustrated pants, her eyes riveted on her son. She didn't fight Jeb, even with all the anguish crashing through her. They were powerless to take Nicky from these men. To do so now, without a carefully orchestrated plan, would result in a disaster that could keep him from her forever.

But soon. Hours, if she could manage it.

The woman held Nicky toward Ramon. He tossed aside the cheroot; with both hands free, he hefted Nicky playfully into the air, his little arms and legs wiggling, his laughter reaching Elena clear across the camp. Her chest squeezed in horror at the sound.

Laughter?

Didn't he miss her at all? Did he have to *laugh* as if he'd already forgotten her?

Ramon kissed Nicky's cheek, then handed him back to the woman. She cuddled him against her ample bosom and took him into the cabin, closing the door behind them. Looking proud and disgustingly satisfied, Ramon found another cheroot and lit it, as if nothing unusual had happened.

The sight revolted Elena. Damn him for acting so— so *fatherly!* And the woman. Who was *she?* How dare she kiss and hug Nicky! How dare any of them so much as even *touch* him!

Nicky didn't belong to them. Nicky belonged to her!

"Come on, Elena." Jeb's low voice pierced through the bitterness roiling through her. "Let's get out of here."

He took her hand and pulled her up the hill, leading the way to their horses when she was so blinded by fury she could barely think for herself. Her feet leapt over the rocky ground, instinctively dodged the dried twigs that could snap and betray their presence. At last, the horses loomed. Jeb turned, hooked an arm around her neck and pulled her roughly against him.

"Did you see how they acted with Nicky?" she demanded into his shoulder, her feelings wounded and in dire need of soothing.

"I saw."

"Fondling him like he was one of them." She huffed a breath of outrage, circled her arms around Jeb's waist. Her world was rocking; she needed to hang on to him. Just for a few minutes.

"Hard for you to see that, I know." Jeb's hand moved down her spine, then up again.

"They don't care where he came from. They think they can just take over his life. As if I never even existed."

"I know, Elena."

"Who do they think they are, anyway?"

"They figure they've got rights to him."

"Well, they don't." She rejected the notion, would always reject it, no matter what. "Pop and I are his family. No one else."

"Elena."

Jeb sounded troubled, but her lip curled, her pique surging strong.

"What does Ramon know about being a father to my baby?" she fumed.

"He's had to learn fast. Looks like he's had help doing it, too."

The memory of the gray-haired woman, of Ramon and Nicky together played again in her brain. She shuddered from another burst of ire. "What I would give to wipe that self-satisfied smirk right off Ramon's face."

"By the time this is all finished, we'll do more than that."

The words rumbled out of Jeb's chest. Barely veiled revenge. After what Ramon put them through, the man deserved all he got.

''Ramon made Nicky laugh. Did you hear him?'' she asked, fighting a pout.

Jeb's arms tightened. ''Yes.''

''I can't believe Nicky would even do it.''

''What? Laugh?''

''Yes.''

''He's a baby, sweet. He doesn't think like adults do.''

''He should be thinking of me. I'm his mother.''

''Would you rather hear him cry?''

Her eyes closed. No, never that.

''Want to know what I think?'' Jeb asked.

He calmed her unsteady world. The heat of his body soaked into her. Heat and the soothing sensation of his hand moving up and down her back, over and over again.

''Yes,'' she murmured. She'd learned to value his opinion. To trust it.

''Things could be a hell of a lot worse,'' he said.

''Meaning?''

''Meaning for as much as de la Vega is being a real pain in the ass, he's taking good care of your son.''

She sighed, long and loud, into Jeb's shirt. She didn't want to admit it. Ramon *was* taking good care of Nicky, she supposed. The gray-haired woman, too. They both were.

Kisses and hugs by strangers were far more preferable than…the alternative. She swallowed down a healthy dose of humility and acknowledged it.

But she refused to accept it.

She lifted her head. The gathering darkness shadowed Jeb's grim features. His scent surrounded her—an alluring blend of wind, sweat, tobacco—and a masculinity that sent an unexpected trill of excitement stirring in her belly.

She felt protected with him. As if his presence formed a shield against all that could go wrong for her and her baby.

"What now?" she asked. The pique had dwindled. She could think again. "Where do we go from here?"

Jeb's hand lifted, tucked windblown strands of hair behind her ear.

"We wait," he said.

"For how long?"

"Long enough for us to watch, learn their routine. See who goes out, who comes in. And when."

"And then we can take Nicky back."

He brought her against him again, rested his chin on the top of her head. "When it's safe."

"Safe, yes." They could do nothing to jeopardize Nicky's life. Nothing. "But how long, Jeb? One day? Two?"

When could she hold him again? He was so close. Knowing he was in one of those cabins in that valley was a torture no mother should have to endure.

"When I say the time is right."

Elena pushed away. "Jeb."

"I know you're hurting to get him back, Elena," he said. "But it's best to leave him where he's at. He's being cared for, and he's happy enough. Until you and I can get him away from de la Vega, you're going to have to let him be."

Her world began rocking again. "I don't want him with them any longer than necessary."

"Neither do I."

She set her hands on her hips, frustration growing in

leaps and bounds. "We can get him tonight. When everyone is sleeping."

"No. We can't."

"We know which cabin he's in."

"Doesn't matter."

"We know who's with him. An old woman who—"

"No, we *don't* know who's with him. That's the whole point, Elena. Could be de la Vega himself—"

Suddenly he stilled.

He'd heard something. Elena listened with him.

Someone, something, was out there. In the dark. Between the trees.

Her heart began a slow, heavy pound. Jeb's hand moved for the Colt at his hip, his long arm sweeping her behind him for protection. A faint light appeared, and Elena blinked in surprise. Unabashed, the glow grew steadily brighter, its scope larger.

Jeb swore under his breath.

A little Mexican man stepped out from behind the girth of a blue oak, not unlike a wraith shrouded in a ghostly dream. He walked straight toward them, a lantern in his hand.

"Put away your weapon, *señor.* I am not one of them," he said.

He kept walking closer, showing no fear. Elena marveled at his confidence that Jeb wouldn't shoot. Or perhaps he didn't understand the possibility of it. But Jeb just let him come as close as he wanted, his only movement being his finger caressing the trigger, ready to fire at the slightest provocation.

Elena stared at the man from around Jeb's shoulder. He wore the clothing of a peasant—sandals, loose cotton pants and a thin shirt open at the chest. She couldn't begin to guess his age, though the years were considerable. Sun and wind had etched deep lines into the leathery skin. His hair was heavy with gray and wild with tangles. It appeared not even a hat could tame its unruliness.

Whatever his eccentricities, he appeared lucid and determined to talk to them. Why else would he search them out, with a lantern no less?

"If I was one of de la Vega's men, you would not be alive right now." He spoke English, the accent of his own tongue thick but not overwhelming. He halted and lifted his lantern high. His black eyes studied Elena for a long moment. "Nor would you, *gringa.*" He shook his head sadly. "Especially not you."

"What the hell's that supposed to mean?" Jeb growled.

"He knows who I am," Elena said, taken aback. She stepped from behind Jeb, no longer afraid to let the little man see her.

"Sí," he said. "You are Nicky's mother."

She sucked in a breath. Just hearing him say her baby's name…

"I know everything that happens here," he said. "Come. Bring your horses. We must talk. I have a place where you can hide." He turned and headed deeper into the trees.

Elena exchanged a glance with Jeb.

"Could be a trap," he muttered.

"I don't think so."

She didn't know why, but she believed the old man. He knew about Nicky, even seemed sympathetic to her plight. Maybe desperation drove her to trust the man, but if he could help in even the smallest way to get Nicky back, then she would let him talk all night.

"He seems harmless, but hell, we wouldn't know for sure until it was too late," Jeb said.

But he headed toward his horse.

"What have we got to lose?" she asked, heading for her horse, too.

"Our lives, for starters."

She kept her eyes on the bead of light ahead of them. "I trust you'll make sure that won't happen. Hurry, Jeb. I don't want us to lose him."

"Let me go ahead of you. First sign of trouble, you turn tail and run, you hear me?"

"Yes. I promise."

The light had grown smaller. Jeb grasped his horse's chin strap and headed toward it, Elena right behind him with the mare.

By the time they caught up with the old Mexican, he had stopped at his destination. He turned the lantern to its highest vantage.

They stood in front of a wall of rock on one side. An open grotto of sorts gave shelter from wind and detection from the south. A thick growth of trees from the north would provide a glimpse of the world beyond the hills. The air was cool, protected from the heat of the sun. Somewhere in the near distance, she could hear the muted trickle of water over stone.

"My name is Simon," the man said, bringing her attention back to him. He laid out a bright-colored rug and set a clay jug on top. A cup. Cheese and a round loaf of bread. "Are you hungry?"

Jeb glanced at Elena. She shook her head, her belly still full from their late dinner.

"Neither of us are," he said.

"Thank you, though," Elena added.

"You have eaten at Berto's cantina, then, eh?" Simon

squatted on his haunches, tore off a chunk of bread and stuffed it into his mouth.

Jeb released his horse's chin strap and strode closer. He still carried his Colt though his grip had relaxed. "How did you know?"

"I saw you coming from San Ignatius. Everyone who visits the village stops there." He shrugged. "There is no other place to get a good drink or a hot meal than Berto and Alita's cantina."

Elena sat on the rug across from Simon. After a slight hesitation, Jeb joined her, sheathing the revolver before he hunkered beside her.

"You are no longer suspicious of me," Simon said, gesturing toward the holster. "That is good."

Jeb grunted, both his weapons visible and in easy reach. "I'm always armed, so don't go getting clever on me."

To Elena's surprise, Simon chuckled. He winked at her. "Is he always so—how do you say it—touchy?"

Her mouth softened. "Most times, yes. His name is Jeb Carson. And I am Elena Malone."

He acknowledged the introduction with a polite bow. "He is helping you find Nicky."

"Yes. I wouldn't be here now without him."

"How do you know of her son?" Jeb asked.

"I told you, *gringo*. I know everything that happens," he said, chewing on a piece of the cheese.

"How?"

"I watch. I learn." Abruptly he dipped his head, lifted one shoulder and contorted his body into a hunchbacked, grotesque *thing*. "And I pretend I am *loco*."

Elena drew back at the horrific sight he made in his tattered clothes and wild hair. "Oh, my."

Jeb breathed a startled oath.

"Why must you pretend to be crazy?" Elena asked, not sure if she should pity him or not.

He transformed himself back and calmly took another bite of bread. "Because Ramon must pay for what he has done. And there is no one left."

Jeb's eye narrowed. "Talk, old man."

He swallowed his food. His black eyes met Jeb's, but Elena could see the pain, the hate, in them. "Ramon rode into our village one night. He brings his men. Zapatistas, all of them. They are drunk on tequila. They steal our money, rape our women. All because of their cause."

"When?"

"Last year."

"Did you fight back?"

"*Sí*, but we were only a few against so many. And we had no weapons. We were only poor farmers. What did we know of fighting? Killing? We fought with what we had, but it did not matter."

"How horrible," Elena breathed, stricken.

Simon swung toward her. "There is no word to describe what we suffered that night."

"Then what happened?" Jeb asked quietly.

"They set fire to our fields and the village. As if what they had done to us was not enough. We were burned out of our homes, our crops. We had nothing left."

Elena bit her lip, the sympathy pouring from her.

"Those of us who could, moved away," Simon went on. "Those of us who could not—" he shrugged "—I buried."

For a long moment, neither Jeb nor Elena spoke. Elena didn't think she could if she tried, not the way her throat was clogged.

"The cemetery," Jeb said. "You take care of it, don't you?"

Simon reached for the jug, filled the cup with water, sipped. "It is important no one is forgotten."

"Your family?"

"They died that night, *Señor* Jeb. My wife. Three sons. One daughter. My father and brother. They are all gone."

"I'm sorry."

"*Gracias.* Me, too."

"But—" Elena hesitated. "Why do you stay? You say there is nothing here for you."

"My family is here." Simon's expression turned fierce. "I should have died with the rest of them. Many times, I have tried to understand why I did not. But I can not leave them. Never."

"I see." She swallowed.

"For them, I must seek justice."

"Against Ramon," Jeb said.

"*Sí.* Against all of them."

"Go on."

"When they come back to Mexico, to their camp, I watch them. I listen to them talk. I learn their plans."

"How?" Jeb demanded. "Do they know you? Trust you?"

Simon rose, strode toward a large straw basket heaped with acorns. He scooped up a palmful, then dropped them on the rug. Elena watched them scatter.

"Have you ever had roasted acorns, *Señor* Jeb?" he asked.

"Yes."

"Ramon has a special weakness for them."

"You bring him roasted acorns?"

"He does not question a crazy man who makes the best roasted acorns on the mountain."

"I see." Jeb frowned. "He doesn't recognize you from the night he raided your village?"

"No. It was dark. So much confusion. So much violence. I can move about their camp freely."

"And that is how you learned of my son," Elena said softly. "When you were in their camp. Bringing Ramon roasted acorns."

"*Sí.*" Simon's troubled glance lingered on her. "He is a fine boy, Elena. Ramon is proud of him."

"I know." Her chin tilted. She had seen that pride for herself.

"His men laugh when he tells them how he takes Nicky from his mother who sells *medicina* from a wagon. Ramon boasts that Nicky will be a great leader for Mexico one day."

"No. Never," Elena grated.

"You must get Nicky away from him before it is too late." Simon leaned toward her, his expression suddenly wild, desperate. If Elena hadn't known his sincerity, she would've been frightened of him. "You must take him back to America where he will be safe again. There is trouble coming. You must believe me."

"Trouble?" Jeb asked sharply. "Does it have to do with the illicit arms shipment?"

Simon whirled. "What do you know of the rifles Ramon is expecting?"

"Just that the deal has been set up. And the men who did it. Nothing more." Jeb's eyes narrowed. "What do *you* know of it?"

"I only know the rifles are coming. No one knows when. Not even Ramon."

"The shipment has got to be stopped," Jeb said, his expression grim.

"*Sí, sí.* It must."

"We've got to find out who's bringing them in. When. Where."

Simon squared his narrow shoulders. "I will do what I can to learn this. But what can we do? We are only two men against dozens."

"I'll find a way," Jeb said.

Simon glanced at Elena, as if he needed convincing. The job would be difficult, even for an entire army of men.

"He's quite good," Elena said, thinking how Jeb had tailed the band of revolutionaries right to their hideout. "You can be assured of that."

"You trusted him to find your son. I will trust him, then, too." Simon rose, quickly gathered the rug and the remains of his meal. "You will be safe here. Ramon does not know of this part of the mountain."

"When will we see you again?" Jeb asked, rising with him.

"I will go into his camp tomorrow, then I will come back to you. You must not let Ramon or his men find you here. They will kill you both."

On that dire warning he left, as quickly as he had appeared, a wild-haired wraith swallowed up by the darkness of the night.

Elena met Jeb's glance. The light from Simon's lantern cast a pallor to his skin, a sheen that made him look more ruthless than usual, his determination as fierce as ever to stop Ramon's revolution and whisk Nicky back into her arms.

If anybody could do it, Jeb could. And with Simon's

ability to infiltrate the revolutionaries' camp and glean key information, the chances seemed better than ever that he would succeed.

It was almost too much to hope for.

Chapter Eleven

Something nagged at Elena. She resisted the feeling—she didn't want to wake up yet. She was too warm, too comfortable, too sleepy. She rolled over to her side and pulled the blanket up higher over her shoulder.

The feeling wouldn't go away. She couldn't define it—an unsettling intuition that something wasn't quite right, an awareness that was instinctive and maternal, like when Nicky was fussy and couldn't sleep, either....

Her eyes flew open.

Nicky.

She sat up, heart pounding, searching for him.

She wasn't in Pop's wagon. Nicky wasn't in his bed. She wasn't in hers.

She blinked at the low-burning fire, remembered she was in a cave of sorts. A gentle breeze stirred the trees beyond. Across from her, Jeb slept.

Jeb.

The unsettling feeling disappeared.

He lay with his back to her, huddled under his blanket, shivering.

Jeb shivering?

Alarmed, she tossed aside her own blanket and scrambled over to him. She laid a hand on his shoulder, gently.

"Jeb, what's wrong?" she asked.

He rolled over to his back. Perspiration beaded his forehead and saturated the dark tendrils of hair on his temple. Glazed and feverish eyes lifted to hers.

"You're sick," she said.

Whatever she'd been expecting, it hadn't been this. He seemed too powerful, too invincible, to fall victim to human frailty.

"Didn't mean to…wake you," he said, his low voice hoarse.

She smoothed away the hair from his forehead. His skin blazed hot against hers, and she clucked her tongue in dismay. "You're burning up. Why didn't you tell me?"

"Not much you can do."

"I can try, can't I? What hurts?"

"You name it, it hurts."

"Oh, Jeb."

She bit her lip in sympathy. How could she help him? They were hiding on a mountain. It was the middle of the night. And a band of rebels was close by.

"Maybe you ate something that disagreed with you," she said.

"Don't think so."

She discarded the notion, too. She'd eaten the same food he had with no adverse effect.

"I'll get you some water," she said.

"Water. Yeah." His eyes closed.

"I'll be right back."

"Not going anywhere."

She found a cup and washcloth in his saddlebag and hurried to the waterfall she'd discovered just beyond their camp, a runoff from some mountain stream. After filling the cup and soaking the cloth, she knelt beside Jeb and helped him sit up. He drank until the cup was empty, then eased back down again.

"Thanks," he whispered.

He looked exhausted. Elena took the washcloth and bathed his forehead.

"How long have you been feeling like this?" she asked.

"Felt it comin' on for a while," he said. "Most of yesterday."

She recalled his heat when he had held her after they'd discovered Nicky in the hideout last night. The pallor of his skin in the lantern light, too, and the sheen of perspiration on his face.

He'd been stoic. Strong. The fever had set in, and she hadn't known.

"Do you get sick often?" The washcloth dabbed over his whiskery cheek, his chin.

"Never." He frowned. "'Cept once, when I had malaria."

"Malaria!"

"Last year. The Philipines." He grimaced. "Heard it could c-come back. Guess it did."

The washcloth faltered. "You think you have *malaria?*"

"Yeah."

"Oh, my God, Jeb."

"Got any…quinine?"

"Sorry. I'm fresh out."

"'Fraid of that."

"I have Pop's elixir, though."

He opened one eye. "No, thanks."

Exasperation at his low opinion of Doc Charlie's Miraculous Herbal Compound rolled through her. He'd never even tried her father's medicine.

"Jeb, it'll help take away the pain," she coaxed.

"Don't n-need it. I'll be better by morning."

Unfortunately, she couldn't force him. Maybe the malady would truly pass in a few hours, as he claimed. He seemed so tired, though. The shivers were uncontrollable, and his fever was alarmingly high.

What if not even Pop's elixir could help him?

"Maybe I should get Simon," she said, worried.

Both eyes flew open.

"The hell you will," Jeb growled.

"He might know what to do."

"You're not going to wander the mountain in the dark…lookin' for him. De la Vega could find you."

That was certainly true enough. And Elena didn't want to suggest the possibility of riding into San Ignatius, either, even though Berto and Alita would know if there was a doctor there who could help.

"I'll wait until morning, no later," she said firmly, giving in. "If you're not better by then, we'll do things my way."

His hand lifted and found hers. He managed to carry her fingers to his lips for a weak kiss. "I'm goin'…to be f-fine."

Her mouth pursed, but she didn't pull away. "People die from malaria, you know."

He rested her hand on his chest, covered it with his own. "Not me, sweet. Got to get that boy of yours…first."

Even feeling this miserable, he hadn't forgotten Nicky. She gave his fingers a quick squeeze, then pulled his blanket higher to his chin. "That's right, Jeb. You do. So you'd best go to sleep and get your strength back.

I'm going to stoke the fire higher for you. We have to stop these shivers.''

"Got a better idea."

She stopped fussing. "Like what?"

"A warm woman goes a long way in helping a man when he's c-cold. Her blanket, too."

It took her a moment to grasp his meaning. "Are you suggesting I sleep with you?"

"Been sleepin' with me every night. Just…too damn far away is all."

"Well." His proposition flustered her. "I'll give you my blanket, but I'm going to sit with you awhile instead. That fever bears watching."

"Don't want your blanket…if you're not going to share it with me."

"I do believe you're flirting again," she said. She retrieved the wool covering from the other side of the fire and draped it over him, making sure he was covered on all sides.

Despite his fatigue, a crooked smile came through. "When I'm feelin' better, I'll show you w-what…real flirtin' is like."

"Oh, shush."

But her belly warmed unexpectedly at the promise. He said nothing more, and after a moment, Elena realized he'd fallen asleep. She added more wood to the fire until it burned high and free, then resoaked the washcloth with fresh water and bathed Jeb's face again.

Afterward, she sat beside him, her knees drawn up to her chest, her troubled gaze rarely leaving him. It was a strange thing having Jeb sick. It frightened her now that she'd grown to depend on him.

To need him.

But he seemed certain enough he'd recover quickly.

Having suffered from the disease before, perhaps he knew as much for a fact. The disease would just need to run its course.

Tomorrow. Tomorrow, Jeb would feel better.

Until he did, she would do everything within her limited means to alleviate his discomfort. And help keep him alive.

Ramon de la Vega leaned a shoulder against the doorframe of his cabin and breathed in deeply of the crisp mountain air. The freshness filled his lungs and chased away the last of the morning's sleep.

He squinted against the rising sun. A flock of Mexican chickadees flitted in the branches of the oaks blanketing the hills beyond his camp. He listened to their song, savored it. So innocent, the little birds. So playful and sweet.

Like Nicky. His flesh. His blood.

His son.

The child had been an unexpected treasure that day in the Texas woodlands. The realization of who he was had stunned Ramon. Excited him. What kind of man would he be not to want the handsome little boy for himself?

Ramon smiled. A treasure, priceless and pure.

It no longer mattered that other women had not given him what he wanted most. Or that it'd been a blond-haired *gringa* who had. All that mattered was that Nicky was a miniature version of himself. He carried de la Vega blood in his veins. He belonged in Mexico with his proud padre.

Sí. Nicky would follow in his footsteps one day. He would finish the work Ramon had started.

Ramon's mind whirred with anticipation of how powerful his son would be. Respected and wealthy. He would devote his life to his beloved Mexico, just like Ramon did.

There was much work to be done first. A revolution was never easy. But Nicky would grow, become strong. Shrewd. He would learn how to rule a powerful nation like Mexico. He would be proud to serve her people.

With Nicky, Ramon had renewed hope. Because of Nicky, his revolution became more important than ever.

Footsteps shuffled behind him, and Ramon's thoughts evaporated. *Doña* Pia handed him a cup of steaming chocolate, rich with cream, just the way he liked it.

He considered her, still dressed in her nightgown, her feet in scuffed leather slippers. The aunt who had taken him in when he was just a young boy, orphaned after his parents died in a political execution ordered by Porfirio Díaz.

Hate curled in Ramon's belly whenever he thought of it.

But, childless herself, *Doña* Pia had loved him, and Ramon had thrived. He loved her, too, he supposed, as much as a man could love a mother that was not truly his own.

Por Dios, he would not have entrusted anyone else with Nicky's care. That much he could not deny. *Doña* Pia treasured Nicky as much as he did.

"Is my son still sleeping?" Ramon asked, testing the chocolate with his lip before sipping.

"*Sí.* But he was restless again. All night." *Doña* Pia glanced at him. "He misses his mother."

Ramon dismissed the concern in her voice. "He will soon forget her."

"She is out there, looking for him." *Doña* Pia's troubled gaze roamed the hills beyond their camp. "Surely you know that, Ramon."

"It does not matter."

"To her, it does. What mother would not fight for her child, eh?"

"She will not find us."

"And if she does?"

"She cannot have him back."

It was not often his *Doña* Pia disagreed with him. Ramon cared little that she did now.

"You must think of the child," she said, frowning. "He has his own family in America. They will be frantic for him."

"*Doña* Pia." Ramon bent and pressed a consoling kiss to her soft, wrinkled cheek. "Why must you be so stubborn? I have carried Nicky in my arms for several days now. He belongs in them. It is his destiny. His birthright."

She reached up and cupped the side of Ramon's face. "When you brought him to me, my heart filled with joy for you. But fear came, too, Ramon. Nicky is American. The United States government will not let you steal one of its children without striking back."

"I am not afraid of the Americans!" Ramon said coldly.

"For Nicky's sake, you should be."

He stiffened. "Enough of your scolding, old woman."

"Ramon, you must listen to me."

Impatient, he nudged her toward the door. "*Por Dios,* I am sick of your nagging. Go. See to my son. Make sure he gets all the sleep he needs."

She resisted, but only for a moment, as she always did. Like his men, she had learned not to fight him too much. Shaking her head sadly, she went inside the cabin.

But his impatience lingered. Her warning would not leave his head.

He did not want to think of the woman who had given his son life. He refused to remember her frantic screams or how she fought to keep him from taking Nicky.

The beautiful *gringa* whose name was Elena. She meant nothing to him.

He sipped the chocolate again. The drink, hot and sweet, slid down his throat and soothed the cold bitterness of his thinking.

She meant nothing.

The low, drawn-out croak of a raven startled Elena awake. An azure sky dappled through the leaves shading their niche, giving her a surprising declaration dawn had long since passed.

Thank God. The night hadn't been an easy one. The water she had given Jeb had come up time and time again until there was nothing left—and still his belly heaved. Elena had done all she could with what little she had to make him comfortable.

Now, at least, he slept, his body curled loosely with hers. She delayed moving away from him, partly from an unwillingness to disturb him. And because another part of her, the feminine one, *liked* lying next to him.

The admission slipped through her subconscious and embarrassed her a little. She'd never slept with a man before but there, well, there was a certain appeal to it. Man and woman, side by side. Comfortable and warm. Together.

In her case, of course, the situation was vastly different. The chills Jeb suffered drove Elena to share her body's warmth. When he'd been racked by the fire in his belly and on his brow, she'd been at his side to soothe both. He had reached for her in the night, and she'd been there for him to hold.

He slept with his chin against her temple, his long arm over her waist. Pleasingly heavy, Elena acknowledged. A bit possessive. Not at all loathsome as she once might have feared.

It should've been, perhaps. Loathsome. But it wasn't.

He had long lashes, dark and thick. She was so close she could almost count them. His skin was still too pale, though, his breathing too shallow. She pressed gentle fingertips to his forehead and discovered the burn of yet another fever.

He stirred, and Elena instantly regretted touching him. She shouldn't have disturbed him. His brows knit in a grimace, and he emitted a restless moan.

His eyes cracked open and caught her staring. He eased away, as if he hadn't known she'd be there. He blinked and tried to focus.

"Creed?" he asked, his voice low, rough.

"Oh, Jeb." She raised up on her elbow, her worry springing in leaps and bounds. Did malaria victims get delirious? "It's me. Elena."

"Elena." He calmed at the sound of her voice. His eyes cleared and he looked relieved. "Elena, Elena."

"How do you feel?" she asked, brushing his sweat-caked hair from his forehead.

"Lousy. I need another dose of quinine," he muttered, and moved restlessly beneath the blanket.

She drew her hand back. "I don't have quinine, Jeb. Remember?"

"No quinine?" He sounded puzzled at that. "Ask Creed, then. He must have it. My quinine."

Alarm rippled through her. He was worse than she thought.

"Find Creed, Elena. He has my quinine," he said, impatient.

''No, he doesn't. No one does. Oh, God. You need a doctor, Jeb.''

She flung the blanket back. She'd have to hurry to San Ignatius to find one. But dare she leave him long enough?

Simon. Maybe Simon would stay with him.

Jeb caught her wrist, jerked her toward him so hard she fell against his chest. The strength in him shocked her. She'd thought him weak, but his strength had easily overpowered her.

What if his fever deranged him so that he became violent?

What if he hurt her?

''No. Too far away,'' he said, teeth bared in desperation. ''Jungle's too thick. You'd never find your way through. You have to stay here with me and Creed.''

Elena bit her lip.

''There's no quinine, Jeb. No Creed, either,'' she said as calmly as she could.

He stared at her. ''He's in the jungle, isn't he? Took my damn quinine with him.''

She drew in a breath. ''Yes. That's it. That's where Creed is.''

''Get my whiskey, will you? I need whiskey for this god-awful pain in my gut.''

''All right.'' She swallowed. ''But you have to let go of me first, Jeb. The whiskey is in your saddlebag. Over there by the horses. See them?''

His head swiveled, his glazed eyes following her direction, then they darted back to her again. He nodded and released her wrist. ''All right. But don't go into the jungle without me or Creed. Too dangerous. Promise me, Elena.''

''I promise I won't, Jeb. I promise.''

He let her move off him. She scrambled to her feet, took a wary step back. He reminded her of a wounded animal, lying there on the ground looking up at her. An animal too ravaged by pain to fend for itself.

Her breath quickened. It frightened her seeing Jeb this way. She hastened toward the saddlebags, but it was her valise next to them that she grabbed and flung open. Let him think she was getting the whiskey he demanded.

He *needed* Pop's elixir.

She rummaged through the clothing crammed inside and found a bottle of Doc Charlie's Miraculous Herbal Compound at the bottom, tucked among a pile of Nicky's soft diapers. It'd been an afterthought that she brought any at all, but she'd thrown in several containers back at the woodlands, just in case.

Thank God she had. She needed it now more than ever.

She hurried back to Jeb, removed the cap and slipped her arm behind his neck to help him sit up. He swallowed a mouthful right from the bottle.

He grimaced at the taste. "That's not whiskey."

"Sure it is, Jeb. The fever must've made you forget. Here. Another swallow. There you go."

She poured a second dose into his mouth just as he was about to refuse, forcing him to swallow or choke. She recapped the bottle and hid it in the folds of her skirt.

He slid his tongue along his lower lip. And frowned.

Elena felt no guilt for deceiving him. "Now try to sleep, Jeb. When you wake up, you're going to feel better."

His eyelids sank lower. "Stay out of the jungle, Elena. Y'hear me?"

"Yes."

"Promise…me." His words slurred. He couldn't fight the fatigue that held him in its clutches.

"I promise. I'll be right here when you wake up. You'll see."

She cradled his dark head on her lap, smoothed the hair from his temple. She had to trust in Pop's elixir. She had to believe his medicine would make Jeb well.

But the worry ran strong within her, and her eyes blurred with tears. She lowered her head and pressed a gentle kiss to his brow.

And prayed that he wouldn't die.

Elena held Jeb for a long time, until the sun crept higher into the sky, until the need to feed the horses convinced her she could leave him for a little while. He slept deeply, his body still, frightfully so. She'd give him a little more time, then administer another dose of elixir.

And if that failed…

She settled the blanket closer around him. She would deal with failure later.

It was cooler here in the shade of the trees, though beyond them, the sun would be mercilessly hot. The thick foliage kept them in a separate world, isolated from the harsh beauty of the Mexican countryside.

From Ramon de la Vega's hideout.

From Nicky.

She watered the horses, her mind heavy with thoughts of her baby. Was he cool enough? He tended to get a rash when he wasn't. Hungry? He was only beginning to tolerate new foods. His stomach would be upset if they gave him something too foreign, too spicy.

Most likely, he had already had his breakfast. Had he eaten his lunch yet? He needed a nap, too. Every day. He was accustomed to one in the early afternoon and liked to be rocked before falling asleep. And Elena always sang his favorite silly song.

The need to see him rose up within her like water surging through a dam. She wanted to know what he was doing. Who he was with. If he was happy. Crying. Playing.

She couldn't take him away from Ramon. Not yet. She accepted that, understood it. But she could sneak a peek of him. Like she had last night.

She *had* to see him.

With the horses taken care of, there was only Jeb to worry about. She didn't intend to be gone long. He'd never know she wasn't there.

The decision made, she left their camp and crept down the overgrown path Simon had used. She found the road they'd taken from the cemetery easily enough, but avoided it for fear one of de la Vega's men might stumble upon her. Or her them.

She kept to the trees, darting from one to another with a nimble step, lower, deeper into the valley. Now that she knew where the revolutionaries' hideout was, she approached with more confidence, assured that with the thick cover of foliage, no one could see her.

The hideout appeared, and she halted behind the trunk of a Mexican oak. The place bustled with activity, women cooking over open fires, men tending to the remuda of horses, children running back and forth. Armed guards patrolled the area on horseback, rifles slung over their shoulders, their black eyes vigilant on the hills surrounding the encampment. Though Elena thoroughly searched each rebel's dark-skinned face, she didn't recognize Ramon or Armando among them.

But she found Nicky.

She almost missed him, sitting in a metal tub in the

shadows of one of the cabins, splashing water. A line of clothes had been strung between the structures, and his tiny red shirt and denim dungarees hung drying.

Her eyes clung to him, her heart swelling with love and breaking from being apart from him, all at the same time. Standing there, watching him, she relived the feel of his pudgy, wet body against her hands as she bathed him. His clean soap smell. His toothy grin as he played.

Nicky *loved* to play in his bath.

The elderly, gray-haired woman was with him again. Elena guessed she'd been assigned as his caretaker, and judging by the way she hovered close, her face smiling and gentle, she was a dependable one.

Even so, Elena steeled herself against the burn of jealousy. This woman had the privilege of being with Nicky when she—his own mother—couldn't.

It wasn't fair.

Though she knew she shouldn't, that she had to get back to Jeb before he awakened and discovered her gone, Elena lingered. It was too hard to leave Nicky just yet, when she'd missed him so much, for so long. She wanted to stay, soak in the sight of him for a little while. Then she would leave.

The staccato of horses' hooves on the dirt trail jarred her resolve. The rider was appallingly close—she could hear the rustle of the leaves upon the branches as they scraped against him, the labored breathing of his mount, the faint creak of saddle leather.

The hooves sounded closer, louder. She froze. One snap of a twig, one flash of movement on her part, and the rider would know she was there.

Oh, God. What then?

Ways Ramon de la Vega would take his revenge upon

her flashed in her brain. Jeb wouldn't know until it was too late. And Nicky…

The horse and rider trotted past. Recognition slammed into her, and with it, deepening dread.

Sergeant Cal Bender was back.

Chapter Twelve

Ramon cracked the shell of a roasted acorn and popped the kernel into his mouth, then considered the map of Mexico spread out on the table in front of him. His finger traced the state lines he already knew by heart. The rivers and mountains. The fertile valleys. The harsh but beautiful desert.

Land. There was nothing more important. Not even the very air he breathed. Or the power and wealth he craved.

He was not alone in his thinking. *Por Dios,* almost all of the Mexican people would agree, from the poorest of the peasants to the wealthiest of the hacienda owners. It was the soul of Mexico—the land. Its spirit.

Without it, a man had nothing to live for. He could not work. Prosper. What would he hand down to his sons and grandsons if he had no land to make them proud?

Ah, land was the prize of his revolution. The reason his men fought by any means they could to destroy the ideals of Mexico's president, Porfirio Díaz, who had taken the *ejidos,* the small tracts of farmland, and given them to the hacienda owners.

Millions of acres of land. Stolen from the poor. Given to the rich.

Just thinking of it fueled the fire of hate and revenge in Ramon, ignited anew his passion to fight.

He wanted the land back for his people. And—he could not deny—he wanted the power and wealth for himself. He would lie, steal, kill to get them. Had he not already done those things?

Sí. More times than he could remember.

Ramon leaned back in his chair. But he needed more guns. As many as he could get his hands on.

Impatience slashed through him. He would get them, if the word of the two United States Army soldiers could be trusted. They promised the shipment would arrive in a few days. A whole wagonful of wooden crates, packed tight with shiny, new Savage lever-action rifles capable of accurate, rapid fire of fifteen shots a minute.

Por Dios. Fifteen shots.

Ramon could hardly wait to hold such a weapon in his hands. The rifles would help him defeat Díaz's armies, which were determined to crush his rebellion, along with the hacienda owners who scoffed at them, as if Ramon and his men were no more than highway hoodlums.

The thinking of fools, eh? It would not be long before they learned how wrong they were.

Hiding here in the valley, waiting for the weapons, was not easy but dangerous. He must keep moving southward, to meet his friend, Emiliano Zapata, whose reputation was growing as fast as his own. Together, he and Zapata would lead the rebellion against Díaz and the hacienda owners.

Joining forces, they would succeed.

Ramon shelled another toasted acorn and returned his

attention to the map. He already knew every twist and turn of the country roads in northern Mexico. Zapata knew the south. They would meet somewhere in the central part. Along the way, Ramon would steal cattle, horses, money, just as Zapata would. He would show the farmers how to fight to get their *ejidos* back.

They would support him. Honor him.

In the future, when success was theirs, they would not forget what Ramon had done for them.

The door to the cabin burst open, and Ramon's head lifted. Only Armando would enter his cabin without knocking first.

"Ramon. We have a visitor," he said, looking grim.

"Who is it?"

"The Army soldier. Sergeant Bender."

Ramon's blood quickened. The sergeant and his partner, Corporal Nate Martin, had arranged the deal for the precious rifles. Had they come to deliver the weapons themselves? It had not been the arrangement for them to do so.

"Is the shipment here already?" he frowned.

"No. He comes alone."

"Without the corporal?"

"*Sí.*"

"Without the rifles?"

"*Sí.*"

Unease filtered through Ramon. Why would the American soldier risk returning to Mexico, then enter his camp without permission first? And why was the corporal not with him?

Ramon had given them the location of his hideout, a necessity for the delivery of the weapons. He'd sworn them to secrecy of the information with their lives.

"Tell him to come in, Armando," he ordered.

Ramon hid his apprehension the deal had somehow fallen through. He *needed* the rifles. Sergeant Bender and Corporal Martin had promised them. Ramon had paid them a generous deposit, and if they did not keep their end of the bargain, he would kill them for their sloppy way of doing business.

Sergeant Bender strode inside. Esteban and Fernando, two of Ramon's cousins, followed him in, their revolvers trained on his back.

"We got trouble, Ramon," the sergeant said without greeting.

It annoyed him that the man used his name with such familiarity. He ran a cold glance over the dusty, disheveled uniform. The soldier's jaw was swollen, too, the skin raw and bruised. He talked with his teeth clenched.

"It seems trouble has found you first, Sergeant," Ramon said. He folded his arms across his chest, over the belts of ammunition. "Where is your partner, Corporal Martin?"

"Dead, I reckon."

"Dead." Ramon's eye narrowed.

"What happened?" Armando demanded.

The sergeant glanced at him. "We got found out. Leastways, I'm figurin' we did."

Ramon uncrossed his arms, sat up slowly. The dull thrum of ugly premonition pounded inside him. "Explain yourself, Sergeant Bender."

"Nate and I got caught unawares a couple nights back. We was just mindin' our business, taking a piss in the Nueces. Next thing we know, here's Jeb Carson, armed to the teeth and itchin' to shoot."

"Por Dios." Such stupidity from the soldiers.

"He forced us into his camp. I managed to get away, but Nate didn't. Waited long as I dared for him to come out. Next thing I know, Carson's wrappin' him up and throwin' him on his horse." Bender spit on the floor. "Nate wasn't movin', either."

Ramon's mind sifted through the details, the possible repercussions. What had the soldier revealed before he died?

"Who is this Jeb Carson you speak of?" he asked.

The sergeant shifted, one foot to the other, as if just hearing the man's name made him nervous. "Hell, Ramon. Ain't you heard of him?"

"No," he snapped. "I have not."

"He's a mercenary. War Department hires him out. Sends him where no one else wants to go."

"He is a soldier?" Ramon exchanged a tense glance with Armando.

"Used to be, from what they say. Now he works on his own. Gathers intelligence for the Army. Undercover." Bender forced a laugh through his injured jaw. "Guess that's why you never heard of him, then."

Ramon was not amused. "I guess not."

"He carries a mean gun. Draws a hard line. Don't make mistakes, either, from what I hear."

"That so?"

"And that ain't all."

Ramon waited, his fury at the two soldiers' ineptitude simmering.

"He had a woman with him. The baby's mother."

Shock rippled through his men. Through Ramon. No one moved. Breathed.

"Describe her to me," Ramon commanded sharply.

"Blond. Green eyes. 'Bout yay tall. Real pretty." The sergeant paused, as if remembering. "Carson called her Elena."

Ramon's nostrils flared. It was her.

He had to think. Nicky's mother was an annoyance.
But this mercenary....

"Why was Jeb Carson with her?" he asked.

"Reckon he's helpin' her find her boy."

"But he is a soldier?"

"Mercenary," Bender corrected. "He's got ways of
doin' things the Army most likely don't want to know
about."

"So he was not riding with the Army? Other soldiers?"

"Nope. Just them two, near as I can tell."

"Where are they now? Texas? Mexico?" Ramon's
demand for answers fueled the rapid-fire questions.

"Don't know. Like I said, I ain't seen 'em for a couple of days." Bender shrugged. "But if Carson's with
her..." He hesitated. "Let's just say, she's got a damn
powerful ally in him."

Ramon digested the information. Elena traveled
around the country and performed in a medicine show.
That much he knew for sure. He did not believe she had
any association with the United States Army. Why
would she?

He had underestimated her ability to find him, however. Perhaps with this Jeb Carson, she would. Still, one
man and one woman should not be too much trouble.
They would not be able to take Nicky, not with so many
of his men to prevent them.

He should have been relieved by that.

Somehow, he was not.

Ramon leaned back in his chair and steepled his fingers.

"I am concerned your stupidity in being caught by
such a clever man as Jeb Carson will affect my shipment
of rifles, Sergeant Bender," he mused. "Should I be?"

"I'm just tellin' you, Ramon, that if she's got Carson with her and she's looking for her baby, and if Nate spilled his guts about the guns, then you got trouble. Carson ain't no one to mess with."

It was all he could do to keep from shooting the sergeant where he stood.

"So what you are saying, Sergeant Bender, is that Jeb Carson would inform your Army of the guns coming across the border to us?" Armando demanded, his voice stern.

"Maybe he would. Maybe he wouldn't. Couldn't say for sure."

Armando glared. "Would he or would he not?"

"I'm saying it's a possibility, damn it. They claim he's as fine a patriot as they come."

"Not unlike yourself, eh, Sergeant?" Ramon taunted, his smile cold.

Bender fidgeted, but he said nothing.

Ramon rose. "Is there anything else you wish to tell me?"

"Reckon there is." Bender slid his tongue around his lower lip. He glanced at Armando, at Esteban and Fernando, and finally, at Ramon himself. "I took a hell of a risk comin' all the way out here to tell you what's happened. I figured you was entitled to a decent warning. Bein's we're in the middle of a business arrangement and all."

Ramon inclined his head. "Your kindness is appreciated by all of us."

"So I was hopin' that—" he cleared his throat "—I was hopin' you could let me hole up with you out here. If Nate spilled his guts about them rifles, the Army's not goin' to be too happy with me when they catch wind of it."

Ramon made a sound of sympathy. "Treason is a serious matter for the United States, hmm?"

He frowned around his injured jaw. "Yeah."

"*Sí.* We can find a place for you here." Ramon smiled.

Relief slumped Bender's shoulders. "Much obliged."

Ramon gestured to Esteban and Fernando, a silent command to take care of the sergeant's slight problem in a quick and efficient manner.

"Wherever you choose, *compadre,*" he murmured.

His cousins nodded in understanding, then prodded the sergeant out the door with the noses of their revolvers. Bender paused long enough to lift his hand in a grateful wave before they pulled the door closed behind him.

Armando spun toward Ramon in disgust.

"*Stupido soldado!*" he spit.

Ramon's mouth tightened. "*Sí.* A stupid soldier."

"Esteban and Fernando will see that he is never found."

"So long as the women and children do not suspect. They will not understand how much trouble the sergeant has brought us with his carelessness."

Armando nodded in somber agreement. "What now?"

Ramon did not know how much of a threat Jeb Carson would be. Perhaps Bender had worried them for nothing. Perhaps Carson, with all his skills as a mercenary, would not even find them here so deep in the hills.

Then again, perhaps he would.

The wild-haired peasant, the *loco* he knew only as Simon, slid a bowl filled with acorns in front of him, his twisted little body moving so soundlessly that Ramon hardly noticed his familiar presence.

He scooped out a handful of the nuts, anticipated their mild, roasted taste. "We watch, Armando. We wait. And we pray the rifles will arrive very soon."

Jeb sat up slowly, a cautious test of his muscles gone tight from too many hours spent on the hard ground. He speared a hand through his hair, ran his palm over his whisker-rough jaw.

The fever was gone. The fire in his belly, too. The chills and headache. All of them gone.

Damned if he didn't feel good.

Puzzled by it, he pursed his lips. The relapse hadn't lasted long at all. Not like he expected. It should have.

Had he been sicker than he realized? Had more days passed than he knew?

He didn't think so. It didn't *feel* like they had.

He tilted his head back and gauged the light falling through the branches and leaves. The hottest part of the day had passed. Nightfall was only a few hours away.

Elena. Where was she?

He was alone in their little hideaway, but her presence was evident. Dishes were stacked off to one side, each one clean except for a bowl of what looked like broth. A pot of coffee simmered near the fire. He spied her hairbrush. Her shoes.

He felt no alarm. Instinct told him she wouldn't have left him. Not now.

He noticed a brown bottle nearby. Next to it, a spoon.

He recognized the elixir, the container half-empty. Doc Charlie's Miraculous Herbal Compound. Bemused, he removed the cap and sniffed. The smell registered in his brain. He dipped a finger into the liquid, tasted it. He knew that, too.

She'd given him doses of her father's medicine when

he'd been felled by the throes of the malaria. He'd resisted, but she had forced them down. Somehow.

Doc Charlie's Miraculous Herbal Compound.

Had it saved his life?

Maybe she'd found some quinine, after all. But there was no evidence of it. And where would she have gotten it?

He tossed aside his blanket, noted he wore no boots, no socks, no shirt. He found them all by his saddlebag, clean and folded neat. The prospect of a bath and a fresh change of clothes appealed to him.

Finding Elena appealed to him more.

He rose, realizing he was amazingly steady. Strong. As if the ravage of malaria had never happened.

But it had.

Puzzled, he headed toward the sound of falling water, his first guess of where Elena would be. He found her just beyond their camp, standing beneath the stream of water babbling from a rocky ridge high above her.

She was washing her hair, her back to him. She wore only a thin cotton chemise, her legs slim, shapely beneath the hem. Water splattered the fabric, made it cling to the curve of her hips. Elena, he discovered, had a fine-looking butt.

Fire leapt to his loins. He strode closer, his focus riveted to the tug and pull of the chemise around her backside while she scrubbed. She turned, her eyes closed against the soap's sting, and tilted her head back into the waterfall to rinse. Suds flowed from the top of her head down over the mane of hair hanging clear to her waist.

The front of her chemise was hopelessly wet. And damned sheer. He swallowed at the gossamer fabric pasted to the mounds of her breasts, darkened at the tips and pebbled from the cold.

The fire in him raged hotter.

She took a step forward out of the water, then bent at the waist to flip the dripping mass forward. She twisted the strands, squeezed out the excess...

Maybe she caught sight of his feet first. Or maybe she sensed his presence before she actually saw him. Regardless, she straightened bolt upright with a gasp.

"Jeb!"

"Don't stop on my account," he drawled. "I'm enjoying the show."

She looked taken aback. "I didn't know you were there."

"I know."

She looked beautiful, water sluicing down her arms, her hair hanging in sodden clumps around her shoulders, eyelashes thick and wet. He took a step closer, his toes finding water. She clawed the hair from her face and reached blindly for a towel.

Jeb plucked it away. He wasn't ready to give up that view yet.

"Jeb," she said, exasperated, and reached for it again.

She missed.

He smiled.

"You must be feeling better." She eyed him warily.

He wondered if she had any idea how naked she looked in that chemise. How damned erotic.

"I am," he said.

She leveled him with an assessing glance, as if to convince herself.

"You scared me, you know," she said, her tone accusing.

"Did I?" He tossed the towel aside, onto a bush, out of her range. "When?"

"Last night. All day today." She tucked a sodden hank of hair behind her ear and crossed her arms over her breasts, hiding them from him. "I thought you were going to die."

"So how come I didn't?"

"My father's elixir saved you."

He grunted. "You think so?"

"I know so."

He cocked his jaw. She might be right, after all. He'd have to do some more thinking on it.

"It's not quackery, like you claim," she said, chin high.

He thought again how good he felt. How *healed*.

"Maybe not," he conceded.

The secrets of the ancients.

"I didn't have quinine for you, though you were certain I did."

"Really?"

"You were delirious, Jeb. That scared me, too."

"Delirious."

"You thought we were in the jungle. That Creed was with us."

"I don't remember." He'd been delirious the first time he'd been taken in by the malaria, too. Last year. Creed had stayed with him. Dosed him with quinine. Saved his life.

Just like Elena had.

Except the quinine hadn't worked as fast. Not like the elixir had.

She clucked her tongue, her sympathy still strong. Fresh. "Your fever was so high, you were burning up."

He patted his bare chest. ''Is that why I'm not wearing a shirt?''

''Yes. I took it off to cool you down.''

''You took good care of me, didn't you?''

''Someone had to.'' She cocked her head. ''Simon brought you some chicken broth.''

''Simon.'' The wild-haired peasant. ''He was here?''

''Yes. This afternoon.'' She hesitated. ''I saw Sergeant Bender, Jeb.''

The soldier's name was a shot of grim reality. He stared. ''Where the hell did you see *him?*''

''Down by Ramon's hideout. He rode right past me.''

Bender's return had something to do with the shipment of arms. Jeb could think of no other reason why he would leave Texas to head back to Mexico and de la Vega.

''They brought him into one of the cabins,'' she went on. ''A little while later, they brought him back out again. I never saw him after that.''

Jeb wondered if he was still alive. He didn't deserve to be. He regarded Elena with a scowl. ''What do you mean 'he rode right past you'? You went down there? Alone?''

She stiffened. ''I wanted to see Nicky.''

He exhaled a slow breath. The risk she'd taken…

''So, did you?'' he said between clenched teeth.

''Yes.'' Her lip curled in a pout. ''They were giving him a bath. I wanted to march right in and take him away.''

''You were a damn fool to go there.'' But some of his irritation left him. It was hard for her to be apart from her baby. ''He doing okay?''

''Well enough, I guess.'' Her expression turned beseeching. "I want him back, Jeb. I don't think I can wait much longer."

"I know, Elena."

With the arrival of the illicit weapons certainly imminent, it was imperative to get the boy out. If they didn't, de la Vega would once more be on the move, committing his acts of vicious banditry, all in the name of his revolution. He would take Nicky with him. Nicky could get hurt, an innocent in all that violence.

Jeb's bout with malaria had delayed the rescue of Elena's son. They'd lost too much time already.

"Tonight," he decided.

"Tonight." She pressed her fingers to her lips at his decision. Fingers, he noted, that had a tinge of blue.

"You're cold," he said, stepping closer. He was responsible for it. He'd taken her towel, after all. His arms took her in, enfolded her wet body against him, absorbing her cold.

"Are you up to it?" she asked, her words soft, worried.

"What? Holding you like this?"

She went still at his teasing. "No, Jeb. Are you up to getting Nicky back?"

He chuckled, low and quiet in her ear. "I've never felt better, darlin'."

Or more desirous of a woman, of Elena, than now.

He expected her to resist, to plant her hands against his chest and push him away in a burst of feminine defiance.

Two days ago, she would have. One.

Surprisingly enough, today, this minute, she didn't.

Maybe she'd gotten used to touching him while he was sick. Or maybe she was so caught up in the prospect of snatching her son from the revolutionaries that she wasn't aware of the lust building inside Jeb with every breath he took.

But the faint tremble that went through her convinced him, yeah, she did.

His head lowered. He traced the curve of her ear with his tongue and drew her lobe between his teeth with a tender nibble.

"Bathe with me, Elena," he whispered. He sucked gently against the curve of her neck. "Then make love to me."

Her breath caught at his bold proposition, and she trembled again. "I can't."

"I want you." He dragged his teeth slowly along her jaw. Licked and tasted her wet skin. "You have any idea how much?"

"Jeb." She'd kept her arms between them, but now they unfolded and moved to his chest, her palms tentative against him, as if she wanted to snake her arms around his neck but held back before she did. "Please."

"Please what? Please make love to me, Jeb? Please strip me naked and get in the water with me, Jeb?" he taunted in a husky whisper.

She pressed her lips together. But her eyes closed and she angled her head, giving him freedom to nuzzle her some more.

"What do you want, Elena?" Persistent, his hands rubbed down her spine and spread to cup her buttocks in his palms. He pressed her against him, let her feel how hard he was for her. "Tell me."

A sound of distress escaped her, and her arms lifted hesitantly to his shoulders. Still she held back, and he marveled at her self-control when his own was disintegrating like smoke in the wind. He dragged hot kisses over her cheek, her cheekbone, the corner of her eye.

He tasted the salt of a single tear snared in her lashes, and he knew, then, he was moving too fast. Ramon de la Vega had tromped upon her womanly needs with his violence and buried them so deeply he made her afraid to feel them again.

Afraid.

Jeb swore inwardly and reined in tight his own needs. Elena had been through hell. He had to remember that. He had to give her the time she needed to heal.

Damn it, he intended to see that she did. A beautiful, vibrant woman like Elena needed a man to pleasure her senseless until she felt so utterly female she would forget that horrible hell she had once lived.

Jeb took her mouth with his in a gentle but persistent assault of kisses. They would be the beginning, his kisses. To break through the barriers of apprehension and resistance until she couldn't deny she wanted him as much as he wanted her.

His hands slid back up her spine and circled her tight. She rose up on tiptoe, letting him hold her, kiss her, over and over. She molded to him, her lips moving, seeking. Wet.

His blood burned hotter. He didn't know how long he could keep his restraints in place with all she made him feel. He groaned, low and not a little frustrated, then pulled back, fisting his hand into the soap-clean tangles of her hair.

"I'm going to make love to you, Elena. Y'hear me?" he murmured against the warm skin at her temple. "Not now. But it's going to happen. I want you to think on it. And I want you to want it and be ready for it because, sweetheart, I'm wanting you so bad it's making me crazy."

She stared up at him, her lips swollen, her eyes shimmering. Her throat worked, as if she tried to speak but couldn't.

"Nothing's going to happen until you're ready. I swear it." He kissed her one last time, long and lingering and sweet.

She drew away and touched his cheek. "Jeb, I'm sorry."

"Don't be."

"You're making me want…something I've never let myself think about. I'm afraid to. I—"

She clamped her mouth shut. Jeb figured it cost her some to admit that much, not only to him, but to herself.

"Then I'm glad it's me who's making you want, and not someone else."

He lowered his head to kiss her again but glimpsed movement in the trees. A familiar face who came to call.

"Go on and get dressed," he said, his ardor fast cooling. He took her towel and wrapped it around her. "Simon's here. Might be he has news to share with us."

Chapter Thirteen

Shadows leapt and lunged against the rocky wall of the grotto in a jerky dance of firelight that cast Simon's features into eerie relief. His wiry hair stuck out from his head like frizzed cotton, and his skin looked tough as cowhide. A bizarre little man, Jeb thought. But a kind one.

He and Elena had become fast friends during the short time Jeb had taken sick. They had talked quietly while Simon taught her to make tortillas, roll the dough to the right thickness, test the heat of the griddle. She made a good-size stack while Jeb ate his dinner of beans and rice, his attention more on her than the food in front of him.

She had a rapport with Simon that Jeb envied. She was relaxed. Smiling. Not as skittish around the old man as she was with Jeb.

But then, if her kisses this afternoon were any indication, she was getting better about it.

The thought consoled him, and he hefted another forkful of rice into his mouth.

"He is hungry, eh, Elena?" Black eyes twinkling, Simon glanced over at Jeb. "A good sign he is feeling better."

"Hmm. His second plate already." She set aside the cast-iron griddle to cool. "Shall I offer him a third?"

"No, no. He will—how do you say it?—explode." Simon grinned.

Jeb grunted and washed down the last of the beans with a gulp of cold water fresh from the falling stream. "Can't remember being so hungry."

"You recovered quickly from the malaria, *Señor* Jeb. I would not have thought it possible."

Elena poured coffee into a tin cup and handed it to him. "That's because I gave him my father's medicine."

"*Gracias.*" Simon sipped, winced at the hot brew on his tongue. "Your father's medicine?"

"He's concocted an elixir." Jeb accepted the cup she gave him and blew once on the steaming liquid to cool it some before drinking. "It's—" He almost said *miraculous.* "Well, it's good. Guess I'm proof of that."

"It's better than good, Jeb," Elena chided, and returned the enamel coffeepot to the fire. She winked at Simon. Jeb saw the pride in that wink. "It's miraculous, actually."

"Made from the secrets of the ancients." The words were out before Jeb could stop them.

He frowned again.

"Is your father a doctor?" Simon asked.

"No. But he's helped heal many people. He's as capable as any licensed physician."

The little Mexican eyed her with sudden sadness. "I think he will be worried about you here in Mexico, no?"

She drew her knees up to her chest, rested her chin on top, and sighed. "Most assuredly. He's in San Antonio. A hospital there."

Simon clucked his tongue in surprise. "Oh?"

"Got roughed up when de la Vega took the boy." Jeb leaned back and pulled a cigarette from his pocket.

"Ramon. Always Ramon." Contempt dripped from Simon's tone.

"He has certainly made our lives difficult," Elena murmured.

"Hell is more like it." Jeb lit the tobacco and thought of all she'd been through.

"Ramon knows you are looking for him," Simon said grimly.

Jeb exhaled with a slow nod. "I suspected Bender told him as much."

"*Sí,* he did." Simon sipped again from the cup. "You know the sergeant came, then."

"Yes, Elena saw him."

"He thinks his partner, the corporal, is dead."

"He is."

"And you killed him?"

"Yeah. Couldn't be helped."

Simon shrugged. "It is better that way."

"What else can you tell me?"

"Bender is dead, too."

Jeb squinted against curling smoke. "You know that for sure?"

"*Sí.* I saw how they killed him."

"A firing squad?"

"No," Simon said with a shake of his head. "Esteban and Fernando buried him to the neck, then galloped over his head with their horses. I am sure Sergeant Bender was happy to die, then."

"Oh, my God." Elena jerked back in shock. "And these barbarians have my son!"

"But not for long." Jeb vowed it.

"When do you intend to take him?" Simon asked.

"Tonight. After dark."

Simon nodded agreement vigorously. "You must move quickly. Ramon has made plans to pull out as soon as his rifles arrive. He has posted more guards around his camp because he knows you will come for little Nicky."

"You know where the guards are?" Jeb asked.

"*Sí*. I was there when he gave them their orders."

"Good." Anticipation began to build inside Jeb.

"My home is not far from here. Elena can wait for you there," Simon said.

Elena straightened. "I'll do no such thing."

Jeb ground out the stub of his cigarette in the dirt. He groped in his brain for a way to convince her to stay behind and let him kidnap Nicky without her.

He failed.

"The boy knows his mother," Jeb said finally. "He'll raise less fuss with her." A corner of his mouth lifted. "Besides, I'd have to tie her to a tree before she'd let me go without her."

Elena was not amused.

"Do either of you really think I'd stay behind after I've come this far for him?" she asked, looking so offended even Jeb regretted entertaining the thought.

"*Por Dios,* it is dangerous," Simon fussed.

The smart thing to do was to go without her, as Simon insisted. She'd be less baggage. Safe. Jeb could move in among the revolutionaries, take the boy and escape without having to worry about her tripping him up somewhere along the way. Any rule book would state a soldier, even a mercenary like himself, would leave a woman behind.

It was what the General would do. Leave her behind.

''She comes, but she follows my orders,'' Jeb said, refusing to acknowledge the rebellion that still ran strong within him where his father was concerned. His stern gaze found Elena. ''But we don't do a damn thing until we come up with a foolproof plan that will keep us all alive, y'hear me?''

''Yes,'' she sniffed.

A moment passed.

''Do you have a plan yet?'' she asked.

''No, Elena,'' he said, mildly exasperated. ''But I will soon enough.''

''Well, I do.''

He regarded her. ''That a fact?''

''Want to hear it?''

The quiet intensity in her voice suggested that, whatever her plan was, she'd thought it through and was convinced it would work. Jeb admitted to a certain curiosity. Hell, at this point, his options were wide-open.

He leaned forward. ''Talk, darlin'. I'm listening.''

Elena carefully pulled the branch down to better see through the leaves into Ramon's camp. She winced at the faint rustle the movement made but assured herself the revolutionaries couldn't hear this far away. Still it would only take one to notice their presence in the trees, then all would be lost.

Jeb lifted the field glasses and peered through the lenses from the opening she'd made. He scanned the camp slowly, methodically, committing each man's location to memory, each woman and child, each stray dog. The horses, the fires, the weapons. Each cooking pot, each bottle of tequila.

And Nicky, she knew, most of all.

He was with the plump, gray-haired woman again.

Doña Pia, Simon had told Elena. Ramon's aunt. Wearing his little red shirt and dungarees again, Nicky sat on a blanket at her feet and played with toys too small to distinguish. He seemed content enough and, for that, Elena was grateful.

The guards, of course, were not as visible. Simon had pinpointed their locations, which were far more discreet—deeper into the trees. They protected their own from afar, under strict orders from Ramon. No one would be able to slip into camp without being seen.

"That is Fernando, there by the twisted old oak. See him?" whispered Simon.

"I see him." Jeb halted the lenses over the unsuspecting Mexican. "He looks about Elena's size."

"*Sí.* I think so."

"All right. I'm going down." He handed the glasses to her. "I'll make this quick. Be ready when I come back."

She nodded. "I will be."

"Simon?"

"I know what to do, *Señor* Jeb."

So did Elena. Jeb had drilled the plan into their heads, over and over again.

"Watch my back. But don't let anyone see you," he ordered.

"That would ruin everything if I did, eh?"

Despite the flippancy of his words, Simon's expression was serious as his gnarled fingers grasped the revolver Jeb pressed into his hand.

A knapsack lay at Jeb's feet. Next to it, a paraphernalia of items he'd removed from the inside. He squatted, slipped a bowie knife between his teeth, then stuffed a long strip of cotton fabric and a coil of wire into a pocket. He worked fast, his movements so brisk and methodical Elena couldn't help knowing he'd done all this before.

He tugged on gloves, pulled his hat lower over his eyes and rose. She sensed the adrenaline coursing through him, the ruthlessness he kept tight inside him. He showed no fear at what he was about to do, at the danger he would be in. He thrived on it, the danger, met it head-on, and he excited her more than any man she'd ever known.

His glance lingered over her but for a moment, then he was gone before she could whisper her worry for his safety. Simon followed, just far enough back to keep him in sight.

Alone, Elena set to work, readying herself for Jeb's return. She stripped off her shoes, blouse and skirt, then swiftly brushed her hair back into a thick knot high on her head, holding the strands snug to her head with pins. She'd already penciled in a thin mustache over her lip from stage makeup she kept in her valise, and the sombrero she would soon have would help hide her face.

She stood bare legged in her chemise and once again peered through the opening in the branches. The fires in Ramon's camp threw off enough light for her to find Jeb in a stealthy approach toward the guard from behind. Elena held her breath, fearful the snap of a twig would betray his intent, but Fernando never suspected Jeb was there until the wire around his throat told him.

With his air choked off, Fernando's eyes rolled back and he crumpled. Jeb released the wire and caught him as he fell, then dragged him into the shadows. Simon appeared one moment; in the next, he disappeared with Jeb. After a short period of time, where Elena's heart threatened to pound right out of her chest, Simon reappeared again, his arms full of the guard's clothes, and

Jeb soon followed. Both of them were safe with Fernando hidden, bound, gagged and thankfully unconscious.

Simon hurried up the hill toward her. "Here you are, Elena. A good fit, no?"

"Yes, I think so," she said, pulling on the black shirt still warm from the rebel's body. "The pants, too." She fastened the buttons of both garments and stepped back into her shoes.

"You look just like one of them," Jeb muttered, and pushed the sombrero onto her head.

"I have to," she said.

It was the only way her plan would work. Fast talking on her part had convinced Jeb to go along with the scheme. He'd been dead-set against her getting anywhere near the revolutionaries.

But one of them had to—to get Nicky.

Elena insisted on being the one. She had the training. The skill. As his mother, she was best suited for it—Jeb had said as much, earlier—and when Simon reluctantly concurred the plan could work, Jeb had agreed. But only after he insisted on being right in the camp with her, in the shadows, heavily armed and prepared to kill to defend her.

Her fingers explored the wide, beaded brim of the sombrero. The sheer breadth of it would take some getting used to, but that same breadth would hide her blond hair and pale, feminine features. She had no choice but to wear the thing.

She was ready to go. A final glimpse into the revolutionaries' camp showed they had lined flaming torches in two rows between the cabins, forming a corridor of sorts. The firelight cast the entire area with daylike brilliance, an advantage she and Jeb needed now that night had fallen.

The anticipation in the camp was palpable. The pleasure of the entertainment to come.

"Ramon was a trick rider not so long ago," Simon whispered. "It is how he met Emiliano Zapata, when they both worked for a rodeo show in Mexico City. They are excellent horsemen. And Ramon likes to remind his people just how good he is."

"His men are bored," Jeb mused, watching the rebels mill about, bottles of tequila in their hands. "They'll do anything for some excitement."

"A little show will help them pass the time until the rifles arrive," Elena mused.

"*Sí*. Ramon can afford the luxury. He knows the men he has posted around the camp will guard him and their families while he shows off." Simon's lip curled in disgust. "See how he struts among them like a rooster?"

"It's time we knock him down a peg or two." Jeb's shadowed gaze found Simon. "You sure you're going to be okay going down there?"

"*Sí*." Simon shrugged. "They will not find it so unusual that I am there, even this time of night." He handed Elena the reins to her horse. "The men will let Ramon begin first. They will wait until he invites them to ride with him. It is then, Elena, you must make your move. To do so sooner will only insult him. Do you understand?"

She nodded, her attention drawn yet again toward the tiny spot of red that was her son, still sitting on the blanket. No longer playing with his toys, he was engrossed, instead, with the horses that had always fascinated him. The men brought them from their corral, saddled and ready to ride.

The time was at hand.

Jeb turned to her.

"Elena," he began.

She heard the rasp of unease in his rough whisper, his reluctance to involve her in their plan. Yet no one knew better than she the risks to her son if she failed.

Quickly she pressed her fingers to his lips. "Shh. This is our own little war against Ramon, Jeb. How can we not fight?"

Something flickered in his dark eyes. His fingers caught hers and squeezed, as if he willed his protection to her in that one touch. Then, abruptly, he released her.

"Wait for my signal. Both of you. When I give it, get the hell out of the camp. I'll cover you." He hooked his knapsack over his shoulder and reached for the reins of his horse. "Any questions?"

"None." Elena shook her head, though her heart pounded ferociously inside her. Her success in the coming minutes would either bring Nicky back into her arms—or keep him out of them forever.

If she didn't despise Ramon de la Vega so much, Elena might have thought him a handsome man. Charismatic, white teeth gleaming in a broad smile as he charmed his audience with his fancy riding tricks, she had to admit he possessed a natural agility on the back of a horse.

She had parted from Jeb and Simon only moments ago, each off to prepare for their part in her plan. She crouched in the shadows on the fringes of the camp and watched Ramon ride down the fire-illuminated corridor. He stood in the saddle at full gallop, balanced on both feet and twirling a rope in each hand. He commanded the attention of his people, and gloried in the praise they gave him. His grace and ability couldn't be denied, she supposed. She had to give him that much.

After he finished his stunt, Ramon rode toward the center of the corridor, swept off his sombrero and bowed with a grand flourish. Firelight touched the wavy hair hanging long and thick to his shoulders. Again, his white teeth gleamed in a broad smile as he reveled in the applause.

He turned, said something to the men clustered at the end of the line, and several mounted up.

There it was. The invitation to his men to join him, just as Simon predicted.

Elena drew in a deep breath. She mounted up, too.

A dozen yards away, Jeb hovered in the dark shadows. Not even she could see him, but she knew he was there. Watching. Giving her enough time to assess the situation, call the shots as needed, but ruthlessly prepared to help her if something went wrong.

Nothing would.

Elena urged the mare out of the shadows. The men were boisterous from their tequila and intent on the rider currently heading down the corridor; no one questioned her approach as she took her place at the end of the line. And why would they? She was dressed in a black shirt and snug-fitting pants, conchos marching down the outside seams, and looked no different than they did.

One revolutionary, then another, took his turn. Well into their spirits, they performed their stunts with a garish lack of finesse and an abundance of humor. Others took the event more seriously, but no one tried to outperform Ramon. Their respect for—or perhaps their fear of—their leader would never allow them to do so.

Finally there was no one left in front of her. Armando

waved his bottle of tequila. ''Go, *amigo*. Let us see if you are as good as Ramon, eh?''

Elena lifted her hand and feigned a drunken wave. It was not her intention to outcompete anyone. If she tried, she would only draw attention to herself. She merely needed a way to get closer to Nicky and formulate a plan to snatch him right out from under everyone's nose.

A simple set of cartwheels would allow her to do that. They'd be easy to manage around the sombrero, and she wouldn't have to concentrate on speed. More important, she'd done them so many times she could perform blindfolded.

The mare broke into an easy run. Elena grasped the saddle horn and one of the handholds, stood in her right stirrup, leaned back and kicked her legs up into the air, straight and spread-eagled. She hit the ground, twisted and rolled over to the other side the same way, then dropped back into the seat.

She pushed the sombrero tighter onto her head, barely hearing the raucous cheers. Her glance caught Simon as she rode by him, meandering closer to *Doña* Pia and Nicky.

Elena reached the end of the corridor, slowed the mare and turned her around. She stole another glance at her son as she galloped back down to the other side, giving a repeat performance of the cartwheels. He hadn't noticed her, but then she looked like any of the other men. Clearly he found Simon's eccentric appearance more interesting.

''You are very good, *amigo*,'' Ramon called out as Elena rode past him into the throng of horses and men. She pretended not to hear. ''Why have I not noticed it before?'' He raised up in the stirrups, strained to see her beyond the sea of sombreroed heads.

Her heart pounding, she continued to ignore him and rode deep into the mass of bodies clustered at the end of the corridor.

"Ramon! It is time for *Correr al Gallo!*"

The revolutionary's attention swiveled between Elena and Armando's call. He apparently dismissed his curiosity about her as not important enough to pursue. He broke into a broad smile and spurred his horse back into the lane.

Relief poured through Elena. Thank God, Armando had distracted him.

There was great excitement for what was to come next. Elena recognized *Correr al Gallo,* one of the oldest displays of riding skills first devised by Spanish vaqueros who had raced past partially buried chickens and plucked them from the ground in a grand swoop. Not a particularly appealing trick, to be sure, but one the revolutionaries seemed to relish.

Elena held back, watched them ride hard toward their squawking quarry, then lean low from the saddle to grab one and hold it high in victory. She had done pickup tricks, too, innumerable times, using handkerchiefs and hats and paper bags filled with sand.

But never a little boy...

The decision slammed into her with a jolt. She'd have to use a different technique than the Mexicans, of course. And ride considerably slower.

But it would work.

It had to. She had only one chance. One single, heart-stopping chance. If she failed, Ramon would know who she was. He would know Jeb was here, too.

He would know everything.

She couldn't fail.

She took her place in the line. She needed a practice

run first. There was too much at stake to misjudge her ability to grab Nicky. One misstep by her horse, a miscalculation of speed, *Doña* Pia…

So much could go wrong.

Nothing would. Nothing would. Nothing would.

Her ears filled with the drunken whoops of the men who cheered their comrades on. The scents of burning torches and sweating male bodies surrounded her, but Elena was aware only of Nicky, still sitting on his blanket, close to *Doña* Pia.

Too close. Why did she have to be so damned *close?*

The mare broke into an easy canter. Not too fast. Not too slow. Elena held her in line with a white-knuckled grip on the reins.

She passed a squawking chicken. Its plight held Nicky transfixed, his wide eyes following each whooping revolutionary as they raced by him. His head swiveled toward Elena, coming up next…

She rode by a second chicken, sat sideways in the saddle and removed her left foot from the stirrup, then replaced it with her right. Grabbing the handholds again, she squatted, her knee pressed against the mare's side.

A third chicken went by. She pushed her knee under the stirrup leather that would help keep her braced against her horse. She let go of the saddle horn, extended her left leg straight and stretched out her left arm.

Hanging this low, she could touch the ground.

She could grab Nicky.

The fourth chicken passed through her range of vision. The sombrero brim fluttered in the breeze, bumped against the mare's hindquarters and went askew. She hastily righted it again.

Elena's gaze lifted, and met Nicky's. Time stopped. A lightning bolt of recognition seemed to pass through him, that intangible bond between a child and his mother forged from birth, powerful and instantaneous. Feeling it, knowing it, incited a flash of emotion in Elena.

A fifth chicken flared up before her, jerking her attention, and she automatically reached out to grab it.

She missed.

The mood of her audience abruptly shifted. The Mexicans booed their disapproval at her error with arrogant jeers. Elena grasped the saddle horn, heaved herself up and sideways back into the saddle.

At the end of the corridor, the mare turned and, unable to stop herself, Elena again sought out Nicky. He pushed himself to a standing position, his black eyes wide and riveted on her. His mouth moved, formed the word *ma-ma-ma.*

"Compadre!"

The bark in Ramon's voice jerked Elena's glance away from her son with a start. The crowd fell deathly still. Ramon rode toward her from the opposite end of the corridor.

"How is it that one who does such beautiful cart-wheels over his horse cannot pick up a single chicken when he rides slow enough that even an old woman can do it, eh?" he taunted.

He drew closer. No one spoke. Moved.

"But you found my son more interesting than the chicken. He distracted you, did he not? What is it about him that fascinates you?"

Her blood ran cold. He knew who she was. Any minute, dear God, any *second,* they would take Nicky away so that she'd never see him again.

"Take off the sombrero, *compadre.*"

The low-voiced command hissed with menace. Ramon removed the revolver from his holster, reined his horse to a stop and pointed the barrel right at her.

"Do not make me kill you in front of our son, Elena," he taunted softly.

Our son.

Hatred exploded inside her at the intimacy his words implied. A loathing, swift and deep, shattered her fear of what he might do and inflamed her need to take Nicky away from him.

Suddenly an object dropped from the air. Glass shattered. Smoke appeared and began to billow and swirl like a cloud of black magic.

Jeb. Oh, God. It was Jeb, creating the diversion she needed, when she needed it most. The women screamed. The revolutionaries scrambled for their weapons, their dark eyes clawing the hills for the source of the attack.

Ramon's lips curled back in a savage epithet and he raised his revolver toward her, his finger on the trigger.

Elena whipped off the sombrero and flung it at him with a sharp snap from her wrist. His arms came up to deflect it, and his shot went wild.

She jerked hard on the reins, turning the mare back toward Nicky and dropping back down to the side. In the chaos, everything moved split-second fast. Or was it slow motion? She couldn't tell, couldn't think, her mind focused only on the red fabric of her son's shirt.

On him stepping off the blanket toward her, his arms outstretched.

On *Doña* Pia coming out of her chair with a cry of protest.

On Simon, hurtling his twisted, old body against her, knocking her facedown into the dirt.

Hanging by the stirrup low to the ground, Elena scooped Nicky up against her with one arm. She might never know the strength it took to take his weight and heave them both up and back into the saddle, to kick free of the stirrup that held her and properly reseat herself all in one swift motion.

It wasn't important. Only that she managed it. That she had Nicky back with her again.

Another object dropped from the sky. More glass shattered. An earsplitting string of *rat-tat-tats* followed—the firecrackers Jeb had lit, sounding like an army of snipers hidden in the trees, shooting into the camp, and the chaos increased tenfold.

The Mexicans fired in the direction of the firecrackers, seeming to forget Elena in their fierce determination to ward off the unseen foe. Smoke billowed throughout the camp. Men coughed and choked, their eyes watering from the sting, their confusion blatant and unchecked.

Then, behind her, a shot exploded, and the burn of it sliced through Elena's body.

Chapter Fourteen

Jeb lit another fuse, drew his arm back and hurled a clay canister containing a combustible mixture of cane sugar and saltpeter into Ramon de la Vega's camp. It was his last smoke bomb, and he grabbed his knapsack. Damn it, Elena was in trouble. He had to move fast.

He should never have agreed to her harebrained scheme. What could he have been thinking, letting her go into the revolutionaries' camp alone? He leapt onto his horse and unsheathed his Winchester. Fear pummeled through him that he wouldn't reach her soon enough. She was unarmed. In no position to defend herself. And de la Vega was on to her.

She was going to make her move for Nicky. Any minute now. When she did, all hell would break loose.

He rode hard through the trees, ignored the branches and leaves slapping against him. He had to get to her. He had to get her and her baby the hell out of that camp.

Within the perimeters, the smoke billowed and built. Jeb kept track of her through the trees as he raced, watched her throw the sombrero at de la Vega, heard his shot go wild. She bolted from the corridor and between the fiery torches, grabbed her son while hanging on to the side of her horse. Jeb caught up with her as she headed up the hill, barely seated in the saddle again.

"Go, Elena! Hurry!" he yelled.

She twisted toward him. Blond hair slipped from the pins and onto her shoulders. If there'd been a shred of doubt among the revolutionaries that she was Nicky's mother, all that hair would be proof enough she was.

"Jeb!" she gasped.

"Go!" He made a savage gesture to keep riding, and she obeyed, spurring the mare into a run until the receding hoofbeats assured him she'd get away safely.

He pulled up, shot a glance back toward the camp. He caught a glimpse of Simon, making his escape, running as fast as his wiry legs could take him to the burro tethered somewhere in the trees.

One of the rebels burst through the haze of smoke, and Jeb lifted the Winchester to his shoulder, took aim and fired. The Mexican screamed and fell from his horse. Another appeared, and Jeb fired again, sending him to the same fate as the first.

Adrenaline pumped through him, the lure of a hard fight. He could taste it, the lure. The danger. The anticipation of hard-won victory or impending death.

He turned his horse and left it all behind. This time, the battle would have to wait. He had Elena to think of. Elena and her baby. It was more important he'd given her and Simon the precious seconds they needed to flee into the night.

He charged up the hill. And then Elena was there, waiting for him, in a small clearing a fair distance from de la Vega's camp. Safe—but not for long. The mountain would be crawling with revolutionaries hell-bent on vengeance anytime now. They had to keep moving.

"Give me the boy," Jeb said, and reached for Nicky.

He had enough to do worrying about Elena keeping up with him without having to worry about her baby, too. He'd feel better with Nicky in the saddle with him.

Elena was breathing fast, shallow. She'd been through a hell of a scare, he knew. Yet she hesitated relinquishing her son, as if now that she'd finally gotten him back, she couldn't let him go.

"Give him to me," Jeb said again, and pulled the little body from her arms. He had no time to give her assurances. Nicky would be as safe with him as with her. She'd just have to trust him on that. "Let's go."

They took off again, their destination Simon's home. Simon had been emphatic they go there first, claiming it was even more secluded than the grotto, farther away from de la Vega's camp and closer to the road that would take them back to the village of San Ignatius.

Jeb and Elena had agreed to the plan. It would be their last stop before they headed back to the United States. Their final opportunity to regroup after their escape from the revolutionaries.

Jeb found the adobe structure easily enough. There was still no sign of Simon, but the burro wouldn't have the speed of a horse. Simon knew these hills inside and out. He'd lived in them all his life. Jeb would give him a little more time to get here.

He sheathed the rifle, hefted Nicky to his hip and dismounted. He couldn't recall holding a one-year old before. Had he ever? Nicky seemed to know what to do, though, and hung on with a fistful of Jeb's shirt. He stared up at Jeb curiously, and though Jeb was a stranger to him, he didn't fuss. Considering all he'd been through this past week, Jeb wouldn't blame him if he did.

He strode toward Elena, still in the saddle. She glanced down at him and eased out a careful breath.

''I might need some help getting down,'' she said.

He frowned at that but lifted his free arm to take her elbow. She slid a foot into the stirrup, swung out of the saddle—and would have collapsed right to the ground if Jeb hadn't caught her.

Alarm shot through him. ''Jesus, Elena. Are you all right?''

''I think so,'' she managed. ''Well, maybe not.''

He had his hands full holding both of them. He shifted Elena to better take her weight against him and felt a damp stickiness on her shirt.

''You're bleeding.'' He gaped at the dark stain on his palm. She'd taken a hit during her escape and hadn't bothered to tell him.

''I'm all right, Jeb,'' she said. ''I'm a little shaky is all. Just give me a few minutes.''

''Few minutes, hell. Won't be long and you'll be feeling worse than shaky,'' he growled. ''Come on. Can you walk?''

''Of course I can walk,'' she said, but she slid her arm around his waist and leaned into him, her eyes full of her son. ''I want to hold Nicky.''

''You will soon enough.''

Taking it slow, Jeb pushed open the thin wooden door and was glad for the lamp Simon had left burning for them. Comprised of only a single room, his home was furnished simply with a bed on one side and a small table and chair on the other. A woven mat covered the dirt floor. In one corner, their gear lay in a tidy heap and waited for their return.

''Lie here on the bed,'' Jeb said.

She eased down onto the straw mattress and released the breath she'd been holding from the effort, then lay back against the pillow and opened her arms for her son. Jeb settled him snugly within them.

"Nicky, oh, Nicky." She fought tears and peppered his face with kisses while Jeb unbuttoned her shirt. "I've missed you so much."

"Ma-ma-ma," he said, and tangled his fingers in her hair.

She hugged him tightly. "I love you, sweetheart. I love you, I love you, I love you."

Jeb pulled the shirt from her waistband and encountered her chemise, soaked with blood. A moment later, his knife's blade slit the fabric wide-open, exposing the wound on the lower curve of her waist. He winced at the small hole torn into her smooth skin.

Elena stopped nuzzling Nicky. She glanced downward with a frown. "This is my only chemise, Jeb. You've ruined it."

"Too bad. Can't fix you up if I can't get to you."

He cleaned away the blood with a damp cloth and examined the damage the bullet had left behind. Gunpowder singed the outer edges. There was no exit wound, and Jeb guessed she'd been almost out of range when she'd been hit. If she'd been closer to the shooter…

She strained to see around Nicky, lying half on top of her. "How bad is it?"

"Bad enough. Bullet's still in you."

"Oh." She swallowed. "Now what?"

"I get it out."

"Jeb, I—" She bit her lip.

"It's just under the skin. I can see it well enough," he said, poking, prodding.

"I'm not so sure about this."

"I am." He strode to his saddlebag and removed the

wooden case holding his surgical tools. He removed his bottle of whiskey, too. As an afterthought, he put it back.

He opened Elena's valise and found her father's elixir instead.

She would prefer it anyway. Besides, the medicine would work as well as the whiskey. Better, most likely.

"Take a dose of this," he said, pouring the dark liquid into a spoon. "It'll help dull the pain." He assisted her in sitting up, and she swallowed from the spoon.

"I know," she said with a half smile and leaned back on the pillow.

The door opened, and Simon stepped inside, looking harried but in one piece.

"Glad you could join us," Jeb said, declining to tell him he'd begun to worry.

"It has been a long time since I ran so fast." Seeing Elena, Simon's black eyes rounded. "*Por Dios.* You have been hurt?"

"Yes, but I'm going to be fine."

"I was just getting ready to take out the bullet," Jeb said, removing long tweezers from the case.

Simon strode toward the bed to see Elena's injury for himself. He clucked his tongue in sympathy.

"You have already been through so much, Elena," he said quietly. "And still you must suffer. But at least now you have your son back, eh?" He reached out a gnarled hand to stroke Nicky's black curls. "A beautiful boy. Beautiful."

"Yes," Elena murmured, and kissed him again.

No one spoke of his strong resemblance to de la Vega, or de la Vega's determination to claim him, or the likelihood their troubles were far from over. Nicky stared with wide-eyed innocence at the wild hair Simon sported, then reached up and grabbed a handful of it.

Simon yelped outrageously and made a game of trying to free himself. Nicky grinned at his antics.

Most likely the boy reminded Simon of his own children, or his grandchildren, Jeb mused. The family de la Vega and his men had killed that fateful night when they had raided his village.

"Thank you for all you did for us tonight, Simon," Elena said softly as Jeb poured elixir on a cloth and dabbed it on the wound, cleaning and numbing the skin.

"I did nothing," Simon said with a shrug. "You were the one who was in the most danger."

"All I did was ride over and pick him up. You knocked *Doña* Pia out of the way so I could."

"*Sí.* But only a small thing."

She reached over and covered his fingers with her own. "They will know you conspired with Jeb and me against them."

"Ramon was wrong to take your son like he did."

"You will not be safe here anymore."

"I live only to avenge my family," Simon said.

"I fear for you—oh!"

She yelped at the sting from Jeb pushing the tweezers into the hole at her waist, going for the bullet. His hand was steady, and the instrument found its mark. He held up the slug.

"You were damn lucky it's a small caliber," Jeb grunted. "Didn't do the damage it could have."

"It still hurt," she said, pouting.

"Would've been worse without your father's elixir," he countered, saying the words before thinking of them.

"True."

Jeb finished bandaging the wound, then cleaned his tweezers and put them back into the wooden case. "You're going to be plenty sore tonight, but if that elixir does what it's supposed to, you're going to feel a lot better tomorrow.''

"I know."

Jeb thought of his recent bout of malaria, and that he, too, knew firsthand how powerful Doc Charlie's Miraculous Herbal Compound was. How quickly it healed. How pretty damned amazing the stuff was.

He stood. "Get some sleep, Elena. Do you have to tend to Nicky first?"

"Yes. He needs a fresh diaper." She sat up stiffly.

"Stay put," Jeb said. "I'll get your valise."

She eased back again. "Thank you."

He brought the case over and laid it within easy reach. Elena assured him she needed nothing else, and Jeb left her to get herself and her son ready for bed. He followed Simon outside, then pulled a cigarette and match from his pocket.

The night air felt crisp. Clean. The skirmish at de la Vega's camp seemed a world away. Not a sound broke the stillness, a peace Jeb knew wouldn't last long.

He scraped the match against the adobe, touched the flame to the end of the cigarette and inhaled deeply. His thoughts whipped into turmoil. Where was de la Vega now? Scouring the mountain, looking for them, furious with revenge? Or back in his hideout, planning his strategy with his men?

Wherever he was, Jeb and Elena hadn't seen the last of him. Jeb didn't know how far he would go to take his son back. Once Jeb whisked Elena and Nicky across the border, saw them reunited with her father in San Antonio, would they be safe even then? Would de la Vega defy the American authorities and hunt them down beyond state lines?

Jeb had the sick feeling he would.

The proud revolutionary wouldn't suffer the humiliation of his son's kidnapping well, not in front of his men, and by a woman, no less. He'd be honor-bound to retaliate. And with the shipment of rifles expected any day, he'd be more desperate than ever to find Elena and Nicky as fast as he could.

Elena was in serious danger. It scared Jeb how much danger she was in.

He couldn't protect her alone. Her injury was a troubling setback in their escape. They should be riding hard toward the border right now, not holed up here in Simon's home.

Jeb scanned the trees that surrounded them, all those branches and leaves that could hide a dozen men so damned easy. If de la Vega discovered them hiding out, Jeb might not know until it was too late.

"You are worried, *Señor* Jeb," Simon said quietly.

"Cards are stacked against us. I'm fresh out of aces right now."

"*Sí.* There is only us against so many."

"Us?" Jeb drew in on his cigarette. "This is my fight, Simon. My responsibility to keep Elena and the boy safe. Not yours."

"How can I not help?" He sounded offended that Jeb would think otherwise.

"You've been a big help already," Jeb said and meant it.

"One of us must go to Fort Duncan across the border to tell the American soldiers."

"Yeah. I know."

Jeb considered going himself. He could ride faster than the old peasant. He had the endurance. A strong horse. He had the knowledge and the credibility to convince the officer in charge that a wagonload of rifles was coming and an American woman and her child were hiding for their lives, and to send a score of men into the Mexican hills immediately.

He thought of Lieutenant Colonel Eugene Kingston and the troops at his disposal. Of Creed, in California by now, halfway across the country. Surprisingly enough, he thought of the General, too.

What would William Carson do in this same situation? Consult his tidy little rule book? Or go by his gut feeling?

Jeb always went by his gut feelings—and they told him he couldn't leave Elena.

Suddenly Simon chuckled. "You do not trust me to take care of her as well as you can, eh?"

Jeb frowned. "It's not that."

Or was it?

"You would only worry about her while you were gone," Simon said, conviction in his tone. "I will go, then. I will ride all night."

"It's too dangerous. And that damn burro of yours won't—"

"You forget I have lived here my whole life. I know the hills and the hidden trails that will get me to Texas faster than you think."

Jeb hesitated. "A shortcut?"

"*Many* shortcuts."

He drew in again on his cigarette. His resistance crumbled. It would be the smartest solution, after all, having Simon go in his place. But, given the old Mexican's eccentric appearance, would the commanding officer believe anything he said?

"I'll send a letter with you," Jeb said.

A missive would be the next best thing to going himself, the documentation the United States Army would need to prove Simon spoke the truth. Jeb had already sent Kingston a wire explaining the circumstances surrounding Corporal Nate Martin's death; the letter would substantiate that the situation had worsened.

"*Sí.* A good idea." Simon's agreeable nod sent his frizzed hair bobbing.

Jeb crushed the cigarette stub beneath the toe of his boot and slipped quietly back into the adobe. Elena was sleeping, lying on her side, her arm around Nicky, sleeping, too.

He found paper and pencil, sat at the table and wrote a brief note, making sure his signature was clear. On an afterthought he added a postscript, demanding that General Carson be contacted should there be a lack of belief in the contents of the note.

Or if Jeb and Elena ended up dead.

Simon tucked the note into a leather pouch of food and supplies he slung over his shoulder. Jeb handed him a pistol.

"Use this if you have to," he ordered.

"It is you who will be in more danger," Simon said, but he found a place in the pouch for it. "I am riding away from Ramon. You are staying near him."

With the truth of Simon's words lingering in Jeb's mind, he watched the old man ride away until the night swallowed him up within its inky shadows.

Jeb reentered the adobe and strode to the bed. In the frail glow from the lamp, he watched Elena sleep.

If only he had shot de la Vega bursting through the smoke screen tonight, and not two of his men, then the revolutionary would be dead now. Instead, he was very much alive, furious and more determined than ever to take Elena out of Nicky's life.

The stakes, already high, had doubled.

They looked peaceful together, mother and son. Innocent and vulnerable and so in need of his protection Jeb's heart pounded from the force of it. Or was it a possessiveness that went beyond his patriotic duty to help an American woman and her child? An unspoken, unrealized, need to keep them alive—just for himself?

Had he fallen in love with Elena?

Maybe. Probably.

He swallowed hard. Yes, he had.

He didn't know what would happen if he succeeded in banishing de la Vega from her life forever. When she had no further need of him. Would he ever see her again?

Elena's eyes fluttered open. Gently removing her arm from around her son, she eased to her back and speared her fingers through her hair with a lazy sensuality that stirred his blood.

"Where's Simon?" she whispered.

"Heading to Fort Duncan."

She frowned. "At this hour? Why?"

"We need reinforcements. As fast as we can get them."

Worry crept into her expression. He didn't want to worry her any more than he had to.

"Got room in that bed for me?" he asked, changing the topic to one more appealing.

She glanced over at her son. Her mouth softened. "I think we can find some."

She gently moved Nicky to the edge, next to the adobe wall where he wouldn't roll off. She scooted to the middle of the mattress with only a small wince prompted by her injury, then patted the empty space she'd made.

"It's not much," she said, apologetic.

The bed was barely large enough for two people, let

alone three. It suited Jeb just fine. He could think of far worse ways to spend the night than being crowded in a bed with Elena.

The mattress took his weight with a crackle of its straw bedding. Jeb shifted to his side and raised up on an elbow. The movement and their low voices evoked a wriggle and a stretch from Nicky. His lips puckered into a frown, and he sighed, as if he resented their intrusion into his sleep.

"Cute kid," Jeb muttered, getting his first real look at him.

"Isn't he?" Elena smiled, lifted his chubby hand and pressed a kiss to the knuckles.

"He's got your mouth," Jeb said.

Elena considered that. "He's frowning right now. How can you tell?"

"It looks soft. Full. Like yours."

Her head swiveled toward him on the pillow.

"Kissable?" she asked in a husky whisper.

"Damned if you aren't learning to flirt with me, woman," he growled, then lowered his head to rediscover how kissable her lips were. She arched her neck, just enough to show him she wanted him to kiss her, was ready for it. He took her mouth hungrily, forced himself to be gentle when he wanted to be rough, to bury himself inside her when she fueled his flames and fueled them high. The kiss lingered, long, deep and deliciously wet.

She had changed into a clean nightgown, the fabric light for sleeping on hot summer nights. His hand moved to her breast, and he filled his palm with the warm, supple mound. His fingers splayed, leisurely kneaded the soft flesh, discovering the fullness, the intense pleasure of it, until her nipple hardened, and she moaned.

He angled his head and kissed her again. Harder, longer, his blood hotter, his desire for her raging through his veins. Ribbons held the front of her nightgown together, and he ached to pull them free, to lick and suckle each rosy crest, but the memory of her bandaged injury was a damned abrupt reminder he couldn't go any further, not if he wanted to keep from hurting her and not with Nicky in the bed with them. Gathering every bit of his restraint, he lifted his head.

Her eyelids fluttered open. Her mouth dipped ruefully in understanding, and he knew she felt his frustration just as much. She traced his lower lip with a fingertip.

"Thank you for all you did for us," she whispered.

"Is that what our kiss was for?" He nipped at her finger with his teeth. "A thank-you?"

"The kiss was for me," she said. "I didn't think of the thank-you part until after."

He grunted, pleased enough with the answer she gave. "You can thank me when I bring you back to your father. We've a ways to go yet."

"That's why you sent Simon for reinforcements, isn't it?" she asked. She drew her finger away. "Because you think the worst is yet to come."

"Yes." Her perception sobered him.

"More lives will be lost. American soldiers. Ramon's men."

"Maybe. Maybe not," he hedged, the allure of their kisses shattered by reality.

"There will be. Because of a little boy."

"And an illicit arms shipment. Two things, Elena. The Army and de la Vega want them both. But only one side can win."

She peered up at him, her eyes troubled. "I just want to be away from this place."

Nicky stirred again, a protest at their hushed conversation. Elena reached over and rubbed his back, and he quieted.

Jeb sat up, peeled off his shirt, tugged off his boots, then removed his holster. He set them all next to the bed, within easy reach. After dousing the lamp, he settled himself beside Elena and cradled her head on his shoulder.

"From here on out, all you need to do is take care of your son. Leave the rest up to me," he said.

He felt her trepidation, but she said nothing more. Eventually her breathing deepened in slumber.

But Jeb lay awake a long time and wondered what tomorrow would bring.

Chapter Fifteen

Jeb woke up to sunlight streaming through the window over the bed. He blinked from the cheeriness of it, needed a minute to remember where he was.

Simon's house. In bed. With Elena.

He lay with his arm draped over her, his chest to her back, her bottom snuggled against his groin. Their bodies were molded and fitted together like a pair of spoons in a drawer.

Not a bad way to wake up.

She'd had an uncomfortable night. The bullet wound pained her, and she needed another strong dose of elixir. Jeb gave it to her, had stayed awake until she fell back to sleep. No fever, though. And her breathing was deep and regular. He hoped the worst of it was over.

He lifted his head to drop a sympathetic kiss to her temple, and discovered Nicky sitting up, watching him.

The boy grinned, rosy-cheeked and wide-awake, and so good-natured that Jeb couldn't help grinning back.

"Ma-ma-ma," Nicky blabbered, and flapped his arms, as if happy that someone else was awake with him.

Jeb put a finger to his lips.

"Shh. Your mama needs to sleep," he whispered.

"Ma-ma-ma."

Evidently babies didn't know what *shh* meant. He eased away from Elena. He couldn't think of a thing he could do to keep Nicky quiet, but he had to do something. Maybe he should just take him out of Elena's range of hearing. He leaned over, swept the child off the bed and settled him on his hip.

One whiff of something downright foul brought him off again.

Jeb held Nicky straight-armed out from him. Whew. The boy had filled his pants but good.

Jeb looked at Elena. She hadn't moved an inch, and he heaved a resigned breath. He didn't want to wake her—she needed the rest. He'd have to change the diaper himself.

He put Nicky back on his hip, found a clean diaper in the valise, a washcloth and, on second thought, a banana from a bowl on Simon's table. He headed to the door. Another thought struck him, and he headed back to find a spare blanket, then stuffed it under his free arm. Couldn't lay the boy in the dirt, could he?

He managed to get the door open with his elbow and shut it again with his hip. The sun shone down bright, already warm. He chose a shady spot on the side of the adobe structure where Nicky could blabber all he wanted without waking Elena.

Working one-handed, Jeb spread the blanket out on the grass and settled the little boy on his back on top of it. He hunkered on his heels and thought of what he was going to have to do next. Nicky watched him with another of his silly grins.

"Think this is funny, do you?" Jeb scowled.

Exuberant, Nicky kicked his legs. Jeb clamped a hand

down on both of them. He didn't want the damage all that wiggling would do to the stuff inside his pants.

Best get started. Nicky was trying to wiggle again. Jeb pulled and tugged at the rubber-coated drawers before he discovered the drawstring that kept them snug to Nicky's waist. Once untied, the drawers pulled down easily, and Jeb muttered a word of thanks for the wisdom of the one who had invented the things, keeping a baby dry on the outside when he was soaked through on the inside.

And Nicky's diaper was sure soaked through. The odor was stronger, too, once the drawers were off. Jeb had smelled plenty of horse manure in his day to tolerate a baby's droppings well enough, but the idea of cleaning it off a naked butt was far less appealing.

He managed it, however, by working fast and not thinking about what he was doing. Until he realized he had forgotten to moisten the washcloth he brought.

Simon had a water pump just a dozen yards away. Jeb would have to leave Nicky long enough to use it. "Stay right here, buddy. Y'hear me? I'll only be a minute."

Placid and agreeable, Nicky watched him with those big, black eyes of his. Jeb had no idea if the little boy understood a thing he said, but he wasn't moving much, so Jeb figured it was safe enough to leave him.

He strode to the pump, wet down the cloth and wrung out the excess. He glanced over his shoulder and found Nicky toddling away, as bare-assed as the day he was born.

Jeb swore and took off after him. Nicky paused, saw him coming, squealed and toddled faster. Jeb scooped him up and tossed him over his shoulder.

The kid was damned quick. Thank God, he'd gotten

to him in time. How would he have explained to Elena he'd lost her son?

Jeb couldn't turn his back on him. Ever. He returned to the blanket, finished cleaning him up and swathed him in a dry diaper the same way Elena had done. Afterward, Jeb sat back, relieved and pleased with himself for getting the job done.

Elena did this every day, and he had stoutly developed a new appreciation for mothers everywhere.

Including his own. Had he been as rambunctious as Nicky when he was this age? Jeb had no idea. His mother had been gone so long he'd probably never know.

He squelched all thought of her, as he always did when she popped into his mind. Sometimes he forgot he'd ever been born of one. But Nicky was lucky. He had a mother who loved him more than anything.

Nicky spied the banana Jeb had left on the corner of the blanket. He crawled over for it, but Jeb grabbed it first. He didn't want the little boy biting right into the peel.

"You hungry, buddy?" he asked, though that part wasn't too hard to figure out. They'd all slept later than usual this morning. It was past time for breakfast for both of them. "Guess we can share this. You like bananas?"

Nicky crawled into Jeb's lap and made himself right at home. He watched him pull back the yellow peel, strip by strip, with his mouth open and ready for a bite.

"Guess you do," Jeb muttered. "Me, too. Always been one of my favorites. Here you go."

Nicky leaned forward and met the banana coming at him. He gnawed off a small piece.

''Hard to chew when you don't have but a few teeth, isn't it, buddy?''

But he was managing well enough. Gumming the fruit to death. The boy had an appetite, for sure. In a few years, he'd be eating Elena out of house and home.

A few years. Nicky would be a fine-looking boy then, just as he was now. He'd grow into a strong man, and she'd be proud of him.

Elena's life would be a hell of a lot different than it was now, Jeb mused. She might even have a husband to help her with Nicky. Another child or two to raise with him.

A husband.

The notion gave Jeb pause. She'd be settled into a comfortable life with another man. He'd have her all to himself, night after night. Elena's kisses, his for the taking, whenever he wanted them.

One kiss. Or a whole night's worth. In bed. Or out.

Jeb didn't like the way all this was making him feel. When before had he thought of the future? Or one with a woman in it?

He gave Nicky another bite of banana and thought of how he'd always lived for the moment. Creed and him, taking it hour by hour. Day by day. Answering to no one but themselves. He'd always liked it that way. A woman had never fit into his way of living.

Damned if Elena hadn't begun to change his thinking.

Elena watched Jeb feeding Nicky. The sight startled her. Warmed her, too, with a curious kind of pleasure.

How strange to see him taking care of her son. Who would have thought a man like Jeb Carson was even capable of it? Yet there he was, sitting cross-legged on the blanket with Nicky sideways in his lap, feeding him with a low-voiced gentleness that tugged at her heart-strings.

He grinned at something Nicky did, and his teeth gleamed white against the dark stubble on his cheeks. He wasn't wearing a hat, and he'd finger-combed his long hair back from his forehead. He wore no shirt, either, and her gaze lingered over the muscles rippling across his shoulders and back.

She was struck by the similarities of the pair. Dark headed, dark skinned, and as dark eyed as her son, Jeb could pass as Nicky's father.

If only he were, Elena mused sadly. Her life would be so very different. She wouldn't be standing here in Simon's home in the wilds of Mexico, on the run from a band of dangerous revolutionaries, that's for sure.

They'd be a normal family—just the three of them.

Well, Jeb Carson had no time for her and Nicky, not with the life he led, traveling the world for the United States government. And he had no desire to be a father, either. If he did, he'd have been one long before now. What woman wouldn't want him to sire her children?

Elena gave herself a mental shake. She couldn't be thinking these thoughts. They were foolish. A waste of time, and she'd dallied watching him long enough.

She went outside, still wearing her nightgown. Jeb glanced up at her approach, and his smoldering gaze drifted over her. As if he liked what he saw.

"Mornin'," he murmured, the word so sultry from his throat that Elena's step faltered. Lord, the man had only to speak to her and her bones turned soft.

"Morning to you, too," she said. "You're taking good care of my son, I see."

Nicky, hearing her voice, twisted in Jeb's lap to

peer up at her. He grinned, banana on his chin. "Ma-ma-ma."

"Hello, sweetheart," she cooed, and tousled his curls. "I hope you're being a good boy for Jeb."

"He is." Jeb extended his hand to help her sit, his fingers warm and strong over hers. "We didn't want to wake you."

"You're very thoughtful." She eased downward to sit cross-legged on the blanket, too.

"How's the injury?"

"Much better, thank you." If not for the bandage around her waist, she would've forgotten the wound was even there.

"The elixir again?" he asked.

"Of course." She searched his face for a sign of his usual mockery regarding Doc Charlie's Miraculous Herbal Compound.

Oddly enough, she found none.

Nicky spied the rice waffle Elena had brought for him, along with his stuffed horse, and he crawled from Jeb's lap onto hers. Elena broke off a piece that he could hold, and he chewed contentedly, watching Jeb finish off the banana.

"He likes you," Elena said.

"Just getting used to me is all." He set the yellow peeling aside.

"He's not often been around men, besides Pop and the performers in our show."

"Mexican revolutionaries excepted?" Jeb asked wryly.

"Yes." She shuddered at the thought of Nicky being with them. "But it was *Doña* Pia who cared for him in the end." Elena cocked her head. "Nicky took to you right away."

"Think so?"

"He feels safe with you. Babies are more perceptive than you think."

Jeb grunted and shifted to his back, using Elena's knee to pillow his head. "Are they?"

"Yes."

She wanted to tell him he'd find out as much someday when he had a child of his own. But she didn't. She already knew Jeb had no room in his life for children.

"Did you have brothers or sisters?" she asked instead.

"No. I was an only child."

"Cousins?"

"I suppose I do. Somewhere. Back East, I think."

"You don't keep in touch with them?"

At the surprise in her tone, he glanced at her. "We moved around quite a bit when I was a kid. My father was gone most of the time, and—" He halted. Frowned. "You might as well know he's a general in the United States Army."

"A general?" Her jaw dropped. "He must be very good at what he does."

"He's a hard-hearted bas—" His glance swung to Nicky. "He's a hard man."

A general in the Army. Elena took a minute to digest the information. A man of his station would be powerful. Highly respected. Intelligent and well trained. *Important.* Yet Jeb seemed filled with resentment when he should have been proud of all his father had accomplished.

"You're wondering how I could be the son of such a distinguished military officer, aren't you?" Jeb asked mockingly.

"I'm thinking you two are very different."

"We're different, all right."

His childhood had shaped him to be the man he was today. How much of an influence had his father been? And was that influence a positive one?

Elena suspected it wasn't. She suspected, too, that Jeb kept his feelings regarding his relationship with the man bottled up tight inside him.

Pop always claimed talking was like pouring oil on troubled waters.

"I'd like to hear more about him," she said softly. "That is, if you'd like me to."

For a long time, Jeb didn't speak. It wasn't too difficult to discern he didn't talk about his father much. If at all.

She shouldn't have asked him to now. She suspected she had ventured into waters too turbulent to calm.

"His name is William Carson," Jeb said. "If he ever loved my mother, I'm not sure she knew it. If she did, she didn't believe it much because I don't remember ever seeing her smile."

Sympathy swelled inside her at the woman's unhappiness. "How hard for both of you."

"She was lonely. She came from a wealthy, cultured family, and she missed them and all the comforts she was used to having. My father would be assigned to a fort someplace, then ride off to join a military regiment stationed God knows where. He'd be gone months at a time."

"And when he came back?" she asked gently.

"The four walls closed in on him. Family life was too sedate. Not only that, he demanded perfection of my mother and me. He had no tolerance for mistakes, not even those of a little boy fresh out of rompers."

Jeb's memories were clearly vivid from such an early age, Elena realized. And her sympathy doubled.

"The General expected strict adherence to the rules he made, just like he did of the men he commanded. He planned every minute of his life, and ours, then made us live them through with military precision."

Nicky nibbled contentedly on his waffle. Elena rested her cheek against his dark head and waited for Jeb to continue.

"One day, before he was due to leave again, they had a hell of an argument. My mother wanted to go with him. Or maybe she wanted him to take her to some city where she could mingle in polite society again, so she could enjoy all the comforts a woman like her missed." Jeb frowned, as if he tried to sort out the details long buried in his past. "It doesn't matter, I suppose, where she wanted to go. Main thing was, she wanted out of the life he forced her to live. But he refused, then he left. He expected her to be waiting for him when he returned."

Elena found herself holding her breath. "And?"

"She wasn't."

Elena's head lifted. "What do you mean?"

"She took off in the middle of the night. Left me in my bed with no idea she was leaving me. Us."

"Oh, Jeb." Tears welled in her eyes.

"Never heard from her after that."

Elena blinked hard. How could any mother abandon her child? "Never?"

"Not a peep."

"And your father?"

"Never spoke of her to me. Just acted like she didn't exist. Which, I suppose in hindsight, she didn't. Not after that."

His head still rested on her knee. Elena touched his

cheek, and his fingers captured hers, bringing them against his chest, holding them there.

"How old were you?" she asked.

"Eight. Even then, I hated him."

She made a sound of dismay. "How can you say such a thing?"

"Nothing I could ever do pleased him, though God knows I tried. I was secretly afraid he would send me away, just like he did my mother, however indirectly. So I tried hard to make him proud of me. I always failed."

"Maybe you just thought you failed, Jeb."

He snorted in disagreement. "Believe me, a kid knows when he doesn't measure up. Eventually, I rebelled. Why should I try to be like him when I despised every breath he took? Came a time when I wanted to be as *unlike* him as I possibly could."

The dam holding in the flood of his memories had cracked wide-open. Elena gave him the time he needed to continue.

"He sent me to West Point Military Academy. He'd gone there himself, so he knew firsthand there was no place better for me to get the discipline I needed," Jeb went on.

"The Academy is quite prestigious," Elena murmured, impressed in spite of everything. "Some of the country's finest military officers were trained there."

"Prestigious, yes. But hard. Being the son of a highly decorated general only made life worse." He spoke matter-of-factly, as if he'd long ago detached himself from the pain.

"Why should that make a difference?"

"Made me a prime target for hazing. Upperclassmen were always trying to test me by humiliating me. They wanted to see if I was as tough as the infamous General Carson was.''

The sympathy coursed through her. It seemed Jeb had spent his entire life fighting to get out from under his father's imperious shadow.

''Met Creed at the Academy, though. He was the one good thing that came out of it all.''

''Yes,'' Elena said. She had seen for herself the bond of friendship between the two.

''Ever hear of hazing?'' he asked.

''Yes.'' She sniffed in disapproval at the practice of initiating a young plebe into military life through the use of cruel pranks. ''Sounds awful.''

Jeb shrugged. ''It was frowned upon by the Academy, but it went on in secret anyway. God knows I endured my share. But one night, some upperclassmen pulled me out of bed and hazed me half the night. Made me do deep-knee bends without losing my balance. I did them—until I collapsed with convulsions.''

''Oh, my God!''

''A congressional investigation was scheduled, but I refused to name names, even though I was ordered to do so. I was court-martialed as punishment.''

Elena gasped.

''By my father, no less. He believed obedience was the basis of all military discipline. Refusal to obey orders would not be tolerated.''

She struggled to stand outside the ring, to remain detached so that she might comprehend General Carson's reasoning for what he did at such great cost to Jeb.

''I suppose it wouldn't do for a man in his position to give special consideration to his son,'' she said thoughtfully. ''Yet, I would think it hurt him as much as it hurt you.''

For a moment, Jeb didn't say anything. His thumb stroked her knuckles absently, as if he considered her words at length. Then he shrugged.

"Yeah, well. I survived it. The day I walked away from the Academy, Creed was with me. We didn't look back. I haven't seen or talked to the General since."

Nicky finished his piece of waffle and reached for another. Jeb released her hand so that she could give him one.

"What happened then?" she asked. "You told me you worked for the military, tracking men like Ramon de la Vega."

He nodded. "Regardless of my experiences with the Academy, I still wanted to be a soldier. More than anything. Guess that's one thing the General managed to impress upon me. There was honor in serving my country. And if the court-martial destroyed my chances of being a soldier in the usual way, I decided to be one of my own making. Without rules and without having to obey anyone but myself."

"Corporal Martin seemed to think you had quite a reputation, as I recall. Sergeant Bender, too," she said, thinking of the night Jeb discovered them just beyond their camp.

Jeb grunted. "Creed and I took risks no one else was willing to take. Hell, we were reckless enough to try. We had nothing else to lose. Got to the point where we could name our own price to the War Department."

Soldiers for hire. He spoke without pride or boast or regret. Two men willing to lay their lives down for America in countries too war-torn to care.

Jeb had his own brand of honor and integrity, and in Elena's mind, there wasn't a finer soldier to be had than he. Except for Creed, and perhaps not even then.

Nicky scooted off her lap and crawled toward Jeb. One chubby hand still gripped the remains of his waffle; the other ventured a curious touch to the scattering of dark hairs on Jeb's chest.

"Give yourself a few years, Nick," Jeb muttered. "You'll have some, too—ow!"

He yelped at the sudden yank and sat up abruptly, bringing Nicky with him, his hands big around Nicky's potbelly, but gentle, too. Jeb stood him on both feet, a few of the curling hairs between the pudgy fingers.

"Oh, I'm sorry!" Elena said, reaching for her son and trying not to laugh. "He has to touch everything he sees, and I'm *sorry* if he hurt you."

"He didn't," Jeb said, rubbing the wounded spot. "Just caught me by surprise is all."

Nicky stepped toward him again, as if he intended to do more of the same, but Elena took his stuffed horse and tossed it to the edge of the blanket, distracting him.

"See your horsey, Nicky?" she cooed. "Go get it, sweetheart. Bring it to Mama."

Nicky fell for the bait and toddled toward it. His drawers began to slip past his hips, and his stride faltered. His face became one of cherubic surprise as he bent downward to see to the problem, but he ventured one more step, and the drawers dropped right down to his ankles, taking the diaper inside with it.

"Oh!" He was pure naked from the waist down, and laughter bubbled from Elena's throat. "Jeb, did you change him?"

"I did," he said, and pondered the sight, as taken aback as Nicky.

Her laughter doubled until her injury pinched, reminding her to have a care and hold her merriment in.

"You didn't pin him up snug enough. I'll show you. Oh, God, you look so funny, Nicky. Come here, baby."

Haltered as he was, he stumbled trying to get to her. Jeb caught him before he fell and laid him on his back in front of her.

"I was afraid I'd hurt him if I got the diaper too tight," Jeb said defensively.

"That's understandable." Impulsively Elena pressed a quick kiss to his lips. "Watch what I do." She made short work of untying the drawers, unpinning the dry diaper and repositioning both around Nicky's hips. Afterward, she gave them a test tug to prove they wouldn't fall down again. "See? Like that."

And she laughed all over again, just thinking of what had happened.

Jeb growled and pulled her to her back next to Nicky. "Think it's that funny, do you?"

He loomed over her in mock ferocity, the dark stubble on his cheeks making him look all the more ruthless— the kind of man she knew he could be.

Yet she'd discovered a gentle side to him, too. Patient, kind and, well, fatherly.

Before she could explore the thought, his head lowered, and she anticipated his kiss with held breath.

"Ma-ma-ma."

Nicky wedged himself between them, wanting her attention, too, and Jeb drew back with a grin.

"You know how good your mama's kisses are, don't you, buddy?" he said, and made room for him. "But I get one first, y'hear?"

His gaze returned to Elena. Lingered. Smoldered and burned. His head lowered again, and his lips took hers in a tender kiss that was both thorough and restrained.

Elena knew he held himself in check, that if they were alone…

He made Elena want more than she should, an impossibility of togetherness, just the three of them. The kiss ended, and she touched his cheek with a stirring of longing she was only beginning to understand. A longing that made her want to lie on the blanket with him for hours. Days.

Forever.

Their time together was fast dwindling away, she thought as Jeb pulled back, distracted by something Nicky did. What would happen after they crossed the border? They'd go in separate directions, Jeb to Fort Duncan, perhaps. Or California to meet Creed. Elena would be heading north to San Antonio.

Would they ever see each other again?

Chapter Sixteen

Elena pulled Nicky's blanket up over his little shoulders and gave up trying to take a nap herself. He slept soundly. A morning of playing and eating and getting reacquainted as mother and son had worn him out.

He'd sleep for a while yet, she knew. He always did at nap time, and she slipped from the bed as quietly as she could. He didn't stir.

The early afternoon stretched out before her. Where was Jeb? Somewhere he wouldn't disturb her, she was sure. He was determined that she rest as much as possible, but she knew he was as anxious as she to leave Mexico.

Concern for her injury was keeping him back. That, and the impending arrival of the arms shipment.

Perhaps she could convince him to leave now. So what if he'd sent Simon for reinforcements? Let the Army fight Ramon. Simon could lead them right to his camp. They could prevent the rifles from reaching the revolutionaries just as easily as Jeb could. Better, most likely. They had the numbers to do it.

Another dose of elixir earlier kept her pain-free. She was on the mend. She was up for the ride.

And she was restless.

But the inevitability of never seeing Jeb again left her pensive and more confused than ever about what she wanted. She had only a day or two left with him. Hours, maybe.

If only she could make time stand still.

She poured herself a cup of coffee and meandered outside. She'd changed from her nightgown into a skirt and blouse, but wore no shoes. The grass felt soft, cool against her feet.

Her steps slowed, her glance snared by the sheet spread and covered with acorns drying in the sun. The final step before Simon roasted them.

He wouldn't be roasting them for Ramon anymore. Not after last night. Simon was as good as dead for helping her kidnap Nicky.

A pair of strong arms slipped around her waist, and startled, she nearly dropped her coffee cup.

"What are you doing up?" Jeb growled into her ear. "You're supposed to be sleeping."

He pulled her against his chest, and she relaxed against him, letting her heartbeat return to normal. He had yet to don his shirt, and the heat from his body soaked into her back, a delicious heat she found herself snuggling into.

"I tried, but I couldn't," she said.

He nibbled at her ear, sent shivers zinging down her spine. "You could've tried harder. You have to get better."

"I am better."

He grunted his skepticism. "Nicky still sleeping?"

"Yes. He was pretty tired." She peered up at him over her shoulder and lifted her cup. "Coffee?"

"Thanks." He took it from her, kept one hand around her waist and lifted it to his lips.

Elena didn't step away from him. She didn't want to, not when he made her feel this warm and secure in her turbulent world. Just the two of them, in this little patch of God's green earth, sheltered in the serenity provided by so many trees.

"It's beautiful here, isn't it?" she murmured, watching a meadowlark flitter in a low branch.

"Quiet," he said with an agreeing nod.

"Simon must feel very alone out here. The isolation— I don't know how anyone could find him."

"De la Vega will, Elena."

She flinched at the grimness in his voice. "We can't let that happen. Not after all Simon has done for us. Or what he's doing even now."

"I'll see that he hides out for a while so de la Vega can't find him. Someplace safe across the border until this is all over."

He evaded her question, but he didn't need to say the words. Simon's life, his home, would never be the same again.

Jeb turned her around. He knuckled her chin gently upward.

"What will happen to us, Elena?" he asked quietly.

He felt it, too. This desperation that their time together was running out. That soon, too soon, their lives, like Simon's, would take a different course, each without the other.

"It scares me what will happen," she whispered.

"Yeah. Me, too."

She cupped his cheek. "These past days, we've taken care of each other. We've worried and planned and risked our lives together, and—"

She couldn't finish. She couldn't say the words, *When this is all over, I won't see you anymore.*

He turned his head and pressed a kiss into her palm. "There's one thing we haven't done yet, sweet."

Her heart skipped a beat. Yes. The one thing that shimmered between them like heat off desert sand, the desire that had been steadily building between them since he found her in the woodlands along the Nueces.

The want.

She wanted him to make love to her. Wanted it more than she ever thought she would. Or could. The intimacy that had once left her revolted and frightened, she now wanted from Jeb more than anything.

Because she might not ever get another chance.

His eyes darkened to sultry midnight. He tossed aside the coffee cup, and the brew soaked into the grass. He slipped an arm behind her knees and lifted her against him.

The blanket they'd used with Nicky this morning was still there, next to the adobe where Jeb had spread it in the coolness of the shade. He carried her toward it and lowered her gently on top.

"You're a beautiful woman, Elena," he murmured. "How can a man not want to make love to you?"

His words circled around her like fine silk, seductive and alluring, captivating her with the promise of what was to come. Her arms slid around his neck, and she eased backward, bringing him down with her. Though he loomed over her, concern shadowed his face, awareness of the violence she'd endured beneath Ramon's brutal hand.

"I'm not so afraid of what will happen, Jeb. Not with you."

He groaned, and his mouth took hers in a gentle assault on whatever threads of resistance might have lingered. He plied her lips with lazy thoroughness, until they were swollen and wet and aching for more.

"I'm going to touch you all over, Elena. Y'hear me? Skin to skin. You and me." He pressed a gentle kiss to the corner of her eye. "Just let yourself feel all the things a woman is entitled to feel. You're going to like it, but if ever you get to feeling scared, you tell me. You tell me right away, and I'll stop."

Already he was making her feel things she hadn't felt before. A languid warmth, deep inside her. An ache for something that wasn't quite there, a promise of pleasure to come.

"Your hair looks kissed by the sun." A corner of his mouth lifted, as if the words amused him, words he wasn't accustomed to saying but that seemed to just come out of him on their own. "Soft and shiny, like glittering gold diamonds." He moved her hair aside, reverently spread the strands across the blanket, then lowered his head and nuzzled the bare curve of her neck. "You smell good, too."

"You certainly know how to woo a woman, don't you?" she murmured, her hands caressing his shoulders. Thick muscle corded them, the skin taut and warm, the breadth a testament to his strength and power.

He chuckled softly. His fingers found the buttons to her blouse, undid one, then another and another. "Just telling it like it is, darlin'."

He nudged the blouse open. She wore no chemise— he'd ruined it the night before—and he gently grazed a trail from her collarbone to her upper arm with his teeth and tongue. Her eyes closed at the seduction, and she wasn't aware he had finished unbuttoning the blouse until he parted the garment wide. Her eyes flew open, and she hastened to bring it closed again.

"Jeb, please," she protested shakily.

"Oh, no, you don't." He pried her fingers away and spread the blouse again. Their gazes locked. "Remember what I said, Elena? Skin to skin. Both of us."

Her pulse floundered, but she allowed him to remove the blouse and toss it aside. Her skirt followed, and for the first time in her life, she lay naked before a man.

A strange thing it was to be surrounded by trees and singing birds, the air a warm cocoon around them. Yet, with Jeb, it felt natural and right, too, and she knew no shame from it.

His gaze lowered to her breasts, her hips, to the joining of her thighs. His breathing roughened.

"Do you have any idea how beautiful you are?" he asked huskily.

A rueful laugh escaped her. She patted her bandage and thought of the scar she'd have. "I'm trussed up from your doctoring. Hardly beautiful."

"Only a small bandage." His brow furrowed. "Does the wound hurt?"

"No, no, no." She pulled him down and touched her mouth to his. "You make me feel something else entirely."

He grunted, and his concern seemed to leave him. "That's more like it. And I'm just getting started."

His hand cupped the underside of her breast and pressed upward, lifting the mound, and he took her taut nipple into his mouth. He suckled, long and strong, his cheeks moving in, then out again, in primal erotic rhythm.

"O-oh, Jeb." The moan that escaped her sounded like a whimper as she fell victim to an onslaught of sensation, a man's carnal pleasure taken at a woman's breast. Nicky had nursed countless times, but nothing like *this*.

The tugging of his mouth sizzled spiraling heat down to the cleft between her thighs. He shifted, repeated the seduction to the other, and her fingers speared into his hair, holding him to her even as she wanted to push him away.

Her thighs loosened. He shifted over her, his mouth open and hungry over hers, his body deliciously heavy. He nibbled her lower lip, licked her chin, nipped and sucked against her neck.

"Elena, Elena."

His ragged whisper fueled her need to have all of him, and her arms circled around him, her hands stroking the cords of sinew along his back. He would know this need she had, but he took his time to satisfy it. She knew, too, his need ran just as strong, for his kisses had grown fevered, passionate, his breathing a little more frenzied.

"Let's get you out of these," she said, her fingers skimming his lean belly and finding the button at the waist of his Levi's. He rolled away and pulled them off, then returned to her with a throaty groan. He lay over her, his chest pressed to her breasts.

"Skin to skin," he whispered. "Oh, yeah...."

She purred at the feeling of lying naked beneath him. He was so warm, so strong. So male. His hand slid between her legs, his thumb pressing and probing her folds, but she drew back a bit in hesitation at this new contact.

"Just feel, Elena," he whispered, the words jagged against her throat. "Don't think about anything. Feel me touch you. Enjoy it."

His manhood quivered against the inside of her thigh, and gently he took her hand and brought it between them. His fingers closed over hers on his pulsing staff.

"I'm going to enter you," he said. "Soon. When I do, I want you to know it's me inside you. No one else. I don't want you to be afraid. I don't want you remembering. What we're feeling, what we're *doing,* is the way lovemaking is meant to be between a man and woman."

"Yes," she whispered.

She understood. Her one experience had been a rending of flesh, an act of terror and pain performed in the dark. Jeb would be vastly different, and his compassion moved her deeply.

A shaft of late-afternoon sunlight filtered through the leaves of the trees, igniting their bodies with fire, painting their skin with mellow gold. Elena stroked Jeb and marveled at his virility, his blatant masculinity. She wasn't afraid, as he had feared. She looked forward to joining her body with his, and the tightening of his jaw indicated the effect she had on him.

Heady stuff, this.

His mouth took hers again, and their tongues mated in wet, erotic play. His hands stroked her hips and thighs. She caressed his back and lean buttocks. She lost herself in his kisses, in his touching, and let the sensations lift her higher into ecstasy.

Her knees had spread, and she cradled his hips between them. The ache he built inside her was almost unbearable, and her hips began to move.

His head lowered to her breast again; his mouth closed over her nipple, his tongue sweeping over and over across the sensitive tip. Her back arched and her breathing quickened. He found the other, laved it lovingly and suckled in that lazy, bone-melting way of his. The fire built in her belly and she whimpered, moving restlessly beneath him.

Again his hand slipped between them. This time,

Elena knew what he was doing. She wanted it, accepted it. *Ached* for it. He kissed her, long and hard and ravenous, then slid one finger inside of her. Two. She was wide open for him. Wet. He kissed her, again and again, his fingers stroking and probing with the same rhythm of his tongue.

She climbed higher still.

When Elena could stand his sweet torture no longer, she grasped his hips and broke the kiss, breathing in quick, aroused pants. "Jeb, I want you in me. Now. Hurry."

"You think anything's going to keep me from it?" Muscles quivering from restraint, he lifted himself over her. "Lord, woman. What you're doing to me…"

He slid into her slowly, filling her. Her eyes closed, and she savored the feel of him.

And then he began to move. Each stroke bumped against that wild sweet spot he'd found with his thumb. Her hips lifted, rocked in the need to pull him deeper. His strokes came faster, harder, bringing with them keening pleasure. Elena climbed and climbed, higher and higher, until a deep, spasming flutter rocked her womb, and she cried out from the glory of it. Then, with one last driving thrust, Jeb peaked with her, held them both on the pinnacle for a single heart-stopping moment, before they floated back down to earth.

Jeb buried his face in her hair and emitted one very male, very satisfied groan.

Elena smiled and kissed the hollow of his throat.

They lay together, still clasped in the rosy glow of what had happened between them for what seemed an eternity. Or maybe it was only a few minutes. It didn't matter, and when Jeb finally rolled off her, she snuggled into him, her breasts against his chest, her legs tangled with his.

"I could sure use a cigarette right about now," he muttered.

"Where are they?"

"Pocket of my shirt. Inside."

"So why don't you get one?" She smiled, having a good idea why he didn't.

"Can't move just yet."

"Hmm." She circled one of his dark nipples with her fingertip. "Nicky's still sleeping. We were lucky he didn't wake up."

"Lots of parents make love while their kids sleep."

Parents.

A series of images loomed in her mind. Jeb and her as Nicky's father and mother. The three of them a happy little family. Night after night of making love while Nicky slept.

She sobered. Jeb meant nothing by it. He was definitely not a family man.

Some of that rosy glow dulled, and she felt chilled from her nakedness. She sat up, drew her knees up to her chest.

"When will Simon come back?" she asked.

"Not soon enough," he said. He eased away from her, handed her her clothes, then reached for his Levi's. "You'd best get dressed again, Elena. It'd be a mite embarrassing for both of us if de la Vega showed up about now."

She draped her skirt over her lap, slipped her arms into the sleeves of her blouse and began buttoning. Jeb rose, pulled on his Levi's and fastened them.

"You don't want to be here, do you?" she asked.

"With you, yes. Just waiting around for trouble? No."

His grim glance scanned the trees beyond Simon's adobe. "We're sitting ducks, Elena. I don't have enough ammunition to fight off de la Vega if he shows up. Never mind the lack of manpower."

"Then why are we?"

His brow arched. "Why are we here? Because you took a bullet last night, that's why. You have to rest from it."

"I no longer have that bullet, remember? You took it out of me. And I was feeling well enough to make love to you just now, wasn't I?"

He frowned. "It's a long, hard ride back to the States. You need time to heal."

"How much time?" she demanded.

"Tomorrow. At least."

"I'm fine today. We can head out now."

He stared at her as if she'd lost her mind. "I'll not hear of it."

"It's my bullet wound, Jeb. And I'm telling you I feel well enough. The farther we can get away from Ramon, and the sooner we do it, the better for all of us. Especially Nicky."

Jeb looked tempted. Elena stood, fastened her skirt and made his decision for him.

"I'll pack up our things. You get the horses ready," she said firmly.

She'd have to take another dose of elixir. As Jeb said, the journey would be hard on the wound, but she could endure the discomfort. It'd only be for a short while. Until she got to San Antonio. To Pop.

Jeb took her arm. "Elena."

She understood his troubled expression, the uncertainty that warred in his dark eyes. She, too, knew the risks of leaving, that they only had a few hours left together.

"Elena, listen to me," he said, his voice rough. He pulled her toward him.

But she would never know what he intended to say. Or do. A noise jerked him to full alertness, and he whirled toward the direction of it.

A wagon lumbered in the distance, beyond the tree line, on a trail Elena didn't even know existed. She could only catch a glimpse of it, but its shape was unmistakable.

Jeb swore. Vehemently.

And Elena knew that the shipment of rifles Ramon de la Vega was waiting for had arrived.

Chapter Seventeen

"I have to stop that wagon," Jeb said.

"Oh, God, no," Elena gasped. "It's too dangerous."

"If de la Vega gets those guns—"

He broke into a sprint back to the adobe. Inside, he grabbed a shirt, his boots, pulled them on. Elena followed him in, the blanket dragging behind her.

"Jeb, you don't have to do this."

"Yes. I do."

Didn't she understand there was no else? That, right now, he alone had the ability to intercept numerous crates jam-packed with weapons that would ultimately kill innocent lives on both sides of the border?

"Let's ride away from here," she pleaded. "We'll find Lieutenant Colonel Kingston if Simon hasn't already. We'll tell him what we saw and where."

"No." Jeb rose, slapped on his gun belt and notched it snug to his hips.

"He'll send his men," Elena said. "They'll be more prepared than you. You're only one person, Jeb! Ramon won't have a chance against the Army."

"We're just outside his camp, Elena. The rifles will

be in his hands in an hour. Two at most. There's no damn time to wait for the Army.''

''He'll kill you in the blink of an eye.'' Her breathing quickened into frantic pants.

''Not if I kill him first.'' He snatched his hat, his gloves.

''Jeb, please don't go.''

He steeled himself against her fear, against the quaver in her voice, against his own worries for her and Nicky's safety while he was gone.

''Don't leave the adobe, y'hear me? Not for any reason,'' he ordered. ''Stay away from the windows. Get your things together and be ready to ride on a minute's notice.''

She swallowed hard. Nodded.

''I'm leaving you a gun.'' He set a Colt revolver on the table and added a knife to go with it. ''Use 'em.''

She made a sound of alarm but said nothing more. He strode toward her. The adrenaline coursed through him, fast and furious, but he held it in check, stealing a few precious seconds to take her into his arms.

''I told you last night, Elena,'' he rumbled into the hair at her temple. ''Just take care of Nicky. I'll do the rest.''

Suddenly she pushed him away. Her nostrils flared. ''You thrive on this, don't you, Jeb? The killing and fighting. It's all you know.''

He stiffened with a swift intake of breath. He refused to remind her it was men like him who kept Americans like her alive. Free and safe. He stepped back and left her alone with her son so that he could do what he had to do.

What he did best.

* * *

Jeb crouched in the shadows of the trees and stared at the buckboard wagon's driver. The shock of recognition slammed into him like a fist to his gut.

What the hell?

The team strained under its load, even heavier to haul uphill. Uneven ground didn't help any, but she slapped the reins again and again in a futile effort to urge the exhausted horses faster.

Margarete Bell had her hands full. The flush in her cheeks didn't come from the thick layer of rouge Jeb remembered her wearing that hot afternoon in her father's mercantile, but from the exertion of keeping a firm hold on the team's leathers. Her fancy curls weren't so fancy anymore, either, and she didn't look bored.

Desperate, though. Yeah, definitely that.

She hadn't spotted him yet, and Jeb let her draw closer before he made his move. He couldn't fathom what she was doing way out here in Mexican hill country, and by herself to boot. Did her father have an inkling of where she was? Or why?

The why intrigued Jeb most. The rig was ordinary. Beat-up some. The manufacturer must've made hundreds just like it, but Jeb had one hell of a strong suspicion it was the same rig the Apache had driven the day he was doing business with Henry Bell in the alley.

What possible connection could Margarete have with the Apache? With the load he hauled? And as heavy as it was...

She had to be bringing the rifles de la Vega expected. She *had* to be. Why else would she be this close to his camp?

Jeb rose from his crouched position and stepped out from the cover of the trees. He lifted his Winchester to his shoulder. Margarete needed to know he meant business, that if she was hauling rifles as he suspected she was, then she was committing a serious offense against her country.

"Pull up, Margarete," Jeb ordered. "You've gone far enough."

She jumped at the sound of his voice and dropped the reins to fumble for the revolver in her lap.

He cocked his rifle. The sound cracked in the air between them. "Don't even think it."

The team blew noisily and dragged to a shuddering halt. Sweat gleamed on their backs.

Margarete stared at Jeb. Her eyes widened. "It's you!"

"That's right. Drop the gun."

"What are you doing out here?" she demanded. She swept a quick glance around her. "Where's your wife?"

She still kept hold of her revolver in an awkward two-handed grip. Jeb figured firing a gun wasn't something she was accustomed to. Still, a nervous woman was a dangerous one, and he didn't trust her an inch.

"Drop it, I said." He took one step closer. Two. "Just so we can have a talk without either one of us getting hurt."

Her glance dropped to his rifle, aimed at her chest. "What do you want to talk to me about? I got just as much right to be here as you do."

"Now that depends, doesn't it?" She was stalling, and Jeb was fast losing patience from it. He halted, only a few yards from where she sat. "Rights and motives are two different things."

"I don't know what you're talking about."

"I think you do."

A moment passed.

"Margarete," he said, his voice a low warning.

Her small mouth thinned. She tossed the gun to the ground in a petulant huff. "There. You have my only way of defending myself against varmints like you. Are you satisfied? Now let me be on my way."

"Not just yet. Get down. I have a strong curiosity what a pretty girl like you might be doing out here in the middle of nowhere."

Her fingers lifted self-consciously to the curls drooping around her face. "I'm doing some business is all. For my pa."

"That so?" Jeb drawled. "He know you're doing it for him?"

"Sure he does."

She was lying. And she still hadn't gotten down from the wagon. Jeb reached up, grasped her elbow hard enough that she knew he had no tolerance for her disobedience. She scrambled for footing, but managed to get herself to the ground well enough. She glared at him.

"Stand over there," he snapped, pointing with his rifle to a spot close enough that he could keep an eye on her. "Don't run off, either. All these trees make it real easy to lose your bearings. You'd just get yourself lost. Might be days before anyone could find you. That is, if anyone bothered looking."

She swallowed at the slur but said nothing. Her eyes jumped from Jeb to the wagon bed and back to him again.

Whatever was in there, she was damned apprehensive about him seeing it. Jeb took a step backward, keeping his rifle trained on her.

A tarp covered the contents. He flung back a corner with his free hand. His glance skimmed over the wooden crates inside, then collided with a pair of eyes blinking up at him.

Jeb breathed a startled oath. The last thing he'd expected to see was a human being inside.

The Apache lay on his back, wedged between the side of the wagon and one of the crates. He'd been bound, gagged and, judging from the dried blood snaking across his forehead, he hadn't seen any of it coming.

"What did you hit him with, Margarete?" Jeb demanded, tugging the bandanna from the man's mouth and eyeing the goose egg he sported. "You could've killed him."

"A rock," she said, defensive. "I wanted him to take me with him. He refused. I didn't have a choice."

"She followed me to my camp outside Piedras Negras." The Apache grunted from the effort of maneuvering himself out of the wagon. His tattered Army uniform carried the dust from his ride. "She wanted to see de la Vega again."

"Again?" Jeb asked sharply, helping him.

"Claims they're in love."

Questions raged inside Jeb's head about her relationship with the revolutionary. He checked the Apache for any hidden weapons, found none, then helped him stand next to her, where he could keep an eye on them both. Again working one-handed, he used his knife to pry open one of the crates.

Inside, rifles gleamed side by side like sardines in a can. Brand new Savage lever-action weapons fresh from a military warehouse. Stolen by one man. Paid for by another.

Jeb whistled, long and low between his teeth. Hell of a lot of money sitting there in that wagon. And one hell of a crime had put them there.

He turned toward his captives. "All right, you two. Start talking."

Margarete's eyes narrowed stubbornly. "We don't have to tell you anything."

His lips formed a hard smile. "If I don't know what you're up to, I can't let you go, can I?"

She glanced uncertainly at the Apache. He glanced at her. His black eyes centered mutinously on Jeb. "What's it worth to you?"

"Depends."

"You take a cut of the profits. You let us go. Deal?"

"Can't agree until I know where those profits are coming from."

The Apache hissed a frustrated breath. Again he glanced at Margarete.

"He knows more than he's letting on, what with him being this close to Ramon and all," she said sullenly.

"Shut up, Margarete!" the Apache snapped.

"Well, it's true, ain't it?" She turned a hostile glare onto Jeb. "I met Ramon last year when he came through Carrizo Springs, all right? He needed a supplier for guns. He figured my pa could find him one."

"Go on."

"Pa didn't want to get involved. Not at first, but I talked him into it. I knew how much Ramon needed them." Margarete's chin lifted. "He's going to be a very powerful man in Mexico someday. He's handsome and exciting and we're going to get married."

"Married?" Jeb snorted in disbelief. "When was the last time he saw you?"

Her chin hiked higher. "I don't—a while, maybe."

"Months, Margarete. He don't care nothing about you except for the guns your pa can sell to him," the Apache snarled.

"That's not so!"

"I kept telling her that when she followed me to my

camp," he said to Jeb. "She wouldn't listen. Stubborn brat was hell-bent on seeing him again."

Disgust rolled through Jeb. Sympathy, too, for the foolish dreams the girl hung on to.

"Ever occur to you de la Vega might be using you to do business with your father?" he asked.

"He's not! Ramon knows how much I hate Carrizo Springs. I've lived in that one-horse town all my life! He can take me places I ain't never been before."

"You got that right. Like a women's prison." Jeb made no effort to sugarcoat the repercussions of the girl's illusions. She needed to know she'd have to pay the price for them. He turned to the Apache. "So how do you fit into all this?"

The Apache shifted. "Nothing you need to know."

"All right." Jeb nodded, agreeable. "I'll do your talking for you. I'm figuring Henry Bell is the middle man for this deal. He works with lots of suppliers. His mercantile is the perfect front. No one's likely to suspect."

Except Roy Marsh, now that Jeb thought of it. The old man had had his suspicions from the beginning. He'd be disappointed to learn the mercantile he'd opened and seen successful had been involved in an illicit weapons deal against the United States.

"You've been in the Army. A scout, maybe. You know Corporal Martin and Sergeant Bender. Between the three of you, you make connections with a gunrunner somewhere," Jeb went on. "He's paying you to take these weapons to Carrizo Springs." Jeb recalled the ruts in the road, the money changing hands in the alley outside Bell's Mercantile. "And Henry's paying you to take them to de la Vega."

"You're getting paid *twice?*" Margarete demanded, eyes wide.

"Had twice the risk, too," Jeb added, his suspicions confirmed.

"So now you're going to play lawman," the Apache taunted.

Jeb's lip curled. "Justice will be served."

"Name your price, Mr. Carson," Margarete said, for the first time looking plenty nervous. "Whatever it costs to let us go."

"Not a chance."

"We've got the money, I swear it." She glanced at the Apache, then at Jeb, her panic growing. "Please, Mr. Carson. Ramon has been waiting a long time. He needs these rifles to help his people."

"He'll kill with those rifles, too," Jeb shot back. "He'll use them to rape and pillage to feed his need to revolt against his government."

"No!"

"And you're a damned fool to get in with the likes of him, Margarete. You're in way over your damned *fool* head."

She jerked back, as if Jeb had struck her with the palm of his hand instead of the sharpness of his words. "No!"

"Carson's right," the Apache sneered. "De la Vega don't have time for you."

"You're lying! Both of you are!"

"Think it through," Jeb said. "While you're at it, think of your pa, too. Think how he'll feel when he finds out you've run off to Mexico to take up with a wild band of rebels."

Her bosom heaved. "I'm a fully grown woman. I can make my own decisions on what I do."

Jeb thought of the rope coiled on his saddle at Simon's place. He'd need it to tie the pair up before transporting them back across the border. He thought of

Elena, too. Alone with Nicky in the adobe. He bettered his grip on the Winchester.

"Start walking." He hated leaving the rifles behind, but he didn't have a choice. He'd have to come back for them. "Take it slow and easy and we'll all be just fine."

"I'm not going anywhere," Margarete said, contrary as ever.

"The hell you aren't," Jeb said, impatient with it.

"I'm not." Suddenly she whipped out a pearl-handled derringer from the folds of her skirt. She held it with hands unsteady. "You should've listened to me, Mr. Carson. Just because I'm a woman doesn't mean I don't have ambitions like a man."

"Put it down, Margarete," he said, and gauged the distance between them. If he was fast enough, he could wrench the gun from her before she could fire a shot and alert de la Vega to their whereabouts.

"Where's your wife?" she asked. "She's around here somewhere, isn't she?"

"No," Jeb said, eyeing the derringer. "Left her behind in the States."

"He's lying, Margarete," the Apache said with a slow grin. "I saw him with her. Crossing the Rio Grande together. The day after he was in your pa's store."

Jeb kept his features impassive. "Must've been someone else."

"You know Ramon's got a son, Margarete? Folks say Carson's woman is the mother." The Apache's grin widened.

Margarete's face drained. "Ramon? And *her?*"

"Shut up!" Jeb snarled.

A glance passed between the pair, a silent message that left Jeb bracing for the repercussions.

"She's here, ain't she?" Margarete said, calmer now.

"Somewhere close. You don't have a horse. You're on foot because you heard us coming and you *walked* up here to find us."

Unease sifted through Jeb. She had more sense than he figured. And she had honed in on his one weak spot.

Elena. Elena and Nicky.

She took a step backward, flexing her fingers over the derringer. "I'm going to find her, you know. If you want her alive, you're going to have to let me bring those guns to Ramon. Now who's calling the shots, Mr. Carson?"

Jeb kept his eye on her and slowly, very slowly, lifted his Winchester. She'd find Simon's adobe easily enough. She knew the general direction. It'd been the one mistake Jeb had made, confronting her from the very direction he came from.

He carried the butt of the rifle to his shoulder and found his mark, right over her heart. "Stop right where you are, Margarete. You make one wrong move..."

Abruptly Margarete spun.

Jeb's finger moved over the trigger.

A pair of fists, bound at the wrists, slammed down in front of him, knocked the Winchester out of his hands, and Jeb's shot went wild. He whirled, but the Apache's fists came up again, hard, and slammed against his jaw.

His head snapped back. He sprawled into the dirt and everything went black.

Dear God, a gunshot.

Elena's fingers flew to her mouth in horror. She ran to the open window and stared through the trees, in the direction Jeb had gone. Minute after heart-pounding minute, she stared, hoping, *praying,* he would reappear,

tall and strong and with a perfectly sound explanation
as to why a gun had been fired.

Stay away from the windows.

His warning popped into her head, and she jerked
back, as if flames leapt through the opening. She pressed
against the wall, tilted her head back and closed her eyes.

Don't leave the adobe, y'hear me? Not for any reason.

He had given her strict orders to stay put, but how
would she know if he was safe if she couldn't see him?
He might need her help. He might be bleeding, terribly
hurt.

Oh, God. Oh, God. Oh, God.

She began to pace, up one side of the room and back
again. If he was hurt, that meant there'd been a con-
frontation with whoever was in the wagon. Who had
fired the shot? Jeb? The rig's driver? Ramon? One of
his men?

She froze.

Nicky.

She spun toward where he lay still sleeping in Simon's bed. Precious and safe and blessedly oblivious to
any of the trouble going on around him.

If Ramon was this close, he would find them.

She drew in a deep, calming breath, blew it out again.
But maybe it wasn't Ramon or his men at all. Maybe
Jeb's gun had misfired. Maybe he had dropped it or
something and it went off.

Jeb would never be so careless.

There was trouble in those trees. Elena could *feel* it.

She rushed toward the window again and took up a
discreet position to watch if anyone approached. If it was
Jeb who stumbled out, he'd need her help.

Movement flickered in the shadows. Heart in her
throat, Elena fastened her glance on it like glue, watched

it draw closer, grow more distinct in shape. And then, suddenly, someone burst through the tree line at a full run.

Elena blinked.

Margarete?

A gamut of emotions and questions swirled in her head, everything from relief at seeing a familiar face, and a female one at that, to disbelief at seeing the young girl, alone and running for her life, to a mix of concern and suspicion about *why*.

Whatever the answers Margarete held, however, she most likely would've seen Jeb. He might even be the reason for her haste, and Elena bolted to the door in renewed fear. Her hand grasped the knob to run out of the adobe, but remembering Nicky, she stopped in her tracks.

Again her worried glance took him in. He hadn't moved. He slept peacefully. And though Jeb didn't want her to step beyond the threshold, in this instance, she had to.

She *had* to.

Nicky would be fine while she was gone. And she wouldn't be *gone*. She'd be right outside the door, just to talk to Margarete to find out what was happening.

In the time it took her to breathe another breath, she was outside and pulling the door closed behind her.

Jeb clawed his way through the blackness. Fire burned through his jaw, and he struggled to remember why he hurt. How he had gotten that way. And where he was. He realized he was in the jungle again, the damned jungle, noisy with the cries from disgruntled ravens and so thick with trees the branches and leaves shut out the sky.

He couldn't remember which country he was in. Or what battle he fought. But he had to find Creed.

Creed was fighting without him. Creed depended on him to survive. It was Jeb's job to watch his back, just as Creed had sworn to watch his.

He had to get up. He was a soldier. A rebel soldier. Like Creed. Fighting for America and her people. Innocents like Nicky and Elena.

The illusion shattered. His eyelids flew open.

Several yards away, the Apache sat on the ground, frantically, awkwardly, sawing through the rope binding his wrists. He was using a knife. Jeb's knife. Margarete was gone to find Elena, and a rage the likes of none other Jeb had experienced before roared hot through his veins.

He rolled to his feet with a snarl and lunged. The Apache's head lifted as he swore, scrambled to get away. Jeb grabbed him by the shirtfront and hauled him up roughly, then landed him a punch to the gut. The Apache doubled over, his wind lost, and a hard cuff to the jaw sent him toppling to the dirt, out cold.

Jeb snatched his knife. He found his rifle a short distance away.

And then he heard it. Horses' hooves pounding the earth. The rumble shimmied through his boot soles, and he knew, then, that Ramon de la Vega was coming, with all his men. They were out there, somewhere, in the deepest shadows of the trees. Jeb couldn't see them, but he could hear them, and they were heading straight for Simon's adobe.

He grabbed his rifle and broke into a hard run.

Sweet mother in heaven. He had to get to Elena before they did.

Chapter Eighteen

"Margarete! What happened?" Elena gasped. "I heard a shot!"

The girl skidded to a halt and struggled to catch her breath. She had a scratch on her cheek, Elena noticed. And pine needles in her hair. She must have snagged branches in her haste, and Elena's alarm doubled.

"I was right," Margarete said, winded. "You *are* here! He said you weren't. He lied!"

"Who?"

"Your husband. He said he left you back in the States."

Jeb had said that? He would've been protecting her. Trying to keep her presence a secret. Elena's heart thundered. "I heard a shot. What happened? Is he hurt?"

"Maybe he is. Maybe he isn't."

Elena went still. What game did she play?

"I heard you have a son," Margarete accused. She stood before Elena, feet spread, one hand behind her back. "Reckon your husband lied about that, too. Back in Carrizo Springs, he said you lost your baby. Made me think he died." She swung her head, defiant. "But that doesn't matter, does it? I could care less whether your baby is dead or not.'' She glared. ''Were you and Ramon lovers?''

''What?'' Elena asked, taken aback.

''Just tell me!''

''That is none of your business!''

''Is he the father of your baby?''

Margarete's voice had turned shrill, her eyes wild, and the realization that she was jealous and nearly hysterical turned Elena's blood cold. One look at Nicky, and the girl would know the truth.

She was in love with Ramon. That was the reason for her jealousy, and Elena knew, then, it was she, Margarete, who betrayed her country and brought Ramon his guns.

Dear God.

She still kept her hand behind her back, hiding the weapon Elena knew she carried. The girl was volatile. On the edge.

''He's the father of your baby, isn't he?'' Margarete said bitterly. ''You're not denying it, so it must be true.''

''Ramon raped me,'' Elena grated.

Shock drained the color from Margarete's flushed cheeks. ''I don't believe you. Ramon would never—''

''Afterward, he stole all my money. You can't possibly want a hateful man like him in your life.''

''You're lying. You're just saying this to make me feel sorry for you.'' Her lip curled. ''You're a beautiful woman, aren't you? Men always want to bed beautiful women.''

''Where's Jeb, Margarete?''

''He's up there.''

''Has he been hurt?''

''I'll take you to him. Then you can see for yourself.''

Don't leave the adobe, y'hear me? Not for any reason.

Elena drew in a breath and shook her head. "I'm not going anywhere with you. Just tell me if Jeb is all right."

The girl bared her teeth, and her arm whipped around. Her fingers clenched over the derringer she'd been hiding.

"You're coming with me to convince him to let me take that wagon to Ramon," she snarled.

Elena braced for the very real possibility she would be shot again. Killed within moments.

"No, Margarete. I'm not. You're wrong to bring the rifles. You're wrong to get involved in any of this."

"Jeb will listen. He's crazy for you. I saw the way he looked at you in Carrizo Springs. He'll do whatever you ask him."

"He'll do everything in his power to *stop* the rifles from getting to Ramon."

"He knows if he wants you alive he'll have to let me go. I *told* him so, and start walking, damn you!"

"Ma-ma-ma."

Elena went still. Nicky was awake, and for his sake, for her own and Jeb's, she had to prevent Margarete from making the biggest mistake in her life.

"All right. Sure. You win. I'll go with you, but I can't leave my son," Elena said. "He's only a baby."

The girl hesitated, clearly impatient with Nicky's intrusion into her plan. She made a sound of capitulation.

"Then you'll have to bring him," Margarete snapped, and pointed the derringer toward the adobe. "Go on. Get the kid. And make it quick. But I'm following you inside just so you don't try anything fancy."

"Certainly."

Elena turned. The door was only a few feet away. An arm's length. She thought of the revolver and knife Jeb had left her. She thought of Nicky, too. Innocent and defenseless inside, and she had to spare him from all of this if it was the last thing she ever did.

Margarete stepped closer. Elena could hear the crunch of her foot on the ground.

And she made her move.

She swung and hurtled into Margarete, her shoulder to the girl's chest. Her hand grappled for the derringer as she tackled Margarete to the ground. The gun fired, the sound deafening in Elena's ears, before it skittered out of reach.

Jeb nearly had heart failure seeing the women scuffling on the ground, the gunshot echoing throughout the valley, and one more signal that would lead de la Vega and his men right to them.

They would be here, within seconds, and then they *were,* the whole damned bunch crashing through the tree line at a hard gallop. He ran parallel with them, ran faster than he'd ever run before. Raw fear clogged his throat. His chest burned from the fire of it.

Elena. He had to get to her before they did. He had to keep them from hurting her and taking Nicky.

"Elena!" he yelled. "Elena!"

The women sprang apart, shock on their faces at the approaching riders. Elena twisted, searching for him. He was almost there, and she bolted to her feet.

"Jeb! Oh, God! Jeb!" she sobbed and her arms opened. He stumbled into them, holding her hard. "I was afraid you were hurt."

He had no time to reassure her—or warn her the worst was yet to come.

"Go inside. Stay with Nicky, y'hear? Arm yourself with my knife and pistol. Hurry." He pushed her to the

door, into the protection of the adobe, and closed it
firmly behind her.

The Mexicans formed a half circle around the structure and prevented any chance of escape. A fierce bunch,
Jeb thought. Armed to the teeth and hungry for revenge
against a mother determined to keep her son.

One of the men rode forward. The brim of his sombrero shadowed his features, making him difficult to distinguish from the rest of the men, but from the arrogant
way he held himself in the saddle, there was no question
of who he was.

"Ramon!" Margarete cried, scrambling to her feet.

His glance flicked over her with no sign of recognition, then returned to the adobe. His gaze seemed to
probe through the door to see Elena inside.

"Ramon! It's me. Margarete!"

His black eyes returned to her again. A slight frown
tugged at his brows.

"The girl from Carrizo Springs." From beside him,
Armando spoke in a low, amused voice. "Remember?
You have done some very important business with her
father."

"Por Dios." An instant smile appeared, as false as it
was charming. "How could I forget? Forgive me,
señorita. It has been a long time since we have seen
each other, eh?"

"Yes! Oh, heavens, yes. It *has* been a long time,
hasn't it?"

She looked relieved that Ramon finally recalled her.
Jeb might've felt sorry for her if he wasn't so infuriated
with all she'd done. She wore her heart on her sleeve,
and the man would only hurt her in the end.

"Why has it been so long, Ramon?" she asked. "You
promised me that..."

"Ma-ma. Ma-ma-ma."

Her words trailed away at the sound of Nicky's happy squeal.

"It seems my son is in a good mood today, eh?" De la Vega said, his glance leaving Margarete to fix on Jeb.

Jeb lifted the Winchester to his shoulder. From here on out, things were going to get real ugly.

"Don't figure you have much right to him," he said. "When this is over, you'll either be dead or headed to prison to live the rest of your sorry life."

The Mexican leader's expression turned cold. "You are the famous soldier Sergeant Bender told me about. Jeb Carson. The American patriot so proud of his country. See him, *amigos?* He thinks he can shoot all of us."

"He don't look like a soldier to me, Ramon," Margarete said, frowning.

"He works for the War Department," De la Vega said and smirked.

She blanched. "The *War* Department?"

"What you've done is a serious offense against the United States, Margarete," Jeb said. "Save yourself while you still can."

"She is only a simpleminded girl, foolishly in love," De la Vega snapped, dismissing her. "Why would you or your War Department care if she saves herself from anything?"

Margarete whirled toward him. "I brought your rifles, that's why!"

Jeb's mouth tightened. He wanted to choke her.

"My rifles?" De la Vega asked, stunned. Shock rumbled through the men. "They are here? Where?" He twisted in his saddle, looking for them, as if they'd be in bold view.

"Why should I tell you?" Margarete said, her small

mouth turned into a pout. "You don't care one whit for me. Not like you claimed you did, and maybe you don't deserve to know about your stupid guns."

Jeb braced for the repercussions. The girl was plenty naive. She was going to learn real quick the Mexican leader wouldn't appreciate her defiance.

He didn't. He pulled a rifle from its scabbard, cocked it and leveled it right at her.

"Forget her, Ramon," Armando said, frowning. "The weapons are here. We will find them."

"Maybe she lies."

"She would not be here if not for them."

De la Vega fired. Margarete yelped. The force of the bullet spun her to the ground. Blood spurted and bloomed on one side of her blouse.

A half-dozen rifles centered over Jeb, convincing him not to retaliate. He wouldn't be much good to Elena dead.

Margarete wasn't moving. He knelt beside her and checked for a pulse. He found one, but barely. He rose.

"If she dies, the noose gets tighter around your neck, de la Vega," he growled.

The Mexican leader barked orders to his men in Spanish, and they scattered in quick obedience.

"Do not return to me until the wagon is found!" he called after them. He turned back to Jeb. "Now give me my son."

"Go to hell," he said.

A muffled thud sounded from inside the adobe. Elena screamed. Jeb spun to bolt in after her, but the door burst open first. She emerged with a revolver pressed to her temple, Nicky clinging with both arms around her neck. Her gaze dropped to Margarete, and she paled.

De la Vega nodded in satisfaction. "Good job, Diego. You have been quick to capture my son for me."

"*Sí*," the man said, and grinned wide.

She held Nicky tighter against her. "I'll never let you take him again. You'll have to kill me first."

De la Vega made a sound of impatience and lifted his rifle. "Bring him to me, Diego."

De la Vega had never intended to let Elena live, Jeb knew, even if she complied with his demand. She'd stolen her son back from him once. Any fool would know she would attempt to do it again.

"Ramon, let the child stay with his mother," Armando said firmly. "We will soon have the guns. They are enough for now."

"You say that because it is not *your* son in the woman's arms." He glared at Elena. "Give him to me."

"What kind of a life can you offer him?" Armando demanded. "You have much work to do yet for Mexico. You will be too busy to watch him grow up."

"*Silencio!*"

"He is a baby. *Leave him with his mother.*" Armando clamped a hand over the rifle barrel. De la Vega tried to wrest his weapon free, and lightning quick, Jeb pulled the trigger once, twice. Both men toppled off their horses. Jeb twisted, rammed the butt of the Winchester into the third rebel's belly. He doubled over, and Jeb hit him again. He crumpled and didn't move.

Clutching Nicky against her, Elena fell into Jeb's arms, and he held them both hard. She closed her eyes and choked on a sob. "Oh, Jeb."

Suddenly, behind him, a horse thundered off, and Jeb whirled. De la Vega was hunched over his saddle and weaving in the seat, badly wounded but getting away.

Jeb swore viciously.

"Let's get out of here," Elena said, bosom heaving.

He released her. "No."

"Ramon's hurt. We can *leave*."

He fished more bullets from his pocket, reloaded the Winchester's chamber. "That wagonload of guns is still out there, Elena. I can't let de la Vega take them. You know that."

"It's not your responsibility right now. You're out-manned. There's no way you can—"

"I have to try."

"You may as well stand before a firing squad!"

Her tears were nearly his undoing, but he held on tight to his resolve. It was in his blood to fight. He knew no other way to win.

He cupped the back of her head, brought her roughly against him, kissed her hard. He had no time for tenderness or for assurances. She had to know what he had to do. She needed to understand it. Accept it.

"I love you, Elena." Funny he'd never said the words before. Ever. But they slipped from his tongue now, for her, like butter. "I love you."

"Oh, Jeb," she breathed. "I—"

The ground shimmied from a new round of hoofbeats, and Jeb's blood ran cold. The horses were close. Damn close. And they weren't coming from the hills.

From around the side of the adobe, Simon appeared. Lieutenant Colonel Kingston. A whole regiment of the United States Army.

And Creed, leading them all.

Jeb stared, stunned.

"Heard you got yourself in some trouble again, *compadre*," Creed said, pulling up. "Need some help?"

He should have been in California with his family,

away from this, another battle on foreign soil. Jeb was damned glad he wasn't.

"Guess I do," he said.

"Mount up, then. Time's ticking."

"It sure as hell is." Jeb walked, then sprinted toward his horse, the adrenaline building with every step.

"What would you have us do, Mr. Carson?" the lieutenant colonel asked, following. "Your call."

It seemed a lifetime since Jeb had spoken to the officer in that Laredo saloon. Damned if fate didn't have a way of changing a man's life. He glanced at Elena. For the better, too.

"Stay with the lady and her son," Jeb ordered. "They've been through a lot. Whatever she wants, see that she gets it."

"Yes, sir."

He left final orders to tend to Armando's body, Margarete's medical needs and Diego's capture, then climbed into the saddle. He took the reins in his hands. "I'll be back as soon as I can."

"De la Vega can't get those guns, Mr. Carson," Kingston said. "President McKinley is most worried about the threat of the revolution."

"I know."

"Stopping that arms shipment would be quite a coup for you and for the United States. An honor, sir."

"An honor." Jeb saw it as nothing of the sort, merely a job that needed to be done for his country. "We'll see."

Creed was waiting, but Jeb held back, burdened with a sudden reluctance to leave Elena. She seemed overwhelmed with the soldiers, the horses, and all the activity around her. He wanted to stay, reassure her that she was safe, that from here on out, her life would be a hell of a lot easier for her and her son.

Her glance lifted, met his. A sudden shot of yearning went through him. A wish that things were different. That no wars needed to be fought, no battles won.

But, of course, they had to be. They would always have to be. Winning them were what made the United States the nation it was.

And him the man *he* was.

Somber in the knowledge, the harsh truth of it, he rode to Creed's side, and together they headed into the Mexican hills, Lieutenant Colonel Kingston's men right behind them.

Elena watched him go, and a part of her died.

She might never see him again. Alive.

She clung to Nicky, her little rock in a world suddenly gone shaky and uncertain. Two soldiers carried Margarete, whimpering, away on a stretcher. Armando lay on the ground, covered with a tarp. And the rebel, Diego, his jaw broken, was being guarded by an armed soldier.

Violence. Death.

How could Jeb survive it? Thrive on it?

She didn't belong here any more than she belonged on the moon. She wanted no part of any war, no matter how urgent the fight had become.

She wanted peace. Security. She wanted to go to San Antonio. She wanted to see Pop.

But most of all, she wanted Jeb.

She could never have him. Their lives were too different.

Tears stung the back of her eyes, and she blinked them away. It wouldn't do to have these men seeing her weakness, not when they were so brave, so strong, so resilient.

"Ma'am?"

Elena scrambled for composure. A tall, barrel-chested officer approached her, sympathy in his expression.

"Lieutenant Colonel Eugene Kingston, ma'am. Is there anything I can get for you?"

"For me?" she asked, taken aback that a man as important looking as he would offer to do anything of the sort.

"Yes." A small smile played on his lips. "Mr. Carson has left me explicit instructions to see to your every need."

She swallowed hard against a welling of emotion. "There is one thing," she said. "Yes. One thing I need."

He inclined his head. "Just name it."

"An escort, please. To San Antonio. I'd like to leave now, if you don't mind. As soon as it can be arranged."

"San Antonio? Now?" The officer cleared his throat. "I'm not sure this is, er, quite what Mr. Carson had in mind."

"I assure you he'll understand. We've talked of it, many times."

"It'll be dark in a few hours."

"I'm prepared to ride all night."

He stared for long moments in the direction Jeb had left, as if he hoped Jeb's sudden reappearance would give the approval the officer wanted. He sighed. "All right. I'll make the arrangements."

"Thank you, sir."

He strode away. Elena dropped a kiss against Nicky's dark curls and fought tears. "We're going for a ride, sweetheart. We're going home."

Jeb and Creed tracked the revolutionary and his men to the brush where they hid like snakes in the grass. Jeb lifted an arm, signaled, and Kingston's men fanned out, surrounding the area, their weapons drawn and ready.

De la Vega didn't have a chance.

"You want to wait him out?" Creed asked in a low voice.

"No," Jeb said.

Night would fall in minutes. Once it did, their chances of capturing the Mexicans deteriorated dramatically. He was impatient to get back to Elena. He didn't have time to wait for de la Vega or anyone else to make their move.

Creed scrutinized the perimeter of the thicket, dense with mesquite. "Broke my share of brush when I was a kid rounding up cattle too stubborn to come out on their own. Hard work getting through it. Dangerous, too."

"De la Vega would have the advantage."

"They'd see us before we saw them."

De la Vega and his men were as lawless as they were proud. They had to be routed out of the brush and captured before they could escape. Jeb made his decision.

"We'll burn 'em out," he said.

Creed nodded. "It'll work."

"Send some men out to light the fires. The rest of us will cover them," Jeb ordered, and Creed rode off.

It wasn't long before the brush began smoking. Jeb raised his Winchester to his shoulder and waited. In the deepening dusk, the soldiers waited, too.

Suddenly the revolutionaries burst through the brush with earsplitting yells and barking weapons. The attack was unexpectedly reckless and frenzied, throwing the soldiers on the defensive as the Mexicans rode right toward the line. It was as if their lives meant nothing, as if...

As if the attack was a diversion for their leader's escape.

Jeb twisted and found de la Vega doubled over in the saddle and breaking out of the thicket just beyond the range of fire. Jeb snarled a curse. He kicked his mount in pursuit.

He caught up in minutes. De la Vega had lost a lot of blood. How he managed to stay in the saddle was beyond Jeb, but it alluded to the man's desperation to get away. And if he did anything, *anything,* Jeb had to keep him from returning to his camp where he would use the innocent women and children there as a shield against the Army's attack.

"Give up, de la Vega," Jeb yelled, riding even with the other horse.

Teeth bared, de la Vega swung his arm outward with his revolver leveled and cocked.

But Jeb was ready for him.

He leapt from the saddle, threw his body into the revolutionary and toppled them both to the ground. De la Vega grunted from the fall, and his gun skittered out of sight. They scuffled like schoolboys in the dirt until, breathing hard, Jeb loomed on his knees over the other man. De la Vega glared up at him, black eyes spitting with hate.

"Give up," Jeb grated again. "It's over, y'hear me?"

"You will never stop my revolution, Carson!"

"We've got your guns. Your men are being killed by the Army. Give yourself up while you're still alive, damn it!"

As if he rebelled against every grain of truth in the words, de la Vega roared and bucked, throwing Jeb onto his back. A knife blade flashed in the Mexican's bloody hand, and Jeb's fingers locked over de la Vega's wrist to prevent its descent.

If Jeb's strength faltered, if his muscles gave way, the knife would plunge into his heart, and the Mexican would win. He would escape, after all. He would find a way to buy more guns and kill more innocents. He would take Nicky, too, all in the name of his revolution.

In the far recesses of his mind, Jeb became aware that the distant gunfire had ended, that horses thundered closer. A single shot rang out. The Mexican jerked, then fell lifeless on top of him.

Ramon de la Vega had finally lost.

Chapter Nineteen

Jeb kicked open the door to Simon's adobe. The interior was pitch-dark. Cold. Abandoned.

She'd left him.

The knowledge infuriated him, left him hurting with a pain so raw and searing he could barely breathe.

Did she care so little for him she couldn't wait to get away? That as soon as she got what she wanted—her son and a way home—she took off as soon as his back was turned?

She hadn't waited.

He never thought it would hurt so much.

"You going to stand in the dark and feel sorry for yourself?" Creed demanded from somewhere behind him. "Or are you going to light a lamp and give me a hand here?"

The words taunted him. Creed was damned perceptive; he would know Elena had left for Texas, would understand why. Would probably even agree with her about it, considering Jeb's brand of living.

A soldier was leaning on Creed, one arm around his shoulder for support. He'd taken a fall off his horse, and

Jeb had a bone or two to set for him. The man had saved his life. It was the least Jeb could do.

He hadn't even known the soldier had followed him when Jeb took off after de la Vega. But he came galloping through the trees and fired when Jeb needed him the most. The man's sense of timing had been uncanny.

"Let's lay him on the bed," he said.

Jeb took one side, Creed the other, and they helped him hobble cross the dark room. The straw in the mattress crackled, and he leaned back against the pillow with a low moan.

Jeb found a lamp and lit the wick. Seeing de la Vega's blood on his hands, Jeb washed up and reached for a towel, folded neatly on the table. Next to it stood several bottles of Doc Charlie's Miraculous Herbal Compound. Thoughts of Elena flooded through him all over again.

She knew he'd need them, if not for himself, then for his men. It moved him that she would even think of it, when she was in such a damned hurry to get out of Mexico.

"She leave you a present?" Creed asked, watching him.

Their skepticism of the medicine back in the woodlands near the Nueces had been mutual. Quackery, he'd thought then. A scam to bilk honest citizens of their money.

Not anymore.

"Stuff's damn good." Jeb tossed him a bottle, his glance skimming the man sprawled on the bed. Blood had seeped through the bandage wrapped low around his head, and he held his left arm gingerly against him. His right knee was swollen within the trousers of his Army uniform. "Give him a double dose, will you? He'll need it when I set that bone."

"You're sure?" Creed asked, staring at the label.

"Positive."

Creed grunted, and he gave the soldier the required amount. Jeb found the wooden kit containing his medical instruments, then sat on the edge of the mattress.

"I'm going to slit your pant leg so I can have a look at that knee, soldier," he said. The scissors snipped through the fabric, worked their way upward. "We'll have to convince Kingston to issue you new trousers, won't we?"

"I'm sure that can be arranged."

His scissors stilled. The hair rose on the back of Jeb's neck.

That voice.

His gaze flew to the man's face. It'd been six years since Jeb had breathed the same air as his father, but they fell away as if it'd been only yesterday. He bolted off the bed and swung toward Creed.

"Is this supposed to be funny?" he demanded.

"Not at all, *compadre*."

"He was under strict orders not to let you know of my presence in the regiment. All the men were," the General said.

Jeb glared at Creed. His friend would pay dearly for the deception. "Why?"

The General answered before Creed could. "Because I wanted to see you."

"And you went along with it," Jeb said, still glaring at Creed.

"He had no choice," the General said.

"And I saw no harm in it," added Creed.

Jeb's nostrils flared. Of anyone, Creed knew best the contempt Jeb had long held for his father. The pain of his betrayal.

''I heard you were leaving the War Department,'' the General went on to Jeb's back. ''There was something I needed to discuss with you before you did.''

''I suppose you told him I was heading to California, too,'' Jeb accused.

''He has his informants,'' Creed said smoothly. ''He knows as much about us as we do. I didn't need to tell him a damn thing.''

Yes, Jeb thought bitterly. Kingston had alluded to as much, back in Laredo. General William Carson was too shrewd to be uninformed about anything—or anyone. Especially his son.

''But I didn't know about de la Vega taking the baby until Creed sent word from San Antonio the next day,'' the General said. ''Told me you took off with the mother to get him back.''

''We met at Fort Duncan. Figured you'd need some help,'' Creed explained. ''After we crossed the Rio Grande, we met Simon. He told us about the guns and led us here.''

Creed had set aside his plans to return to his family for Jeb's sake. Elena and Nicky's, too. Some of his irritation faded.

''Now. You going to talk to him directly?'' Creed set his hands on hips. ''Or are you going to stand there with your back to him and talk through me instead?''

Jeb hated it when Creed was so damned reasonable. And when it came to his father, Jeb never felt reasonable.

He allowed his pride to slip a little and turned. Below the bandage, eyes as dark as his own watched him. The General's skin was a shade pale from his injuries, his hair grayer at the temples, but his expression was as stern and brooding as ever.

Or was it?

The faint furrow in his brow revealed—Jeb strove to define it—apprehension? Concern? Worry?

Of Jeb's reaction to seeing him again?

Well, hell. Imagine that. The General was human, after all.

Jeb couldn't remember him being apprehensive about anything. Ever. The man had always been made of stone, always so sure of himself and the others around him, always *right*.

Maybe the years had mellowed him some.

Or had *he* done the mellowing?

He gave himself a mental shake. He didn't like feeling this…confused.

"You've grown into a fine soldier, Jeb," his father said, voice quiet.

"That so?" He willed himself to sit on the edge of the bed again, resume cutting open the pant leg. It was easier that way. Giving his hands something to do, his eyes something else to look at, besides the man who had so unexpectedly returned into his life. "Bet you never figured on that, did you?"

"I've always known you would be. You were born with nerves of steel. Not many young men would've had the courage to walk away from an appointment at West Point and a father who was a general, no less."

"You court-martialed me, for God's sake."

"For disobeying orders. I had no choice, under the circumstances. But you could've been reinstated. You wouldn't have been the first cadet to be, or the last, but you were too proud to stay until the hearings began." The General hesitated. "I don't blame you for still being angry with me."

"Angry?" Jeb growled. The word didn't cover the

anger, the hate and bitterness, that had eaten him inside out over the years.

"It was damned hard seeing you walk away. Don't think I didn't have my own regrets. But there wasn't a man on this earth who wasn't prouder of his son than me."

Jeb swallowed. The words were turning him to mush. He felt eight years old again, hungry for his father's love and approval.

"Who do you think recommended you to the War Secretary to be sent overseas?" the General asked.

Jeb had always suspected as much. He recalled the battle-scarred places he'd been to—South America, Cuba, Africa—and the bone-chilling danger he'd endured in each one of them. He recalled the success, too. The gratification he and Creed had felt in serving their country in a way few men could.

"I damn near lost my hide everywhere I went," he said.

"But you didn't. You survived. Honorably, I might add."

Jeb glanced at his friend. Creed was grinning like an idiot. He sighed. "Well, you killed de la Vega. Not me. Secretary Alger will need to know that."

The General grunted and rubbed his injured arm. "De la Vega was half-dead by the time I got to him. You had the worst of it. And Alger does *not* need to know I was felled by a damned tree branch." He scowled at his injuries. "If I'd been watching where my horse was leading instead of being scared for you, I wouldn't have been knocked clean from the saddle."

"You? Scared?" He'd never thought the General would be afraid of anything, and certainly not for *him*.

"De la Vega had you in a rough fight. Not that you

weren't holding your own.'' He shifted on the mattress, then grimaced. ''Seems I'm getting too old to skirmish.''

After the revolutionary had been shot, the regiment came riding in. His father had quickly been tended to, and Jeb hadn't had the opportunity to show his gratitude for saving his life.

Until now.

''Thanks,'' he muttered grudgingly. ''For all you did.''

''Forget it. You'll get the credit you deserve from Washington for keeping those rifles out of the rebels' hands.''

The credit meant nothing to Jeb. The War Department knew what he was capable of. He didn't need acknowledgment from them.

''Still painful?'' Jeb probed the swollen knee, tried to determine if it was dislocated or sprained.

''Getting better.'' The General picked up the bottle of elixir. ''Doc Charlie's Miraculous Herbal Compound. What's it made of?''

''Secrets of the ancients.''

Creed snorted.

Jeb glowered at him.

''Think it's funny, do you? Elena says—'' He clamped his mouth shut. He refused to talk about her when just saying her name hurt.

''She's a beautiful woman,'' the General said quietly, shrewdly.

''Lots of beautiful women in this world.''

But none like her. None as caring or gentle or alluring as Elena.

''I'm sure she's grateful for what you've done, getting the boy back for her and all,'' he mused.

''Yeah, well. She has a funny way of showing it,

doesn't she? She couldn't get out of Mexico fast enough.''

"There you go. Feeling sorry for yourself again." Creed exhaled, loud and long. "What's the matter, Carson? You afraid of her?''

His chin jerked up. Afraid of a woman? Of Elena? "Hell, no.''

Or was he scared out of his mind she'd never want him in her life?

"Never known you to back down from a good fight. And I'm thinking she's one woman you might want to fight for.''

Jeb swallowed. Hard. Yeah, she was.

"What's the harm in going after her? Say goodbye proper, you know?''

He grappled for a solid excuse. California. He had to go to California. The trip had already been delayed once, and Creed was long overdue to get back to his family.

But a side visit to San Antonio could be arranged easily enough. A day at the most. What was a few hours to see Elena anyway?

A few hours. That was all. Mere minutes in the grand scheme of things.

"Sure." Jeb cleared his throat. "I—yeah, sure. I could do that. I guess.''

"You guess." Creed shook his head and headed for the door. "Carson, you're so crazy about her, you can't think straight.''

He left, pulling the door closed behind him. Jeb glanced at the General, watching him with twitching lips.

"He's wrong," Jeb said, defensive. "I can think just fine.''

The General nodded somberly. "Sure you can.''

All his trepidations fell away. His mind cleared,

snagged on a comment his father had made earlier. "You said you had something you wanted to discuss with me?"

His father smiled. "As a matter of fact, I did."

One Week Later

Pop glared at the walking cane with fierce dislike.

"I'm not going to use that thing any sooner than I have to, Lennie," he said stubbornly. "Push me to the doors. I'll walk out with it then."

"Pop." Elena exchanged an exasperated glance with Toby. "There's nothing to be embarrassed about. Lots of people walk with a cane every day."

"That's right, Doc," Toby said, his hair sticking out around his ears from beneath his cap. "Your leg has some healing to do yet. You need the cane to—"

"I know full well why I need the cane." From his seat in the wheelchair, he reached for Nicky. Elena reluctantly settled him in his lap, away from his tender shoulder. "C'mon, Nicky. We'll ride this fool thing together. What do you say about that, my little man?"

Nicky gurgled something happy and agreeable, and Elena gave in. If Pop was so insistent on using the wheelchair to get himself out of the hospital to finish recuperating at the small apartment she'd rented, there was no real harm in it, she supposed. But the sooner he started using the cane, the less foreign it would feel.

She hooked the stick on the back of the wheelchair and pushed him down the hall, Toby beside her, their pace leisurely. It had been difficult seeing her father felled by his injuries, pale, confined to bed and virtually helpless in so many things. But since her return from Mexico with Nicky, his spirits had raised in gigantic proportions. Every day, he was moving about more, and

Elena knew it wouldn't be long before they both put the nightmare with Ramon behind them.

Well, almost.

Except for Jeb. She missed him terribly.

The longer she was away from him, the more she thought of him. It'd been a mistake to leave like she did. Unfair, too. He had deserved a decent goodbye. A hug, maybe. A long, soul-destroying kiss that neither of them would *ever* forget.

She didn't even know where he was or if he was dead or alive. She didn't have an inkling of how she could go about finding him, or if she should even try. Or if he'd want to see her if she *did* find him.

"Elena." Toby waved a hand in front of her face, and she blinked back to reality. "I'm talking to you."

"Were you?" She hadn't heard a word. "I'm sorry. I wasn't listening."

"I know. You've been doing that a lot lately. Not listening. You sure you're doing okay? Ever since you came back from Mexico, you've been—" he shrugged "—I don't know. Different."

Had it been so obvious? Jeb had changed her. Made her want things she had never thought she'd want or need.

Like having a man in her life. Jeb. Forever and ever.

"I'm sorry," she said again. She had to stop thinking about him. She had decisions to make. Pop's injuries and Nicky's kidnapping had brought the medicine show to a grinding halt. Bookings were canceled. Troupe members had left, understandably, to find jobs elsewhere. Only Toby stayed, out of loyalty to Pop, and Elena felt guilty for it.

She had nothing to offer him. Not anymore. He was young yet. He needed to move on, for his own good.

They approached the hospital's lobby. Three men stood in front of one of the windows. The midmorning sunlight accented the fine cut of their clothing, the glint of smartly polished shoes. The men looked important, Elena mused as she pushed the wheelchair closer to the doors. One especially, with his tall stature, his back straight, shoulders square. Though his arm was in a sling and he held a cane, he wasn't a patient here. He looked too healthy, too important. Clearly he was waiting for someone with the others.

The shortest of them turned and smiled. He had a portly belly and a round face. A thick mustache covered his upper lip.

"Malone?" he asked. "Doc Charlie Malone?"

Pop was as surprised as Elena. The wheelchair rolled to a halt. "Yes. I'm Charlie Malone."

The man walked toward them, his hand extended. "Patrick Morrow. Morrow Pharmaceuticals. Philadelphia. Glad to meet you."

For a moment, Pop didn't move, his shock rendering him speechless. Then he handed Nicky to Elena, went for his cane and scrambled out of the wheelchair, all in one motion. He took the man's hand in a firm grasp. "Likewise, thank you, sir."

"We've a matter to discuss with you, if you don't mind?" The second man spoke as he drew nearer, his gait graceful despite a faint limp. His features looked familiar, but Elena was much too distracted with curiosity to dwell on it. "In the hospital garden, perhaps."

Pop exchanged a glance with Elena. "Of course, of course. The garden will be fine."

"Name's William, by the way." He smiled, and for the first time, he looked at Elena. His eyes were clear.

Sharp. And twinkling. Something about those eyes pulled at her.

"Ma-ma-ma."

Nicky wiggled and Elena shifted him to her hip with a soft "shh." William studied him.

"A handsome boy," he murmured.

"Thank you," she said.

"My daughter and grandson, Elena and Nicky," Pop said, by way of introduction.

"Yes. I know."

Pop frowned.

Morrow stepped back and graciously extended an arm toward the door leading out to the gardens. "Shall we?"

"Certainly," Pop said.

Canes clicked on the tile floor as the men meandered outside, Morrow slowing his pace to allow for the other men's handicaps. He spoke animatedly, and Elena lingered in the doorway, her curiosity raging.

"I guess I can bring the wagon around while they're talking," Toby said.

Elena had forgotten he was there. "Yes. Good idea."

"Elena, before I do, I—"

At the hesitancy in his voice, she peered up at him, at the freckled face she'd always held dear. He was trying to grow a mustache, but the pale fuzz over his lip showed the attempt was lacking. At two years younger, he was like the brother she never had.

But the blatant adoration in his expression told her she meant much more to him than a sister.

Why had she never noticed before? Had she been so busy shutting men out of her life after Ramon's attack that she was blinded to one's affections?

"Elena, I know things are looking pretty bleak for you right now, what with the medicine show gone belly-up and all. But I—I care for you. I always have. We get along, and Doc likes me. Nicky, too, and well, I want to stay with you. That is, if you'll have me.''

"Stay with me?" As in be her *husband?* "Oh, Toby."

''Maybe now isn't the right time to be mentioning it,'' he said, taking a step back as if he feared her rejection. ''But think on it, will you? We'll talk later. I'll get the rig, and we'll talk…later.''

He turned and fairly bolted from the hospital. Elena stared after him, knowing how much courage it had taken to reveal his feelings.

''He's not man enough for you.''

At the low growl, Elena spun with a squeak of surprise.

Jeb stood with one side of his coat swept back, his thumb hooked in his waistband. His shirt was stark white against his sun-dark skin, his suit perfectly tailored to fit his broad shoulders. He'd cut his hair. Shaved. And if she thought him dangerous and exciting in the wilds of Mexico as a mercenary, he was doubly so now, dressed as a gentleman in civilized society.

Her heart squeezed at the sight of him. She loved him, no matter where he was or what he wore. She loved him, for he was a man like no other she'd ever known.

And he'd been blatantly eavesdropping on her conversation with Toby.

''I—I didn't know you were there,'' she said. ''I didn't recognize you.''

He scowled. ''Obviously.''

It occurred to her he might be jealous. ''I've known Toby most of my life. He's a good person.''

''He's just a kid.''

She clamped her mouth shut. She refused to defend Toby or his tender feelings for her.

But a bevy of questions got her talking again.

"You were with those men, weren't you?" she said, glancing out into the garden. "Who are they? What do they want to discuss with Pop?"

He grunted and took her elbow. "You're a damned chatterbox this morning, Elena. Funny. You couldn't even say goodbye in Mexico."

He pulled her out of the hall and into the nearest room, then shut the door behind them. Sunlight filtered through white cotton curtains on the window. The room was cool, hushed, empty. Seeing the crucifix on the cloth-covered altar, Elena realized they'd slipped into the hospital's chapel.

She deserved the rebuke. "I was upset that day—"

"Upset."

"—and Lieutenant Colonel Kingston was trying to be helpful."

"Helpful."

"You were so determined to go after Ramon, and I never wanted to see him again. I just wanted to go back—" She halted. "Did you capture him? Ramon?"

"He's dead, Elena. His men, too. The whole damned bunch. Dead."

"Oh." She pressed a hand to her breast in relief, then remembered they were standing in a chapel. "Thank God."

But then, she should've known better than to think Jeb would settle for less than victory over the revolutionaries. He was as driven for justice as she'd been.

Nicky squirmed and strained against her, his arms reaching for Jeb. "Ma-ma-ma."

"We're going to have to teach him a new word,

Elena," Jeb said, taking him and tossing him into the air. Nicky squealed in delight. "Like 'Daddy,' for starters. Isn't that right, buddy?" He tousled Nicky's curls.

"We?" Elena was afraid to breathe. To hope. "Daddy?"

Jeb held her son in one strong arm. "That's right. He needs a father."

Her mouth softened; she cocked her head in consideration. "Hmm. True. Toby would do well enough, I suppose. Nicky has known him all his life, and—"

Jeb went still. "Toby?" He swore—clearly, he didn't care they were in a holy chapel—and hooked his arm around Elena's waist. He hauled her roughly against him. "I didn't mean Toby, Elena. Me. *I* want to be Nicky's father."

She feigned surprise, her heart bursting. "You?"

"I want to be your husband, too." His head lowered. "Marry me, Elena. Make us a family for the rest of our lives, because I love you so much I don't want to be away from you ever again."

"I love you just as much." Her fingers slid into his hair. "Being your wife would be an honor, Jeb. I'll follow you wherever you need to fight, and if I can't, I'll wait until you come back. Nicky and I both will."

At her avowal, his mouth took hers in a hungry kiss that banished all thought from her mind but the feel of him in her arms and the love in her heart. A lifetime of kisses and happiness wherever they would be, so long as they were together, taking care of each other. Loving each other.

Slowly he ended the kiss, then dropped little nibbles against her jaw. "There's a thing or two I haven't told you yet."

Elena drew back. His dark eyes smoldered with a mysterious light.

"I've been offered a position in the War Department. I'll be advising President McKinley in Washington. A revolution in Mexico is inevitable. Killing de la Vega and confiscating the arms shipment was only a small hitch in Zapata's plan."

Pride swelled through her. He would serve his country well in Washington, too.

"That's your father in the garden with Pop and Patrick Morrow, isn't it?" she asked.

"Yes. We've spent a lot of time talking the past few days. He was quite impressed with the elixir, by the way."

"Was he?" Jeb would've given him some, then. For his injuries. The news pleased her.

"Morrow's company supplies medicine for the Army. He has a sizable contract with the government, and the General requested we meet with him here in San Antonio. Morrow is prepared to place a large order of Doc Charlie's Miraculous Herbal Compound for both military and civilian hospitals." He kissed her temple. "Your father will soon be a very rich man, Elena."

"Oh!" She pressed her fingers to her mouth; her eyes shimmered with tears.

"He can open that apothecary you've always wanted," Jeb went on, wiping a drop of moisture off her cheek with his knuckle. "No more medicine shows, no more traveling. For either of you. I'll buy you a real house. You can see him every day if you want."

"How can I ever thank you?"

"Marry me. Today. Now."

She smiled, happier than she'd been in her entire life. "We're in a chapel, you know. All we need is a priest."

''Well, hell. What are we waiting for?'' He took her hand and headed for the door.

It wasn't long before he found one.

* * * * *

PICK UP A HARLEQUIN HISTORICAL AND DISCOVER EXCITING AND EMOTIONAL LOVE STORIES SET IN THE OLD WEST!

On sale July 2004

TEXAS BRIDE by Carol Finch

Join the fun when a brooding Texas Ranger reluctantly escorts a spirited beauty on a hair-raising adventure across the Texas frontier!

WEST OF HEAVEN by Victoria Bylin

When a desperate young widow is pursued by a dangerous bandit, she finds shelter and love in the arms of a grief-stricken rancher.

On sale August 2004

THE HORSEMAN by Jillian Hart

A lonely horseman eager to start a family jumps at the chance to marry a beautiful young woman. But could his new bride be harboring a secret?

THE MERCENARY'S KISS by Pam Crooks

Desperate to find her kidnapped son, a single mother enlists the help of a hardened mercenary. Can they rescue her child before it's too late?

Visit us at www.eHarlequin.com

HARLEQUIN HISTORICALS®

HHWEST32

FALL IN LOVE WITH
THESE HANDSOME HEROES
FROM HARLEQUIN HISTORICALS

On sale September 2004

THE PROPOSITION
by Kate Bridges

Sergeant Major Travis Reid
Honorable Mountie of the Northwest

WHIRLWIND WEDDING
by Debra Cowan

Jericho Blue
Texas Ranger out for outlaws

On sale October 2004

ONE STARRY CHRISTMAS
by Carolyn Davidson/Carol Finch/Carolyn Banning

Three heart-stopping heroes
for your Christmas stocking!

THE ONE MONTH MARRIAGE
by Judith Stacy

Brandon Sayer
Businessman with a mission

www.eHarlequin.com

HARLEQUIN HISTORICALS®

Savor the breathtaking
romances and thrilling adventures
of Harlequin Historicals

On sale September 2004

THE KNIGHT'S REDEMPTION by Joanne Rock

A young Welshwoman tricks Roarke Barret into marriage
in order to break her family's curse—of spinsterhood.
But Ariana Glamorgan never expects to fall for the
handsome Englishman who is now her husband....

PRINCESS OF FORTUNE by Miranda Jarrett

Captain Lord Thomas Greaves is assigned to guard Italian
princess Isabella di Fortunaro. Sparks fly and passions flare
between the battle-weary captain and the spoiled, beautiful
lady. Can love cross all boundaries?

On sale October 2004

HIGHLAND ROGUE by Deborah Hale

To save her sister from a fortune hunter, Claire Talbot offers
herself as a more tempting target. But can she forget the
feelings she once had for Ewan Geddes, a charming
Highlander who once worked on her father's estate?

THE PENNILESS BRIDE by Nicola Cornick

Home from the Peninsula War, Rob Selbourne discovers
he must marry a chimney sweep's daughter to
fulfill his grandfather's eccentric will. Will Rob
find true happiness in the arms of
the lovely Jemima?

www.eHarlequin.com

HARLEQUIN HISTORICALS®

HHMED08